Cats
Undercover

Cats Undercover

by
GED GILLMORE

deGrevilo
Publishing

Copyright © 2016 Ged Gillmore
First published by deGrevilo Publishing in 2017

www.gedgillmore.com
www.degrevilo.com

Cataloguing-in-Publication details are available from the National Library of
Australia www.trove.nla.gov.au

ISBN 97 8-0-9941786-2-6

Cover illustration: Felipe Van Rompaey.
Editing: Helen Masterton, Oliver Sands.
Copy-editing & Proofreading: Bernadette Kearns.
Formatting: Oliver Sands.
Set in Times New Roman.

This is a work of fiction. Names, characters, businesses, places, events and
incidents are either the products of the author's imagination or used in a
fictitious manner. Any resemblance to actual persons, cats, rats or Pongs, living
or dead, or actual events is purely coincidental.

In loving memory of Major

WARNING!

Well now, I hope you're not picking up this book thinking it's all cute and furry and about sweet little puddycats. If you are thinking that, you should put the book down immediately and go and put on a nappy. Because this is not a sweet little story. It's a terrifying tale about rough characters and rougher places. It's scary and spooky, exciting and kooky. Just don't come crying to me when the whole thing gives you goose bumps, laughing fits, and nightmares about giant rats.

It's not like I didn't warn you.

WHAT A START!

Once upon a time, not that long ago, there was a farm deep in the middle of the countryside. This farm lay in a hollow called Dingleberry Bottom and bordered a great dark forest called The Great Dark Forest. The farm had been abandoned many years before and now its fences were mostly collapsed. Its fields, once grazed by fat dairy cows, were overgrown and full of weeds. The main gate hung at a strange angle from just one hinge and, in the night when the wind blew, its eerie creaks echoed across the yard.

Cripes, what a sight! If you or I had looked at this farm we might have thought, '*Goodness, what a desolate, dilapidated and downright decrepit dead-dairy dump.*' At least I'd have thought that, because I'm learning lots of long words and I'm up to 'D' in the dictionary. But maybe you're ahead of me? Maybe you'd have thought, '*Far out, that flipping farm is fairly forlorn, fully forgotten and frankly forever forsaken.*' And that would have been a fair conclusion. But it would have been a wrong one. **Because on this farm lived three cats.**

How the cats came to live on the farm is another adventure altogether. What I will tell you is that there had once been *four* cats living on the farm: a big ginger cat called Ginger (think you can remember that?), an athletic black cat called Tuck, a mild and mellow old mouser called

Major, and a rather precious and very furry cat called Minnie. Don't worry, you'll get to meet them all in good time, and then you'll learn who is who. At least, you'll get to meet three of them but, alas, you will not meet Major. For cool, calm, collected Major departed for Purrvana before this story begins. This, I suppose, was a happy ending for him, because Purrvana is the lovely place where dead cats go to await the ones they love. And who did Major love? Major loved Ginger. But whilst many gruesome, gruelling and grievous things were yet to happen to Ginger, at the start of this story she was still very much alive.

Ginger was an extremely experienced cat. She'd travelled all over the world and wherever she'd travelled she'd had adventures. She'd chopped chillies with children in the chillier parts of Chile. She'd played a pongy bongo wrongly in the Congo. She'd used a loudhailer to bail a whaler in Venezuela, and she'd had a seizure of amnesia in breezy Indonesia. She'd even been a world-famous street fighter. In fact, when she wasn't pining for her lost love Major, or counting all her bellies (she had a total of six), Ginger spent a lot of her time being amazed at how clever and experienced she was. The trouble was, as well as making her a bit arrogant, this also made her think of all the adventures she was now missing out on. Ginger liked life on the farm—most of the time—but it was rather quiet and boring for such an adventurous cat as herself. Unfortunately, for reasons which will soon become clear, she felt she couldn't leave.

Tuck, on the other hand, absolutely loved living on the farm. He was a very handsome black cat and could run faster than any other cat you've ever seen in your life anywhere in the world **ever**. As a result, he was an amazing hunter. Tuck's ability to catch food had helped him and Ginger survive previous adventures and—no matter what Ginger might say—it was thanks to his talents that the two cats had once crossed the Great Dark Forest and arrived at the farm in the first place.

Unfortunately, though, Tuck wasn't the brightest crayon in the box, if you know what I mean. For example, Tuck was convinced he'd been to the moon, although because he couldn't spell, he normally thought, '*Woww, I've beeeen to the moooon.*' Also, it has to be said, Tuck (with all due respect) was the biggest scaredy-cat you've ever met. He would have loved to have been a brave hero, but he was afraid of his own shadow, afraid of the dark, and even afraid of his own poo (really!). Tuck believed in King Rat, the Bogeyman *and* the Cookie Monster and he was terrified of all three of them.

Nowzen, Tuck's girlfriend, Minnie, couldn't have been more different, either in looks or in personality. Whereas Tuck was a model of manly monochrome magnificence, Minnie was a crazy confusion of all the colours a cat can be. Her mixed cultural heritage was reflected in the countless tones of her extremely long hair. If you met Minnie in the mall you might think, '*Far out sister, that's one brave choice of highlights!*' unless of course you were thinking, '*Goodness, what inappropriately* *long hair!!!*' For Minnie's fur did lead to a lot of exclamation marks. It was long all over, not only on her body, but also coming out of her ears, protruding from between her toes and sticking out all along her tail. And don't start me on the length of her whiskers. They were so long they drooped, so long they—No, I said don't start me!

Minnie had four favourite things she loved to do, and the most favourite of all of these in the world **ever** was eating. Oh boy, was this a cat that liked a snack! Minnie didn't just eat all the normal things cats like to eat, like fish and milk and cream and cat food. Oh confusing culinary concoctions, no! Minnie liked to eat **anyfink**. At least **anyfink** which could be eaten, plus a few extra things besides. She liked lime leaves and liquorice, peanuts and periwinkles, eels and erasers and, once, she even ate a piece of Tuck's tail, but we won't go into that.

Minnie's second most favourite thing to do in the world **ever** was watching television. The farmhouse had no front wall left and gaped open to the elements like a doll's house. But what it did have, amongst the dusty and dirty furniture on its open-fronted second storey, was an ancient black-and-white television. Oh, how Minnie loved that television! You didn't want to get between her and the screen when the Press Paws Network was showing *I'm A Cougar, Get Me Out Of Here*, or if *Cattyday Night Live* was on the Feline Broadcatting Company. But most of all, you didn't want to make a sound when Minnie was watching *Kitten's Got Talent*. For *Kitten's Got Talent* was the highpoint of Minnie's week. Oh, how she loved that show! She would watch it avidly, shuddering her bottom jaw at the screen and pointing out all the performers' mistakes. In fact, the nights on which Minnie watched *Kitten's Got Talent* were the quietest on the farm. Can you imagine the scene? The only noise or light for miles around coming from a black-and-white screen flickering high in the open-fronted farmhouse, making the ferrets flee and the weasels worry and the bunnies in the fields wonder what was on the sports channel.

Minnie's third most favourite thing to do in the world **ever** was taking care of her long and lustrous fur. She plaited it and braided it and cleaned it and licked it and flattened it and admired it all day long (when she wasn't sleeping or eating or watching television). It was extremely unlikely that Minnie was a princess, for she had been born under a house in a horribly rough town, but that didn't stop her behaving like one when she was doing her hair.

'Ooh, Tucky,' she might miaow in a very girly tone, 'I want some mossy mouse mousse to muss up my messy mane.'

Or, 'Tuck, darl, run and fetch me a pine cone to use as a curler.'

Or, 'Tuck, baby, I need a bit of broken mirror to check out this weave.'

It was, 'I want this,' and, 'I want that,' all day long.

And Minnie's fourth most favourite thing in the world to do **ever** was sleeping. And why did she love to sleep? Minnie loved to sleep because she loved to dream. It was the same dream every time she slept: a dream of herself as an all-singing, all-dancing entertainment superstar. Fame! Glory! Mirrors with light bulbs around them! Sometimes Minnie dreamed so hard she sang and danced in her sleep, imagining crowds screaming her name and begging for a pawtograph. Oh, poor Minnie. Every day she awoke to find herself on a dirty, deserted and derelict dairy farm was a dreadful and dreary disappointment.

As you can see, the three cats who lived on the farm each had very different personalities and, as a result, they didn't always get along. In fact, on the day this story starts, Minnie and Ginger had the most terrible fight. Soon afterwards they forgot all about it, what with all the other craziness going on. Later, however, when they looked back, they realised this fight was the start of all the adventures that followed.

WHAT A FIGHT!

Now, before I tell you about Minnie and Ginger's big fight, I have to explain to you the importance of the smokehouse. The smokehouse was Ginger's idea, and she had it during the first winter the cats spent on the farm. Oh dicey icicles, what a terrible time that had been! It was a horribly long and cold winter with deep, deep snow and the cats had all gone very hungry. Tuck might be the best of hunters, but when winter comes and the ground is covered in snow, a black cat is not at an advantage. He knew where the squirrels hid their winter stores, but, being a polite cat, he knew never to touch anyone else's nuts. So that winter, the poor pussies had to resort to dreadful measures to survive. They took turns licking an old can of cooking oil they found in the barn. They nibbled on a dead bat that had fallen to the floor of the stables. They even lived off the whiff of an oily rag for a few days. But, on other days, there was nothing at all and the cats had to satisfy themselves with sniffing each other's bums.

'Next winter,' Ginger had promised them, when even Minnie was as skinny as a long, thin thingy, 'we'll be better prepared.'

As ever, Ginger was true to her word. She realised that every winter would be as bad unless they found a way of preserving some of the food they caught over the warmer months. There was no freezer on the farm, and so the cats couldn't preserve their food that way. But did you know that smoke, if handled carefully, preserves meat just as well?

Ginger got the idea of what to do from sniffing around the only building on the farm that wasn't a ruin. It was a small round brick building with a slate-grey roof, and it stood on the edge of the farmyard beside the stables. Ginger could tell by its smell it had once been used for smoking meat and—**bingo!**—that's when she had her idea. As soon as spring came, she convinced some hard-rocking fireflies to hold a party over some kindling she'd prepared inside the little building. And boy, did those fireflies like to party! They were mad, bad, and dangerous to glow. They buzzed and shone and sparked until the whole place was *smoking*. From that day on, the 'funny, round brick building' became 'the smokehouse', always chuffing away and leaking a thin trail of smoke into the sky. All Ginger had to do after that was make sure every time any of the cats caught some food, there was always a portion put aside and preserved for winter. All through spring and summer the system worked well, but in the last days of autumn, Ginger began to grow suspicious. Every so often, she would hear a noise from inside the smokehouse which sounded like someone moving around in there. Who else would it be, she thought, but Minnie? She could just imagine Minnie mooching for a munch of mouse mortadella, or rustling away a rabbit rarebit. She had even discovered a loose brick in the smokehouse wall. The only trouble was, by the time Ginger had ever trotted her six bellies over and opened the door, there was never anything to see. Nothing, but all the food stored for winter, smoking nicely and sending off a lovely aroma which even she found difficult to resist.

But then, on the day this story starts (which—thank you for your patience—is **right now!**), Ginger figured she'd caught Minnie red-pawed. Or, as cats like to say, with her head stuck in the cat-food tin.

It was the very last day of autumn, when a cold wind was blowing, and all but the stubbornest leaves had fallen from the trees. Late in the afternoon, Ginger was walking between the smokehouse and the ruined stables when she heard, yet again, a noise from the round brick building. This time there was no doubt about it. That noise was Minnie.

'Mm, push, two, three, four,' Ginger heard. 'Mm, push, six, seven, eight.'

'Jumping junipers,' thought Ginger. 'I've caught her at it at last!'

And without a second thought (which is always the better one in my experience), she ran around the building. There, on the other side, she found Minnie, leaning with her two front paws against the warm brick wall.

'Gotcha!' shouted Ginger. 'I knew you were nipping in and nicking num-nums. Just try and deny it!'

'You what?' gasped Minnie, who was clearly out of breath. 'Deny what?'

Well, the innocent look on Minnie's face would have

befuddled almost anyone who thought they'd caught her doing something naughty. Unless, of course, they'd met her before. For, as anyone who *has* met Minnie will tell you, the wide-eyed innocent look is her speciality: 'Me? Lick that trifle? Oh no, officer.' Ginger was unimpressed.

'You've been stealing from the winter stores,' she growled.

'How dare you?!' said Minnie. 'I haven't been takin' any food, **akcherly**.'

As you will have noticed, Minnie's spelling became somewhat haphazard when she was upset.

'Oo put you in charge, any'ow?' she continued. 'You're such an arrogant, 'orrible old moggy, I'm surprised any of us ever listens to you at all.'

Ginger flicked her tail and stared at Minnie.

'So what *were* you doing, then?' she asked with a gingery smirk on her face. She was looking forward to Minnie trying to talk her way out of this one.

'I was exercising, innit? Working out. Unlike *you*, Ginge, I take pride in my appearance. This might surprise you, but I was Miss Junior Slums 2014, the **bestest**-looking cat in my school.'

'What surprises me,' growled Ginger, 'is that you went to school at all. Do you really expect me to believe you ever do any exercise? Is that the best you can come up with?'

'Aggh!' screamed Minnie, with the 'G' pronounced. 'Nag, nag, nag, you make me want to gag, you craggy old scrag-bag. You're just a sad saggy dag, like a hag in raggedy-drag.'

Across the farmyard, in the open-fronted farmhouse, Tuck was cleaning the television for that night's viewing of Minnie's favourite show.

'*Uh-oh*,' he thought, as the noise of the argument reached him. '*I better go and break that up.*'

And he wasn't wrong. By the time he had taken off his apron, gone downstairs, remembered what he was hurrying off to do, started hurrying again, crossed the farmyard, gone past the stables and remembered where the smokehouse was, Ginger and Minnie were having a proper old catfight, spitting and scratching and tumbling through the windblown leaves in a screaming furry ball.

'Stop it,' said Tuck quietly.

He was, after all, a rather unassuming cat. Minnie and Ginger ignored him.

'That food's for the winter,' Ginger screeched as she and Minnie tumbled past Tuck one way.

'Please stop it,' said Tuck a little louder.

But he was drowned out by Minnie snarling, ''Oo made you the boss?' as she and Ginger tumbled back the other way.

'Stop it now!' Tuck said a little louder still.

'I could be off travelling and having adventures if I didn't have to make sure your ugly face got fed over winter,' Ginger spat as she and Minnie tumbled back the first way again.

'I could be a star if I didn't have to live on this boring farm with boring you and your boring rules,' miaowed

Minnie as she and Ginger tumbled back towards Tuck again.

'STOP IT!!!' Tuck yelled.

Well, that surprised all three of them. It wasn't often you heard Tuck yell anything, let alone in capital letters. Minnie and Ginger stopped fighting and, panting and feeling grotty all over, sat glowering at each other.

'Enough,' said Tuck. Then he couldn't think of anything else to say, so he said 'Enough,' again because it had sounded quite good the first time.

'It's 'er fault,' said Minnie. 'Accusing me of all sorts.'

'It's—'

But Ginger never finished her sentence. Instead she put her head on one side, pricked up her ears and listened carefully. Then she sat up straight, the wind blowing her fur up from behind as she stared down the overgrown driveway.

Tuck followed her stare and gasped. And, then, last of all, Minnie also turned and saw what had left Ginger lost for words.

WHATEVER NEXT?

Old MacDonald had a farm, ee-ay ee-ay oh!
Then Old MacDonald lost an arm, ee-ay, ee-ay, eugh!
With a spurt-spurt here, and a spurt-spurt there,
Old MacDonald died of blood loss, ee-ay ee—aw, that's
sad.

Now, I know what you're thinking. You're thinking I've lost the plot and started making up gruesome versions of nursery rhymes instead. But fear not, dear reader. The plot is still exactly where I left it (unless it's down the back of the sofa again), and it wasn't I who changed the nursery rhyme, it was the nasty children who, years before, had lived near the farm. And why did they do this? Because what they described in their horribly insensitive manner was the truth. The farmer who had once farmed the farm was, indeed, called MacDonald and he was, indeed, old. But he was not old and wise. Oh dimming dementia, no! Old MacDonald was a bit stupid actually, and he believed you could operate farm machinery without taking due precautions. This is how he lost his arm, and it is also—I hasten to add—how he came to die. I'd love to tell you all the gory details, but it's a long and gruesome tale which we really don't have time for. You'll just have to make do with the moral of the story: never keep your phone in a pocket you can only reach with one hand.

Anyhoo, once Old MacDonald died, the farm—as I may have mentioned—fell into wrack and ruin. The old milking shed crumbled and became overgrown with weeds; holes formed in the sides and the roof of the stables, and the farmhouse lost its entire front wall. Only the smokehouse survived intact. No one ever visited, not even the postman. No one ever popped in, for few people knew the farm still existed. And almost no one ever drove by, for the nearest road to the farm was a quiet road with nothing much else of interest on it. In fact, the farm was so incredibly quiet and forlorn that it was easy for a cat living there to forget human beings and cars and cities even existed.

So, can you imagine Minnie and Ginger and Tuck's surprise as they now watched a very large, high-sided truck driving towards them down the overgrown driveway? At first they stood dumbstruck, failing to believe their eyes. Then they all spoke at the same time.

'Run!' miaowed Minnie.

'Hide!' hissed Ginger.

'Mummy!' squealed Tuck.

Then the three of them bumped into each other as they got confused about which way to run and hide and cry for their mummies.

'Quick!' said Minnie. 'Let's get inside the smokehouse. Ginger, where's the key?'

'I don't have it on me,' said Ginger slyly. 'Maybe there's another way in?'

'What about the stables?' said Tuck. 'Let's run in there instead!'

Well, Minnie and Ginger didn't even respond. Instead they both turned and bolted for the nearest hole in the stables' wall. The hole was the shape and size of a cat holding a bazooka, and first Ginger and then Minnie jumped through as quickly as they could. But what's faster than a fat and a fearful cat? An athletic and fearful Tuck, that's what. He'd got inside the stables so quickly I didn't even have time to describe it.

'Ooh, ooh, ooh,' he said to Ginger and Minnie as they landed either side of him. 'What if it's King Rat come to eat us all?'

Ginger rolled her eyes and licked her chest coolly, as if she too hadn't just bolted in.

'Tuck,' she said. 'King Rat doesn't exist, and, even if he did, I doubt he'd drive a human-size truck. Come on, let's go up to the gable window and see what this is all about.'

'Don't want to!' Tuck miaowed sadly. 'I want to run and hide and be safe.'

'Safe all alone?' said Minnie. 'Good luck with that. We're going upstairs.'

Aw, bad luck Tuck. The only thing he hated more than Minnie and Ginger fighting was when Minnie and Ginger ganged up on him. He looked around fearfully at the stables and thought they had never looked *less* safe. High above he could see the huge hole in the roof, and high above that the top of the giant oak tree that stood outside, its branches whipping back and forth in the late autumn wind. All around him, dead leaves rustled in the shadows, like creatures waiting to bite him on the bum. Unsure of what to do, he looked back at Ginger and Minnie and saw they'd started climbing up an old plank to the remains of the attic above.

'Wait for me!' he yowled. 'I want to go up to the gable window and see what this is all about!'

Well, needless to say, Tuck was first to arrive at the little round window built into the wall facing the farmyard. As he stared through it, fearful of how high up he now was, the gigantic human-sized truck pulled up below him. Pumping pistons, it was loud! **Chugger, chugger, chugger** it went, belching black smoke out its two huge exhaust pipes and vibrating like a giant metal jelly.

'Ooh,' said Tuck. 'It's so big.'

'Let me see,' said Minnie coming up behind him and pushing in on his right for a look through the window.

'I need to see it too,' said Ginger, squeezing in on his left to get the best view.

Minnie pushed in harder on the right and Ginger pushed in harder on the left and soon poor Tuck found himself unable to move at all. Which was probably quite fortunate for otherwise he would have soon run away from the horrible sight unfolding in the farmyard below.

'Ooh, eugh, eek,' he said. 'It's so horrible and ugly!'

Tuck had not seen many humans in his life, so the sight of the tall, pale, skinny man who now climbed out of the giant truck's cabin was quite a shock to him. As I'm sure it would be to you too if you were used to cute and furry animals about the same size as you.

'Agh!' he said. 'It is King Rat!'

'Oh shush, Tucky, it's just a human,' said Minnie.

'It's a man,' said Ginger, keen to show her expertise. 'And *that* is a woman.'

She was talking about the short and dumpy person who was climbing her way down from the driver's door of the truck, scratching her ribs and, once she'd arrived safely on the ground, rubbing her nose on the sleeve of her pullover.

'Humans normally find me perfectly adorable,' said Minnie. 'Maybe they'll take me in and love me and let me share their bed.'

'Ssh,' said Ginger. 'Watch.'

For the two humans had opened a door in the trailer behind the truck's cabin and were now pulling out long pieces of wood. They were clearly chatting and laughing as they did this, but their voices were inaudible over the chugging of the truck's engine. The wind blew its exhaust fumes towards the stables until the three cats' noses were full of nothing but its stink. Tuck, with better eyes than either Ginger or Minnie, was fascinated by what he'd seen inside the trailer. For past the pieces of wood, attached to the far wall, he thought he'd seen a row of cages. And for a split second he thought he saw a shadow inside the cage opposite the door. A black shadow with four legs.

Once the humans had taken all the wood, a ladder, and a toolbox out of the truck, they slammed the door shut and started hammering the pieces of wood together into a huge wooden structure. When it got too tall for them to work on from the ground, the man held the ladder for the woman to climb to the very top of the construction so she could bang with a hammer up there too. Thud, thud, thud went the hammer; chug, chug, chug went the big truck's engine, on and on and on for so long that Tuck began to feel quite sleepy. It was, after all, rather warm and cosy with Ginger on one side and Minnie on the other. He even closed his eyes for a second and thought maybe this wasn't so scary after all—unless he'd suddenly become extremely brave and no one had thought to tell him. Then he opened his eyes again and was amazed to see the humans had stopped hammering and building and banging and were now unfurling an enormous roll of paper between them. As Tuck watched, the woman climbed the ladder again and stuck the piece of paper to the front of the wooden frame. Then, without so much as a cursory look at the farm, the two humans gave each other a high five, jumped back into the truck, reversed it over the brick-paved farmyard, turned and **chug**, **chug**, **chugged** up the driveway and away towards the road. The silence they left behind them was such a sudden surprise that, for a while, even the leaves forgot to rustle in the wind.

It was ten minutes before Ginger and Minnie dared to leave the stables, and another ten minutes after that before Tuck dared to join them. He found them sitting side by side, staring up at the huge wooden structure the humans had left behind. It was shaped like a flat screen on giant wooden legs.

'Is it a cinema?' said Tuck. 'Just for us?'

'It's a billboard,' said Ginger, her lips moving slowly as she read the human writing.

Tuck asked Minnie what the billboard said, but Minnie was silent for a while before admitting she'd skipped school the day they learned to read as there had been an important beauty contest on. Now, both Tuck and Ginger knew this was a complete lie. Minnie was a very good reader, but she was far too vain to ever wear her glasses. Ginger rolled her eyes, then read aloud what was written on the sign:

LAND ACQUIRED
Dingleberry Bottom Farm has been acquired on behalf of Pong's Pet Products
Construction work to start next week
No trespassers, no hawkers, no poppers-in and absolutely no animals!

'No animals!' said Tuck. 'But what about the poor bunnies in the fields?'

'Bother the bunnies,' said Minnie. 'What about us?

'Ooh, ooh,' said Tuck, running around in a circle. 'What about us? What about us!! Ginger, what are we going to do?'

'What we are *not* going to do is panic,' said Ginger calmly. 'It looks like we're going to have company, and human company at that. But that could be a good thing.'

'Hang on!' said Minnie. 'Pong's Pet Products? They make those new Pongs Party Pies for Pets? You know, like the adverts on the telly?'

Much to Ginger and Tuck's surprise, Minnie burst into song:

> *'Put down a Pong pie for your pussy or pooch,*
> *And they will thank you very, very mooch!'*

'Oh, this is fabulous news,' she said. 'Humans with pet food. Oh, they're going to love me so **mooch!**'

'But on the other paw,' said Ginger, narrowing her eyes, 'it does say "no animals".'

Well, that shut Minnie up, which at least had the effect of improving Ginger's mood.

'Come on,' said Ginger, 'let's get inside. It's getting dark and there's nothing we can do about it now.'

'Getting dark?!' said Minnie, noticing the fading sky above them. 'Flippin 'eck, what's the time?! Oh no! Oh no, no, no, no. I mustn't miss *Kitten's Got Talent*, not tonight of all bloomin' nights!'

And with that she ran towards the house, even faster than she'd run for the stables. Oh, Minnie in flight—what a fur-filled and magnificent sight.

Watching her go, Ginger shook her head, sighed and padded back to the smokehouse. But Tuck sat where he was as the evening grew dark around him, staring up at the sign and wondering why a pet food company wouldn't like animals.

WHAT A PALAVER!

Minnie stared anxiously at the tiny white dot in the middle of the television screen. As I may have mentioned, the television set was pretty ancient and—as you may or may not know—in the old days (when your grandparents were young and everything was in black-and-white), televisions didn't click on instantly like they do today. Oh woeful wait-times, no! You had to sit around picking your nose until they'd warmed up. Yes, really! And, as there were no cables or satellite dishes; to get a picture you had to keep rearranging the metal aerial that stuck out the top of the television set. Oh yes, you did! If you don't believe me, ask an old person—quickly before they die.

Bennyway, while the television was warming up, Minnie herself was cooling down. As darkness had fallen, the wind that had blown across the countryside through the Great Dark Forest and into the farm all day had grown even stronger and even colder. Minnie bristled her thick fur and stared at the screen as at last it came to life.

'That's right, toms and queens,' said a voice from the television, 'you'll want to make a beeline for this feline, for it's time to meet the host who can boast the most. Put your paws together because heeeeeeeeeeere's Mickey!'

The screen blurred as the camera panned across an audience of screaming young cats to the host of *Kitten's*

Got Talent, a Manx cat called Mickey Manx. Now, Manx cats have ridiculously short tails and are very rare outside the Isle of Man. Maybe it was this exoticism that explained Mickey Manx's appeal, or maybe it was his perfect grey stripes and his glittering white teeth. He was very popular with a lot of cats, particularly female cats, and *especially* particularly with female cats who watched television.

'Hello Mickey,' Minnie purred under her breath.

'Hello out there,' Mickey Manx said to the camera and Minnie felt the same little thrill she felt every week. As if Mickey Manx were talking to no other cat in the world but her.

'And let's not forget folks,' Micky Manx was saying in his dank accent, 'tonight is a big, big night for some of you out there …'

'Yes, it is!' said Minnie.

'… because tonight's the night when we—'

Just then a gust of wind blew through the room, bringing with it big crunchy leaves and even a few fair-sized twigs from the oak tree that stood over by the stables. Most of these rattled onto the floor in front of the television set, but one of them smashed into the aerial on top of it. Minnie held her breath as the screen went blank, then exhaled loudly as it came back to life again, although in a furrier and fuzzier version than before.

'But first,' Mickey Manx was saying, 'let's meet our opening act. All the way from the coast, it's a trapeze act with a difference, it's—'

Again the screen went blank. Only this time—as Minnie stared in disbelief—it stayed blank.

Now, I don't know if you've ever visited the Chinese opera, or set off a car alarm, or put an accordion in a blender, but if you can imagine a combination of all three of those things, then you can imagine the noise which now came out of Minnie.

'**MIIIAAAOOOOUUUUEEEEEWWWW!** Agh! Help!' she screamed. 'Tuck, help, help, help!!!'

Tuck was still near the bottom of the driveway staring up at the sign, but when he heard Minnie's horrendous scream, he bolted for the farmhouse, shot up the stairs and tore into the television room. For although Tuck was a very cowardly cat, he always forgot his fear if others were in danger.

'What is it?' he asked Minnie. 'Are the leaves getting dangerous? Did King Rat decide he does exist after all? Are you having a nervous breakdance?'

'It's worse than all them **fings** combined,' cried Minnie. 'The telly's not working.'

Then, thinking Tuck looked relieved, she started to sob loudly, struggling to speak through her tears.

'Most important … *sniff* … night of the year … my big chance … *sniff* … nobody loves me or ever has … *sniff* … if only we could get the aerial working … *sniff* …'

'I love you,' said Tuck. 'You know I do.'

'Oh good,' said Minnie, suddenly not crying or sniffing at all. 'Well 'urry up and fix the aerial then. C'mon, darl, look lively! Just jump up there, that's it. Then hold it up, that's it! Yes! Yes!!!'

As Tuck jumped up and rearranged the aerial, the

television screen once again flickered to life. Immediately Minnie was transfixed, the screen's black-and-white images reflected in her eyes.

'Can I stop now?' Tuck asked after a few minutes. He was balanced on three legs, his fourth one hooked around the base of the aerial whilst his tail pushed against it to stop it from toppling.

'No!' said Minnie gruffly. 'Look at this double act, they're dreadful. I don't know what they did to their hair stylist but, OMG, the revenge is 'orrible. Gasp! They're so off-key!'

Tuck said nothing for another minute or two, listening to the singing from the television below him. Then he said, 'This isn't very comfortable, actually. Can I stop please? The wind's blowing up my bum and it makes me want to sneeze.'

Minnie ignored him. She was giggling at the caterwauls from the *Kitten's Got Talent* studio audience as it responded to the act on stage. Suddenly the audience was interrupted by Mickey Manx's Isle of Man accent.

'Ho, ho, ho, dearie me, I think that's a resounding 'No' from the audience. I did warn you, they're a catty bunch! But, anyway folks, this is the moment you've all been waiting for. This is the moment when we tell all of you out there in your dull and dreary little world, if you'll be joining us in the glamorous exciting fun-filled world of show business. Here comes the list. We're ready to—'

'Achoo!' sneezed Tuck.

And then, because he never sneezed once, 'Achoo! Achoo!'

Tuck heard a strange rattling noise and looked down to see that he'd dropped the aerial onto the floor.

'**NOOOOOO!!!** No, Tuck, go back to 'ow you were, go back to 'ow you were! Why are you ruining my life?'

'You have to say "Bless you",' said Tuck. 'It's only polite.'

'Fix the furballing aerial, you moron!' screamed Minnie, which – you have to admit – doesn't sound like 'Bless you' in any language. But then Minnie must have seen something in Tuck's face, because she quickly said, 'I mean bless you, bless you, bless you times a thousand. Oh, Tuck, please, you're not a moron, I am. But please, please, pretty-please with cheese on top, please fix the aerial.'

Well, Tuck might hate being called stupid—or dumb, or an idiot, or a moron—or anything which implied he was nearly as academically ungifted as he really was, but he did also really adore Minnie. So he jumped down from the television set, picked up the aerial in his teeth, and jumped back up again.

'Even better!' said Minnie. 'The picture's perfect now. Whatever you do, don't blooming move!'

Bad luck Tuck! Now he had to stand with the aerial clutched between his teeth, looking like a rather tacky cat-shaped aerial you might find in a novelty television accessory store.

'Oh, oh, oh!' said Minnie, popping the reading glasses she was normally too vain to wear onto the end of her nose. 'Sssh!!'

Tuck stared down at her and saw, reflected in her lenses, a long list of writing scrolling on the television screen.

'Mmf,' he said, the aerial clutched between his teeth.

'Ssshhh!' said Minnie. 'I'm reading… oh, they're up to 'R' already. Tiddles Ridell, Fluffy Rifferty, Felix Rimmington. Here it comes… wait… YES!!!!! OH MY COD!!! Oh, did you see, did you see?'

Tuck *thought* Minnie was talking to him, but he wasn't completely sure. For one thing, there was no way she could expect him to have seen anything on the television screen very well. And, for another, she knew he couldn't read. And for yet another on top of that, she was dancing around the room, with her glasses fallen to the floor, and leaves flying up into the air around her. Maybe she was having a nervous breakdance after all?

'Whoopee!' she was screaming. 'Woohoo! Oh, Tucky, Tucky, I did it!'

'Mmf,' said Tuck, and he said it again and again until at last Minnie calmed down and told him he could drop the aerial now.

'I don't understand,' he said as she danced him around the room, closer to the open front of the house than he was comfortable with. 'What happened?'

'Oh, it's so exciting!' said Minnie, twirling him around and around, closer and closer to the drop to the farmyard. Then she stopped suddenly, and a strange glow appeared in her eyes.

'Oh, let's go and tell Ginger!' she said. 'I can't wait to see the look on *her* face.'

Without another word she turned on her heels and ran to the top of the staircase.

'Come on,' she said mischievously. 'I want an audience for this.'

WHAT A
NASTY NIGHT!

Outside the open-fronted farmhouse, the wind was bolder and colder than ever. Tuck realised the heat from the old black-and-white television set had been keeping him warm while he held the aerial for Minnie. He also realised the brightness of the television screen had disguised what an inky-black night it was outside. There was only a slither of moon high above.

'Ooh, what a nasty night,' he miaowed after Minnie. 'Let's go back inside and be snuggly.'

Minnie turned and narrowed her eyes at him. With the violent wind blowing her fur in all directions, she looked like a tangle of tights in a tumble dryer.

'Don't be silly, Tuck,' she said. 'It's only a bit of wind. Let's go and see if Ginge is in the stables.'

But it wasn't only a bit of wind; at least, Tuck didn't think so. For one thing, it was full of all the smells of the Great Dark Forest. It smelled of foxes and wild dogs and snakes and badgers and ferrets and weasels and all sorts of cat-eating monsters. And it was full of leaves and twigs too, not to mention grit, which got into Tuck's eyes and made them sting. Things weren't much better when he and Minnie reached the stables, for although there was less wind between the broken stable walls, there were far more leaves and—worst of all—thousands of shadows that danced and leapt as the huge oak tree overhead bent back and forth in the wind.

'Ginge!' called Minnie. 'Ere, Ginge, want to 'ear somefink exciting?'

But Ginger wasn't in the stables. Not downstairs in the stalls—which still smelled of horses after all these years— nor upstairs in the creaking attic where she normally liked to sleep at night.

'Maybe she's gone to a nightclub,' said Tuck. 'Let's go back to the farmhouse and tell her in the morning.'

'Nah,' said Minnie. 'She'll be in the barn.'

The barn was the largest building still standing on Dingleberry Bottom Farm. It stood across the farmyard from the stables, but was so riddled with woodworm and damp and damage that it leant backwards at a steep angle, like it was waiting for one good push to topple it over. The cats generally avoided going inside in case it fell over and squashed them.

'Oh, do we have to go to the barn?' said Tuck. 'Isn't she more likely to be at the smokehouse?'

'Of course!' said Minnie. 'The smokehouse! I'll bet she's guarding the blooming stores, marching back and forth with a gun on her shoulder like it's the crown jewels or somefink. Come on!'

Poor Tuck! He was totally terrified by the storm blowing around them, but had no choice other than to follow Minnie even further away from the farmhouse and into the grassy shadows south of the stables. He'd forgotten about the visit by the humans, and when he saw the huge wooden structure they had left behind, he screamed out loud.

'It's a giant monster!' he yelled. 'It's a—

'Billboard,' said Minnie. 'Remember? Try and keep up, darl, you'll miss the show.'

But when they arrived at the smokehouse, there was no show to be had. For although they both walked all the way around the little brick building, Ginger was nowhere in sight.

'That's strange,' said Tuck, forgetting his fear for a second. 'Normally I'm out hunting by now, and Ginger always waits for me to bring the food here first. Oh, I'm not supposed to tell you that.'

But Minnie wasn't listening. She was staring at the smokehouse door with a huge grin on her face.

'I know where Ginger is,' she said. 'Look!'

As we all know, the door to the smokehouse was normally kept tightly locked, but not on this windswept and inky-black night. When is a door not a door? When it's ajar.

'Ginger!'

It was Tuck who called this time. He couldn't explain how he knew it, but he knew something was wrong. It was as if he could smell it, or—he suddenly realised—not smell it.

'Ginger?'

He walked over and pulled the door open, the noise of its rusty hinges competing with the creaking of the oak tree over the stables. As he did so, there was a gap in the clouds crossing the moon, and both he and Minnie gasped at the moonlit sight which met their eyes.

WHAT A DISCOVERY!

Brace yourselves!

Because if you want to know what had happened to Ginger, we need a flashback so we can go back in time. Not very far, don't worry. No fancy costumes and horse-drawn carriages, we just have to go back a couple of hours to when Minnie ran into the farmhouse to turn on the television, and Tuck stayed back to look up at the sign, and the light faded from the sky. Whilst all of that was going on, Ginger walked slowly back to the smokehouse. The fight she'd had with Minnie had bothered her, and she wanted to have a good think about it. Not that she was upset at a bit of fisticuffs. Oh flying furballs, no—she was an ex-street fighter, after all! Nor was she upset that Minnie had fooled her. No, in fact the opposite was the problem. For Minnie's reactions to her accusations had convinced Ginger that Minnie was, for once, telling the truth.

Now you might wonder how on earth Ginger could be so sure, but let's not forget what a clever and experienced cat she was. After all, you don't get to be the first ginger cat in history to win the National Poker Championships without knowing when someone's bluffing. So, as soon as their fight was over, Ginger knew Minnie had been neither stealing, nor planning to steal, from the smokehouse. This bothered her for two reasons. Firstly, if Minnie had not removed a brick from the back of the smokehouse wall, then who had? And secondly, if Minnie was not on a fitness regime so she could squeeze through the smallest possible hole, then why was she on a fitness regime?

It was as Ginger was pondering these two questions that Minnie let out her pitiful howl because a windblown twig had knocked down the TV aerial and stopped her watching *Kitten's Got Talent*. From her vantage point outside the smokehouse, Ginger could clearly see what had happened. She rolled her eyes, sighed a big gingery sigh, and turned to walk along the long and crumbling stable wall which ran away from the farmyard. Ginger didn't mind Minnie laughing at her and teasing her about how strict she was—without the food store they would all starve to death—but she hated seeing how Minnie took advantage of Tuck. After all, if anyone should take advantage of Tuck, it should be Ginger herself and—

But whatever Ginger was about to think next was blown away by the full force of the wind as she rounded the back of the stables. Winter, she realised, was even closer than she'd thought. There was snow on the way, and she thanked her lucky stars—not to mention her forward planning—that there was enough meat in the smokehouse to get them through it alive. But then Ginger smelled something strange on the wind: something eerie and unsettling. It was the smell of change. She shivered and ran to shelter behind the ruins of the old milking shed. Ginger closed her eyes and curled up tight. In the distance she could hear Minnie's television with that manky Manx and his too-tight pants. Then the wind came through the forest again. She heard dry leaves crackling in the air, twigs clattering as they fell onto the stables and the loud whisper of something saying 'Push it!'

The voice shook Ginger out of her thoughts. She pricked up her ears even more than normal (which is a lot for a cat, considering how upright their ears always are) and listened carefully. Crackle, crisp, crunch went the leaves. Rattle, tumble, tattle went the twigs.

'I am blooming well pushing it, aren't I, so?' said a second whispery voice.

Ginger cautiously opened one eye; then she cautiously opened the other one; and, moving only her head, looked all around her. There was nothing in sight to account for the voices, but even so she heard the first one again as it grunted, 'Well, push harder then.'

The whispers were coming from beyond the ruined wall Ginger was leaning against, inside the tumbled remains of the old milking shed. Even more cautiously Ginger stood up, turned and jumped onto the top of the wall. As she did so, she dislodged a bit of crumbled brick.

'What was that?' whispered the second voice. 'Did ye hear something there?'

'I did not, so. Will you please push this thing?!'

'I'll push if you— There it was again! I heard something!'

And the second voice was right: its owner had heard something. For Ginger, who had never been particularly light on her paws, was creeping slowly along the wall. Still she couldn't see the source of the voices, but her ears—not to mention her feline sixth sense—told her she was moving in the right direction. On and on she crept, guided along by squeaky grunts and what sounded like something heavy being pushed along the ground. Then, at last, as she climbed over a particularly high-jutting brick, she saw them. Three rats! Three big, fat, squeaky rats. Except, as Ginger looked again, she realised the middle one wasn't a rat at all. Oh round rodents, no! It was a lumpy bag, which the two rats—who actually *were* rats—were pushing (from behind) and pulling (from the front) along the ground.

'Now there's something you don't see every day,' thought Ginger.

And she decided to sit and watch and see what she could learn before she had the rats for an extra helping of dinner (minus a portion for the smokehouse).

'Listen to me, Fleabomb,' said the first rat. 'If you don't push this thing, we're never going to get it back to the boat, and the others will go without us and, more importantly, they'll go without paying us, so they will. They managed all the other bags, I can't see why you can't push this one. What's wrong with you?'

'Please keep yer voice down, Bumfluff,' said the rat called Fleabomb. 'Ye know full well there are cats living here. What if they hear us? This being the last one, that's when it happens, ye know. No one ever stole anything after they were killed.'

Ginger heard the rat called Bumfluff sigh a ratty raspy sigh.

'The quicker yer push, yer eejit, the quicker we'll be out of here with the loot. So just *push*.'

Ginger let the two rats and their heavy load get another metre through the ruins of the milking shed. They were working their way towards an old oil sump which sat beneath a pile of twisted machinery. Then, just as the rats were about to disappear into the field beyond, she leapt.

Now, as you no doubt know by now, if Tuck had been in this scene, he'd have caught those two rats in a jiffy, killing them so quickly it would make you feel squiffy. But Ginger was not nearly as fit, nor as athletic, as Tuck. In fact, she was as dumpy and lumpy as a flump with the mumps, and as she jumped, her rump bumped an old milk pump with a harrumphing thump which sent the two grumpy humpers running past the sump before Ginger could catch even a clump of them.

'Aw, rats!' she said to herself, blushing in the dark at having let them get away. She licked her tail, just to remind herself who was in charge, and then she wrinkled her nose. **Mmmmmm**, something smelled **goooooood**. She wrinkled her nose again and, following its lead, stepped towards the bag the rats had been heaving away. It smelled like dried lark shanks. Ginger put out a paw and opened the mouth of the bag. It *was* dried lark shanks! And she'd thought she was the only cat in these parts who knew how to prepare those. She had a few in the smokehouse and—

Hang on a **secondominium**! Something here smelled fishy, and it certainly wasn't the contents of the bag.

Ginger closed the bag again and sniffed the ground along which it had been dragged. The trail was easy enough to smell, and as Ginger sniffed her way along it, she moved deeper and deeper into the overgrown ruins of the milking shed until soon she found herself inside a bit of a tunnel. On and on Ginger sniffed until suddenly the sky opened above her, and she found she was no longer under the ruins at all: she was in the overgrown patch of field behind the smokehouse. And yet, still the trail didn't fail. In fact, if anything it got stronger. Now it wasn't just lark shanks she could smell. There was a whiff of wilted worms, an odour of offal hors d'oeuvres, even a pong of pickled parrot. Ginger followed the trail on and on, right up to the backmost wall of the smokehouse, right up to the hole she'd discovered that afternoon.

'No!' she miaowed aloud. 'No, no, no, no!'

And without a second thought (or a sixth 'no'), she ran at full speed around to the smokehouse's front door. Struggling to remain calm she found the right key, dropped it twice, then jammed it into the lock and turned. But when she did so, you know what she saw? The smokehouse was empty! All the dried stores—all of the cats' canapés for the coming winter—were gone!

'Rats!' said Ginger, in a very different tone from the one she'd used ten minutes before. 'Rats!!!'

And with that she ran back the way she'd come. Back outside, back around to the hole in the wall, back into the tunnel under the ruined milking shed, back along the winding path towards the sump. And did she stop at the dark bag of lark shanks? Blistering bags of booty, no. Because the bag of lark shanks had now disappeared too.

'Rats!' said Ginger for a fourth time.

Then she put her nose to the ground again and followed the trail on past the sump, across the overgrown fields, and towards the Great Dark Forest.

WHAT A THING
TO SAY!

That night Tuck and Minnie had such a fierce and frightening fight that it drowned out the noise of the storm outside. Even the bunnies, sheltering wearily from the wind in their warm dry warrens, heard Tuck and Minnie's screams and shouts and—not for the first time—wondered what had happened to the neighbourhood.

Tuck and Minnie's fight erupted outside the smokehouse, snarled across the blowy farmyard, growled into the farmhouse, hissed up the stairs through each open-fronted storey and ended up screaming and shouting in the house's attic. Unlike the roof of the stables, the roof of the farmhouse was completely intact, and it was up here that Tuck and Minnie generally spent the night. The attic was normally warm and always dry and, best of all, contained an old chest of drawers full of Old MacDonald's winter clothes. Tuck and Minnie shared the middle drawer, and it was as Minnie jumped up into this drawer that the fight reached its peak. Until now, it had just been two cats bickering about what they had seen in the smokehouse. But here, with Minnie exhausted, unfed and desperate for bed, and Tuck feeling guilty for being inside, the fight turned nasty. Now, to you or me—or your average rabbit—Tuck and Minnie's fight would have sounded like screeching and yowling and meowling and hissing. But cat language is far more subtle than that. There's a huge difference between a hiss and *a hiss*, after all.

'She'll be fine' said Minnie for the hundredth time. 'Don't you worry about Ginge. If ever there was a moggy what could look after herself, it's that big bossy boots.'

'How can you say that?' said Tuck, aghast. 'Something terrible must have happened. Someone must have—'

'Tuck, please. She's fine. Don't be silly.'

'I'm not being silly.'

'You are being silly; you're being silly and stupid. Please let me go to bed.'

Uh-oh. Can anyone see Minnie's strategic error here? Don't ever tell Tuck he's stupid.

'Well,' he hissed (as opposed to *hissed*), 'at least I'm not lazy and lumpy and losing my looks! You're bigger than Ginger's ever been!'

Minnie, who had lain down to go to sleep, now jumped up on all fours again, her fur standing up on end. Or, at least as 'on end,' as it ever got, what with it being very long and rather heavy.

'You take that back!' she screamed at Tuck. 'You take that back this second.'

'No. Shan't. Can't make me, won't do it, na-ah, no!'

'No?' Minnie looked like she was going to choke. 'No?! 'ow … 'ow dare you. I didn't crawl my way from under a house, I didn't escape from a cattery, I didn't risk life and limb to come to this dump of a farm to have someone say 'no' to me. I could have been … I could have been …'

'Thinner?'

'A star!' said Minnie. 'I 'ad the looks, I 'ad the voice; Cod nose, I 'ad the ambition. And now look at my life. **AOEIOOOH**, it's too depressing.'

'But why does that mean you can't help me look for Ginger?' said Tuck. 'Something's obviously happened to her. We have to help.'

'A star,' said Minnie dreamily. Her expression softened and she held out a paw. 'Oh, Tucky, let's run away in the morning. Just you and me. Let's go to the city and make our fortune there.'

'But what about Ginger?'

Minnie caught the expression on Tuck's face, and her own features hardened again.

'Ah, don't bovver,' she miaowed at him. 'I'm gonna sleep.'

'But you can't!' said Tuck.

But he was wrong: she could. For, even though Tuck stood miaowing at Minnie at the top of his voice, within five minutes she was snoring softly and dreaming her dream of being a star. Tuck could tell by the little ballet kicks her front paws were doing in her sleep.

Tuck got to bed very late that night. He spent hours scouring the farm to see if he could find even a clue of what had happened to Ginger. Then he spent hours sitting in the television room, looking out at the windy night.

Eventually, long after midnight, he climbed the stairs to the attic and crept in beside Minnie, who was snoring 'When Will I Be Famous?' gently in C minor. '*Oh well*,' he thought, '*maybe everything will be better in the morning. Maybe Ginger will be back and maybe Minnie will be in a better mood.*'

But Tuck was wrong. For the next morning, everything was worse, not better. Not only had Ginger failed to return, but now Minnie had disappeared too.

NOT MUCH TO CROW ABOUT!

Tuck sat sadly next to the one-hinged gate. This was the furthest part of the farm from the farmyard, where the long, overgrown driveway ran out of the hollow and met the road. It was two hours since he had woken up and found himself alone and he had arrived at the gate intending to set off on an adventure: to discover what had happened to Ginger and Minnie. But now he was here, it didn't seem like such a good idea. For one thing, he already felt an awful long way from the safety of the farmhouse. For another thing, from up near the road, if he turned and looked past the farm, he could see the massive expanse of the Great Dark Forest.

'What if I end up in there?' he thought. 'Surely I'll die of fright before I can rescue anyone?'

He turned again and looked at the tarmac of the road instead, trying to think of a better idea than an adventure of discovery and rescue. After all, Minnie had disappeared overnight once before. On that occasion she'd turned up the next morning in a wonderful mood, refusing to say where she'd been or why she was so tired. But Tuck knew, in his heart of hearts, this time, things were different. Swallowing his fear with a gulp, and reminding himself Ginger and Minnie were probably in danger, he stepped out onto the road. He turned left and told himself he was being brave.

The weather was very different from the night before. The stormy wind had completely disappeared, leaving behind an empty blue sky and quiet air beneath it, as if all the birds and insects and rustling leaves had blown away somewhere else. Tuck looked around him as he walked down the road and thought he'd never seen such a still day. Nor had he ever been so lonely. On and on he walked, away from the farm where he lived and along the borders of other, better-kept properties. There were furrowed fallow fields, carefully cropped crops and great green growths of grass.

'Goodness,' thought Tuck. 'Having a scary adventure isn't half as bad as I thought it would be. In fact, it's rather pleasant.'

Half an hour later he was crying.

'**Woooh**,' he wailed. '**Waahaaah**. I've run out of idea,' (he'd only had one to start with) 'and don't know what to do. Boohoo-hoo. Baa, baa, ha, ha.'

Now, I know what you're thinking. You're thinking 'Baa, baa, ha, ha' sounds like a sheep laughing, not a cat crying and, I must admit, it's possible I got a bit mixed up there. You see, as Tuck walked and wailed, he wandered past a field of sheep, all of whom were rather brainless. No sooner did they hear poor Tuck crying than they all ran over to the fence which separated them from the road and started laughing at him. Which, of course, made Tuck cry all the more.

'Maaaaah,' he cried.

Well, of course this made all the sheep join in saying 'maaah' too, just to mock him and because they didn't know many other words. You know what sheep are like.

'Maah!' he said.

'Maaah,' said the sheep.

'Oh, stop it! Maaah,' said Tuck.

'Maaah,' said the sheep.

Now, this could have all gone on for several pages, and in the pre-edited version of this book it did, but at that moment (phew!) Tuck heard a lovely voice calling to him.

'Oh, my goodness,' it said, in a soft and rather old-fashioned way. 'What a to-do and a hoo-ha! Whatever's the matter, you poor little pussycat?'

Well, I'm sure if you heard anyone talking to you in such a patronising and creepy way you'd run down the road screaming 'Stranger danger!' But Tuck was not you. Unless, Tuck, you've learned to read and this is you reading the book, in which case it *is* you. But for everyone else, I can categorically state: Tuck was not you (even if, coincidentally, your name happens to be Tuck). So Tuck stopped his crying and looked around him. But could he see anyone? Well, do you think I'd be asking if he could? He could not.

'Oh!' he sniffed. 'Has the invisible man come to help me?'

'Hoh, no, ha, ha,' chortled the rather patronising voice. 'I'm not invisible, you're just looking in the wrong place.'

So Tuck looked under his tail, at each of his paws, into the ditch beside the road, into the hedge and, lastly, into the field of sheep.

'Behind you!' said the voice.

Tuck turned around and around, but there was no one on the road, no one in the ditch, no one through the hedge and no one in the bare brown field behind him but a raggedy old scarecrow.

'Give up,' said Tuck, who was never very good at guessing games and generally got a headache before they were over.

'It's me, you funny little thing,' said the voice.

Tuck looked up at the sky, down at the tarmac, up and down the road.

'Over here!'

Tuck looked... well, there was nowhere else for him to look, so he just looked stupid.

'It's me, the blooming scarecrow, you muppet!' said the voice, losing its patience before remembering it was supposed to be a nice kindly character. Tuck does tend to have that effect on people.

'Oh! 'said Tuck. 'A scarecrow!'

And he looked up in time to see the scarecrow stop rolling its button eyes and start rearranging its pillowcase face into a smile. Tuck jumped over the ditch, through the hedge and ran over the furrowed ground to the scarecrow. But then he stopped with a start (never easy).

'Ooh!' he said, looking at the scarecrow's ragged brown coat and torn black trousers with a rag hanging from one pocket. 'Are you a scary scarecrow?'

'Are you a crow?' said the scarecrow, with something of a strain to the lovely lilt in its voice.

'Er... no?' said Tuck, who hated difficult questions.

'Well, I think you'll be fine, then. Now, what's all that dreadful fuss about? Are you lost, you poor wee thing? Can I help you?'

Two difficult questions at the same time!

Tuck thought for a long time and then said no he wasn't. But he had lost Ginger and Minnie and that was even worse. And with that he started crying again, blubbing through the entire story which you've read so far and which—I have to be honest—I cannot be bothered repeating.

'Oh dearie, dearie, do,' said the scarecrow. 'What's your name, you poor darling little puddy-wuddy cat?'

'Tuck,' said Tuck.'

'Well, my name's Sheryl,' said the scarecrow, thus revealing herself to be female which, I have to say, came as a surprise to me, but who can tell these days?

'And let me ask you this,' she continued. 'Is Minnie a rather plump pussycat with long hair of lots of different colours?'

'Yes,' said Tuck sadly. 'Oh, if only someone knew what had happened to her!'

The scarecrow smiled knowingly. 'Well, I think I might know someone who saw what happened. Someone who stands here all day and sees everything that happens down there on that road. Someone who's happy to help.'

'Ooh,' said Tuck. 'Will they be back soon?'

There was a brief silence whilst the scarecrow took a deep breath and struggled to maintain her composure.

'It's me!' she said at last, nice as pie, which isn't always *that* nice, but generally is.

'What is?'

'For goodness sake!' said Sheryl, losing her rag, which fluttered down and lay beside Tuck in the field. 'I saw the whole thing. Your friend Minnie walked past early this morning, not looking very happy, and when I called out to her she was rather rude.'

'Why?' said Tuck.

'What do you mean, why? I don't know. I'm a helpful scarecrow not a blooming psychic. I mean, er … hoh, no, I don't know.'

'Oh. Well, who would know then?'

Sheryl the scarecrow looked a little annoyed by the question. It looked to Tuck like she was struggling to keep the smile on her pillowcase face.

'Try the wise old owl,' she said with a huff, 'he generally knows everything.'

'And where does he live?'

'In the Great Dark Forest.'

'Oh no!' miaowed Tuck. 'I couldn't go in there, it's far too great and dark and foresty.'

'Well, what do you want me to do for you then, you silly cat?' snapped Sheryl. 'I'm supposed to be kind and give you good advice, and then you turn out to be a fairy or a witch or something with magical powers, and you're so grateful you turn me into a human again and we all live happily ever after. But you're not, are you? You're just another cat, walking on legs without realising how grateful you should be for them. Nothing at stake for you, is there? Whereas me—here for fifteen years now and counting—a stake is all I've got. And you can guess where I've got it!'

'But …' said Tuck. 'But …'

But the scarecrow's good nature had apparently worn off. She narrowed her button eyes at Tuck and said 'Boo!'

'Agghhhh!' Tuck screamed, forgetting he wasn't a crow. 'Aggghhh … which way?'

Sheryl the scarecrow turned as if on the wind and pointed along the road.

'Run on, little one,' she said, in a tone which, I think you'll agree, sounded rather false by now. 'Run like the wind. Run. No, faster than that. Faster! Oh, for goodness sake, get out of here! BOOOOOO!'

And so Tuck ran, as fast as only Tuck can run, back to the road, not sure whether to scream or cry or shout out, 'Minnie, my darling, I'm coming for you.'

Needless to say, he then turned the wrong way.

WHAT A BORE!

Meanwhile, three miles to the south and half an hour to the east—so basically south-east if you think about it (do make an effort)—Ginger was waking up and trying to remember where she was. There was sunlight in her eyes, which meant she couldn't be in the stables. And it was very quiet, which meant she couldn't be on the farm, where there were always birds twittering about. Then she remembered.

The night before, she had needed less than five minutes to catch up with the two rats and the bag of lark shanks they'd come back for. Resisting the temptation to eat the rats then and there, she'd followed them carefully. All night long she tracked them across the overgrown fields behind the ruined milking shed, where the grass competed with wild flowers and tangled weeds. Until then, Ginger had assumed the fields were unpassable and had always given their messy mangled mishmash a miss. But now, as she followed Fleabomb and Bumfluff, she found that below the grasses and flowers and weeds was a network of paths for smaller animals. Tiny lines of paths for ants and insects, larger strips for voles and field mice, slithering stripes for snakes—eek!—and one particularly padded path along which she now followed the rats. Oh meaty munchies, this path smelled good, and Ginger was in no doubt that all the missing food had been dragged along it, just as Fleabomb and Bumfluff were now dragging their load. On and on she followed them, through the stormy night, while the two rats bickered constantly.

'Sure it stinks something horrible down here,' Bumfluff kept saying. 'Like dead bodies, so it does.'

To which Fleabomb replied 'Still, it makes ye hungry, don't it?'

'Yer always hungry so yer are, Fleabomb McGee. Would yer push harder from the back there?'

'And ye're always stinking, Bumfluff McGuff. Would ye like to pull at all?'

All night long they went on like this, which was fortunate as their arguments covered up the noise of Ginger squeezing her ample frame along a trail made for smaller animals than herself. What Ginger couldn't understand was how these two rats had managed to steal so much food so quickly. Only a few days before she'd checked on the smokehouse and found it full. Wherever the rats were going, surely they had to get there soon, otherwise on previous journeys they would never have had time to go back and steal some more. It must be around the next bend, Ginger told herself, or over the next rise in the path, or just a few metres more. But then the path would straighten out again and still there was no end in sight.

It was hard work following the rats. Ginger had to make sure she was far enough behind so they wouldn't hear her, but close enough so she didn't lose them. At the same time, she had to resist all the other tasty treats she saw around her. Voluptuous voles and meaty mice, crunchy cockroaches and wiggling worms. And, more importantly, she had to keep her six cat senses on high alert to be sure not to become dinner herself for a snake or a fox or a weasel. By the time the rats decided to rest for the night, she was utterly exhausted.

'Is me back not hurting me more than I can say?' said Bumfluff. 'Cheeses, Tia Maria and processed, I'll never bend over again.'

Fleabomb nodded in agreement. 'Are me shoulders not aching like me front paws are coming out their sockets, so?'

Bumfluff pointed with his nose at a hole in the ground. 'Here, this hole here will happily hold us the night, so it will. Shove the bag down first and then we'll scamper down after it.'

'Ye do it,' grunted Fleabomb. 'I'm done in.'

And so, as Ginger watched, the two rats set about bickering again until, at last, they and the bag were down the hole. Only once she heard them both snoring did she look for somewhere to sleep herself. It was the first time in hours she had taken her attention away from the rats and the stolen food and she was amazed to find where she was. There were no long grasses nor tangled weeds nor fallen stems nor brambles overhead. Instead there were huge great pine trees reaching up towards the black sky. Ginger realised with a shiver she had followed Bumfluff and Fleabomb right through the wild field and into the Great Dark Forest.

And now, half a day later, here she was waking up in the GDF. Yikes! Just the idea of it made her tremble. But then Ginger remembered she was a bad-sass brave-cat, not a sissy scaredy-cat, and she had a quiet word with herself. Everything was going to be OK. For one thing, she'd had the foresight to climb into a tree before settling down for the night. And for a second thing, the forest floor looked quite welcoming with the morning light coming gently through the trees. And for a third thing … But Ginger couldn't think of a third thing. She was too hungry. Oh rumbling tummies, was she hungry. Not only had she trailed those two rats through the night, she'd also trailed the smell of nine months' worth of missing food. And even up here, on the third branch of a pine tree, she could smell the bag the rats had taken down the hole with them. She wasn't alone. Her stomachs could smell it too and one after another they grumbled, 'Feed me, feed me, bubbleburp.'

Ginger sighed and looked down at the hole in the ground below her, wondering if she could leave it unguarded while she went to find some food.

'Don't worry,' said a voice. 'They're both still in there.'

Ginger froze. She had thought there was no one else around. But now, looking to the right of the rats' hole, she saw a strange grey animal the same shape and size as a pig. But, unlike the short-haired and pink pigs she had met on her travels, this animal had thick grey and bristly fur, a black nose and tough little horns either side of its snout.

'Yikes!' said Ginger. 'You can't climb trees can you?'

'Good morning,' said the animal, staring up at her. 'At least, I suspect it is morning. It may, in fact, be afternoon. Morning finishes at midday, and it is now possibly later than that, judging by the time of the year and the position of the sun. I notice you sleep in late. Well, that's the joy of being a cat, I suppose; whereas the rest of us have to work day and night just to stay alive. You arrived here after midnight, obviously following those two rodents, and here you are still, still looking at their hole, and I can only assume you're keen to check they're still there. And—'

'Thank you,' said Ginger. 'But what kind of animal are you?'

The grey animal puffed herself up and snuffled huffily.

'I'm a wild boar.'

Ginger decided not to comment on that, given the sight of the boar's frightening tusks. It might be against the law, sure, but it would be neither chore nor sore for the boar to gore her from jaw to paw. Instead, she asked the boar her name.

'Noreen,' said the boar. 'Noreen is the diminutive form of Nora. Nora means light or honour and is most likely from the Latin name Honora—'

'Fascinating!' said Ginger, with her sweetest possible smile (which, I have to admit, wasn't all that sweet). 'And how do you know the rats are still in their hole?'

'I've been watching them for you all night' said Noreen, the boring boar. 'I judged from your careful tracking of them, combined with your self-restraint in not eating them, that you might want to know exactly where they went and when. I considered it my citizenly duty to assist you in this endeavour, although you are a total stranger to me. However, as a good citizen of the Great Dark Forest, I must also warn you of the immense danger of pursuing the rats any further. You see—'

Ginger suppressed a yawn. 'Don't mind if I have a quick wash as I listen, do you?' she said, sticking one of her legs straight up in the air and licking the back of it. Now, most of us would take that as a very clear sign to snuffle off and mind our own business, but not Noreen. She was, after all, a complete bore of a boar.

'Not at all, please continue. I am aware of how much cats like to keep clean. As I was saying, you face an immense danger in following the rats. They are not working alone, but are part of a network of … Oh!'

Noreen stopped talking as suddenly as she'd started and wandered off into the trees.

'Great,' said Ginger quietly. 'Thanks, for that. See ya. Wouldn't want be ya.'

But then, two seconds later, Noreen the boring boar's words finally penetrated Ginger's skull.

'Hang on!' she shouted after the boar. 'Wait up, what do mean "immense danger"?'

She jumped down from the tree, landing rather painfully on a sticky-up pine needle, and ran after Noreen.

'What do you mean "immense danger"?' she repeated when she'd caught up with her.

'Truffles!' said the boar, her flat nose to the ground.

'Truffles? How can truffles be dangerous?'

'No, I can smell truffles. Mmmm, truffles! Where are they, where are they?'

Ginger ran around in front of Noreen, but the boar just sniffed her way right over her, like a hairy vacuum cleaner with tusks. Her eyes had glazed over and she was singing under her breath:

'Oh, there might a scuffle!
Or even a kerfuffle,
But when things get tough, you'll
Just have to snuffle a truffle!'

Ginger picked herself up and dusted herself down. Then she miaowed at the top of her voice, 'I know where there are lots of truffles!'

Well, that got Noreen's attention. She stopped snuffling in the undergrowth and looked up at her.

'How could you possibly know? A cat's sense of smell is refined, but pigs, dogs and boars have far better noses. Despite the olfactory structure of the—'

'Why is following the rats dangerous?' said Ginger.

'Oh,' said Noreen, who, despite being a boar on any subject, was remarkably easy to distract. 'Because they work for …'

She looked around, coughed, and took a step towards Ginger. She didn't look any less scary that she had before, and Ginger had to summon up her courage not to turn on her tail and flee to the safety of the nearest tree. Closer and closer Noreen came, until she could say in a tiny whisper.

'They are not working alone.'

'Yes,' Ginger whispered back conspiratorially, 'you said that bit already.'

'They,' Noreen looked around again, as if she was afraid the very trees were listening. 'They're working with the Riff Raff Sewer Rats on a job for …'

The boar hesitated again, as if ellipses (look it up!)

were going out of fashion. Finally, she swallowed and, clearly summoning up great courage, said '… for King Rat!'

'King Rat!' said Ginger with a laugh. 'King Rat? Nobody believes in King Rat!'

Noreen the boring boar put a trotter over her mouth, clearly shocked that anyone could say such a thing.

'The evil king's existence is a well-documented fact-'

But she got no further, for now, with her foot near her mouth, she detected something hotter on her trotter than a regal rodent rotter.

'Oh!' she said instead. 'Truffles!'

And with that she turned away again, nose to the ground.

Ginger let her go. She walked back slowly to the tree where she'd spent the night and climbed back up to her viewpoint.

'King Rat!' she said, resigning herself to hunger and settling down for a light snooze. 'Nobody believes in King Rat.'

But just the mention of his horrible name, now she was alone again, was enough to give Ginger a shiver along her spine.

WHAT A DITCH!

Well, no doubt you're wondering what happened to Minnie. No? Well, tough, you're going to find out anyway. What do you think this is: a movie where you can fast forward to your favourite bits? Well, you could, I suppose. I mean, why not flip forward a few pages and find out how Ginger singed her fringe? Or flip further and discover how Tuck, with more pluck than luck, felt yuck about a clucky duck's muck? I'll tell you why not. Because neither of those things happen. And serves you right if you jumped ahead before reading that last bit about how they didn't. Ha!

So, this is what happened to Minnie. Needless to say (but I'll say it anyway), Minnie was **FUUUUUURIOUS** after her argument with Tuck. She had never felt so undervalued or underappreciated in her whole life **ever**. Admittedly, this was because until then she'd never done anything worthy of valuation or appreciation **ever**, but earlier that night, watching television, she had discovered the most marvellous piece of news. She had, weeks before, applied for an audition on *Kitten's Got Talent*. Since then, she'd exercised for at least three minutes every day, spending an equal amount of time writing songs and dancing. Then, just before her big fight with Tuck, as he held the aerial for her and the storm raged outside, she'd received the news she'd wanted for so long. *Kitten's Got Talent* had selected her (and several thousand other cats) to come for an audition. That was why she'd been so excited! But had Tuck been excited for her too? Had he been grateful she'd set herself on the path to stardom? He had not. And had he shown any appreciation for how tough it was going to be for her, all that fame and glory? Nope. He had acted as if Ginger was more important. Poor Minnie, being a star is so tough! If you don't believe me, you find a star and ask them. I bet they'll say 'Bells, yes! It's SO tough!' And if they don't, they're probably just being sarcastic—you know what famous people are like.

Anyhoo, Minnie was still not in the best of moods when she woke up early the next morning. In fact, she was in the worst of moods. Or at least in the worst mood since the day she'd seen her reflection in a piece of bent metal in the farmyard, and laughed at how much rounder it made her look, until Ginger came along and pointed out the metal wasn't bent at all. Ouch! That had been an eight-out-of-ten bad mood. But her mood on the morning after the fight was even worse, eight-point-nine-out-of-ten at least, which is very high on the Kicked-Her Scale. So when she woke up in the drawer beside Tuck, just the sight of him set her seething again. Without a second thought she jumped out of the drawer, grabbed her teeny-tiny suitcase (which was always packed in case of a need to flounce out), padded down the stairs, strode across the farmyard and stomped up the overgrown driveway. Shocking, I know; she hadn't even washed her face! And when she reached the road, did she pause to peruse the pores in her paws? She did not. She turned left and carried on stomping along the road.

'Maaah,' said the sheep in the fields as she passed.

'Get lost,' said Minnie, as she stomped past.

'Oh hello, you beautiful darling,' called out a scarecrow.

'Lick my tail!' said Minnie, as she stamped on down the road.

In fact, she stomped and stamped all morning long until, finally, she was stumped.

'Oh, what am I going to do?' she said. 'How am I going to get to my audition?'

Poor Minnie. She was tired and hungry, down and depressed, a fat cat and a flat cat all at the same time. She sat by the roadside and had a little cry, just a tiddy-tiny one because no one was looking, but a proper cry all the same.

But if you think Minnie sat in this slump of self-despair for long, then you don't know Minnie at all. For Minnie Themoocha Ripperton-Fandango was, let us not forget, a cat whose cunning had careered her from cattery to countryside. A moggy whose mentality had mangled mighty monsters and made mincemeat out of massive men. Or, at least, that's what she'd tell you if you asked. For when they were handing out self-confidence, chutzpah and optimism, Minnie had cheated her way to the front of the queue each time. So, now, after no more than eight minutes and thirty-two seconds, she stood herself up, shook out her fur, picked up her teeny-tiny suitcase and carried on walking.

'Minnie, me gal,' she miaowed out loud, 'you din't get where you is today by relying on no one else. If you 'as to walk, you 'as to walk. So you may as well put a brave face on it and remember how good walking is for your figure.'

Minnie was practising brave faces to see which one felt the bravest when she heard a noise and looked up at the road ahead of her. She couldn't see very far as the road went around a bend, but the noise was definitely that of an approaching vehicle.

'Oh!' she said to herself. 'It's probly some 'oomans what will find me irresistible and will take me to the city. I'll play 'ard to get, but, ooh, it'll be nice to get off me paws.'

The noise got louder and louder and still there was no vehicle in sight.

'Must be a right flash car to make so much noise,' thought Minnie. 'There is justice after all!'

Then, at last, the source of the noise appeared. But it wasn't a car at all. It was a huge high-sided truck driven by a short dumpy woman, with a tall thin man in the passenger seat.

'Cor,' thought Minnie. 'It's them 'oomans again! They must've spotted me yesterday and found me irresistible. Now they've come back to get me!'

She bristled her huge fur coat so that she looked like an old-fashioned movie star or a fat pom-pom on legs, depending on your point of view. But as the lorry approached, did it slow down for her? Oh rudely ripping rubber, no! If anything, it seemed to speed up and even head a little in her direction as if it meant to run her over.

'Cor, limey lummocks!' screamed Minnie, throwing herself at the last minute into a ditch beside the road to avoid being flattened. And then she said, 'Coorrghi limechy lumoccchs,' as she coughed up the dirty ditch water she'd swallowed. Climbing slowly back up to the road she was so upset she couldn't even raise a clenched paw to shake after the lorry as it sped back the way she'd come.

'Oofee!' she wailed. 'Look at me, I'm fill-fee! Ooh, me beautiful coat, it's gritty, not pretty, it's not lush or plush, it's just a mushy bush!'

And it was true: she did look quite a sight. She was a daggy, claggy, baggy, saggy, boggy, soggy moggy. And, worst of all, there was nothing she could do about it. Her teeny-tiny suitcase, with all her combs and ribbons and hairclips and bows, had burst open when she dived into the ditch, and now its contents were floating in the dirty water. All she could reach—apart from the teeny-tiny suitcase itself—was a tube of paw-paw lotion.

'Oofee,' she said out loud. 'Sometimes life can be a real ditch!'

She stood looking at her belongings floating in the dirty water and thought for a second that maybe she should give up on her ambitions and head back to the farm. Maybe she should accept she was never going to be a star and settle for the quiet life of a country cat. But, thoughts being far faster than words, she'd already rejected those ideas before you even got to read about them.

'*Nah!*' she thought. And then, just to be sure, she miaowed it out loud. 'Nah!!! I'm going to get to that audition if it's the last thing I do. And I'm going to get through it, and I'm going to be a star! Watch out world, Minnie is on the way, and you might want to get your tickets early because it's going to be a sell-out show.'

And on she walked again, not even thinking about crying.

WHAT A PONG!

A few minutes later, Tuck also heard the lorry approaching. He was, by this time, only a short distance behind Minnie. He had run all the way back to the farm, realised his mistake and then run all the way in the right direction, while Minnie had just plodded and stomped and dawdled and huffed and puffed and done her hair a few times. Indeed, had the lorry not approached, Tuck would probably have caught up with her in a matter of minutes and this whole story would have taken a very different turn. But the lorry did approach, and the story didn't turn. Nor did Tuck, which you have to agree has a certain splat potential.

Have you ever heard the expression 'a rabbit in headlights'? Well, you have now. It's a metaphor to describe someone so frightened by something approaching that they stand still and stare at it instead of jumping out of the way. I'll be honest and say I've never seen a rabbit do this, but I have seen Tuck do it. And on this day, when the huge high-sided lorry came charging around the bend towards him, he did it again.

'*Uh-oh,*' he thought.

He sat watching the lorry getting bigger and bigger and listening to its brakes hiss and squeal and its tyres screech and scream until it came to a stop right above him. That's right, *above* him. The lorry's front left wheel had gone to the left of him and its front right wheel had gone to the right of him and now its juddering, spluttering, vibrating cabin sat right above him.

'*Uh-oh*,' he thought again.

Then he heard the lorry's doors opening and saw a long pair of thin human legs climb down to the road on one side of him and a rather dumpy pair of legs climb down on the other. Then, on the first side, he saw the pale long-nosed face of the male human bending down to look under the lorry. It was at this point that Tuck started to think something other than 'Uh-oh'.

'*Agh!*' he thought. '*Eek!*'

The male human reached in one of his long thin arms and stuck out his long thin fingers towards Tuck's fur.

'Miaow!' said Tuck. 'Eek, eugh, miaow, help!'

Now, at last, he started moving. He crawled slowly backwards as he miaowed, wondering what this evil being with its hideous tentacles was going to do with him. But before he could wonder any further, or wander any further come to that, he felt himself grabbed firmly from behind. He'd been so intent on escaping from the male human that he'd forgotten about the female human and he'd crawled backwards to within her reach.

'Oh furry-purry-dumkins!' she said as she grabbed him, her voice deeper than you'd expect. 'My, aren't you beautiful! We nearly ran you over you, silly pussycat.'

Tuck tried to stick his claws into the road to stop himself being picked up, but, of course, that didn't work, and within seconds he found himself pulled out into the brightness of the day. Then he was lifted up and held tight.

Well, Tuck hadn't been held by a human since he was a tiny kitten. What a strange, frightening and rather high-up sensation! He closed his eyes tight, miaowed even louder and was about to stick out all his claws again and even bare his teeth too, when something stopped him. Was it:

a) Because the woman smelled very nice, like your best friend's mum when she's getting ready to go out?

b) Because his flight/ fight/ freeze mechanism had set itself to 'freeze' again?

c) Because the woman immediately started rubbing his neck with the knuckles of one hand and tickling his tummy with the fingers of the other?

d) Because it was so nice not to be under the lorry?

The answer, dear reader, we will never know. Not because I haven't done my research—how very dare you—but because Tuck himself has never worked it out. It might well have been:

e) All of the above

Whatever the correct answer, suffice to say Tuck did not stick his claws through the woman's bright yellow and surprisingly-light-for-the-time-of-year dress. Instead, he lay in her arms, looked up at her narrow green eyes and said, 'Ooh, purry-purry purr-purr. Hee, hee, hee, that tickles.'

'OK, William, open the door,' replied the woman in her thick and throaty voice.

Except, of course, this wasn't a reply at all. It was an instruction to the man who'd walked around from the other side of the truck and who—I'll save a lot of time by telling you now—was her husband. His name was William Pong, and he was, as you may have noticed, very tall and very thin. He was so tall and so thin, in fact, that if you passed him in the street you would probably say to a friend, 'Staggering stick insects, look at how tall and thin that man is!' In fact, he was taller and thinner than that. He was so tall and thin that if you saw him in the street, and you weren't with a friend, you'd have grabbed a random stranger just to point out his height and his thinness. Which would be quite rude, but there you go; sometimes you just can't help yourself, can you?

'Yes, dear,' said Mr Pong.

Then, as Tuck watched, he pulled a face as if he'd just smelled a pool of vomit. He walked in a very wide circle around his wife, and started opening a large door in the side of the trailer behind the lorry's cabin. Actually, thinking about it, I better tell you the woman's name too, hadn't I? Her name was Frances Pong, and she was the prettiest human being in this entire story (there aren't any others). As stated, she had narrow green eyes and bright red hair. She also had a lovely strong nose and generally all the bits of her face in the right place. The only downside to her appearance was her teeth, which were shockingly yellow. None of which particularly interested Tuck at that moment.

'That's enough now, thank you,' he said.

Something was ruffling his feline sixth sense, and he thought it might be time to think about rescuing Minnie and Ginger again. But Mrs Pong ignored his miaowing, and moved from rubbing his tummy to tickling the top of his head.

'Ooh, stop it, that's lovely' said Tuck. 'I mean—don't. Put me down! Ooh, up a bit, just there … purr, purr. I really should be going—try the ears.'

As Tuck tried to resist Mrs Pong's gentle yet firm fingers, he could hear Mr Pong opening the side of the trailer and pulling something down to the roadside. When Mrs Pong tickled under his chin, so he could put his head back and see what was happening behind him, Tuck saw it was a set of metal steps. And now, as he watched in an upside-down (and not entirely unpleasant) kind of way, he saw Mr Pong's tall and skinny frame climb the steps and enter the trailer. Tuck couldn't see much more, but suddenly he could smell ever so much, because coming out of the trailer was the unmistakeable odour of cats. Lots and lots of cats. Whether it was these scents, or his sixth sense, which sent him back to his senses, Tuck did not know. But what he did know was that all of a sudden he was finished with fuss.

'Thank you very much for having me,' he miaowed politely, 'but I have to go now.'

And he wriggled and turned in Mrs Pong's arms hoping to get away. But Mrs Pong merely held him tighter, and then tighter still, until it really was quite uncomfortable. Tuck twisted and turned and wriggled again, until, at last, without thinking, he stuck out all of his claws, piercing Mrs Pong's plump pale person ten times through her thin dress.

'Aaah,' she screamed, her yellow teeth on full display. 'This little monster just scratched me!'

Which wasn't strictly true, given that Tuck's super sharp claws had all gone straight into her flesh with not a scratch in site. Still, Mr Pong seemed to understand. He reappeared in the doorway of the trailer wearing a huge pair of green oven gloves. He descended the steps in two strides, reached out with a nauseous look on his face and pulled Tuck from his wife's grasp. Mrs Pong screamed as his ten claws came out of her body less cleanly than they'd gone in.

'Eugh, foul thing!' shouted Mr Pong in a nasty nasal voice, as Tuck stuck his claws out again, each of his four paws searching for something else to scratch and help him get away. 'Oh, how these things disgust me!'

'**Miiaaaaooooowwwwwww**,' yowled Tuck. 'Let me go!'

He had never been so terrified in his entire life. He just wanted to be dropped so he could run away again, but Mr Pong had grabbed him in such away than his claws found only air, no matter how he kicked or reached or wriggled. He miaowed and miaowed for help, but it was no good. Soon he found himself carried roughly up the steps and into the darkness of the lorry.

WHAT A RAT!

Ginger dozed on and off in the pine tree until halfway through the afternoon, the soft smell of the tree's needles almost sending her into a trance. Each time she woke, as soon as she'd checked the rats were still in their hole, she remembered how hungry she was. She had, of course, been hungry in her life before, but hunger is not something you get used to by doing it several times. Quite the opposite, in fact. If you've ever been really hungry for a long period of time, for all of your life you'll feel new hunger pangs more than anyone else around you.

Ginger tried to console herself with the fact she was having an adventure. She was away from the farm, footloose and fancy-free. But she was also foodless in a trancey tree and, oh how her bellies were complaining. They grumbled and rumbled, like a fumbling juggler tumbling his dumb-bells. She told them to be humble, to mumble not rumble, but even when she pummelled them, they would not be still. Eventually, nervous their noise would wake the two rats and alert them to her presence, she climbed to a higher branch. She'd been there little more than an hour, watching the early winter sun cross the sky, when at last there was movement below her. One of the rats had left the hole.

'Nnngg, eek, yawn,' he squeaked, stretching himself. 'It has to be said, from my head to my toes, there's nothing

69

I like more than a good doze.'

Ginger recognised by his voice that this rat was Bumfluff McGuff. In the light of day, he proved to be short-haired and brown with tiny ears and a tail which seemed to have been chopped off halfway along. His friend, Fleabomb, who now appeared beside him, was slightly larger. He had dark shiny eyes, was black rather than brown, and was much fluffier than his friend. Well, can you imagine a more impressive feat of self-discipline than Ginger's right now? Here she was, as hungry as a hippo who hasn't had his healthy helping of hummus, and looking down at two rats, stretching themselves and half-awake. She could have easily jumped, landed on top of them and squashed them flat. Then she could have spent the rest of the afternoon eating them. But let me tell you a secret, dear reader, something you must remember for the rest of your life: self-discipline is the key to all success. Without self-discipline you will never achieve anything you want. All successful people know this and all successful cats too. Was Ginger going to be satisfied with catching two thieving rats? Oh stolen stores, no! She wanted all her food back, her entire Spring/ Summer/ Autumn collection. So she swallowed the saliva that was pooling in her mouth and told herself food could wait.

Within a few minutes, brown Bumfluff with his tiny ears and black fluffy Fleabomb with his shiny eyes, had pulled the heavy bag out of the hole where they'd slept and continued on their journey. Naturally, Ginger followed. For the rest of the afternoon she trailed them, always staying far enough back to ensure they wouldn't hear her. Always downwind to ensure they wouldn't smell her. Always behind trees and low shrubs to ensure they wouldn't see her. And always not eating them to ensure … well, you get the picture.

Ginger had been in the Great Dark Forest only once before in her life and, on that occasion, she had come face-to-face with a fox. But the forest seemed less frightening this time. Maybe it was because now she was the hunter; maybe because she was so concentrated on the two rats and their heavy bag; maybe because she was too hungry to feel anything but hungry. Whatever it was, the hours passed quickly, and it was beginning to grow dark when she heard a strange rushing noise.

'Do yer hear that?' she heard Bumfluff say. Despite his tiny ears, he had obviously noticed the noise himself. 'Are we not nearly there? Oh, cheeses in heaven, I don't think I could have gone any further.'

As Ginger watched, Fleabomb stopped pushing the bag, stood on his furry hind legs and started clapping his front paws together.

'Nigh!' he said. 'Sure, let's run down and find the others. We'll let them drag this blooming bag the last little way.'

And with that the two rats scurried off toward the rushing and racing sound. Ginger crept after them, but only as far as the bag of dried lark shanks. Without thinking too hard about it, she bit through the bottom of the bag and started in on the food. Yum and a quarter. Yum and a half. Yum and three quarters. Yum, yum!

'Must. Stop. Eating,' she thought. 'Before. Rats. Get. Back.'

But have you ever seen a cat try to stop eating? Even Ginger, a mighty mistress of self-mastery, couldn't do it. Yum, yum and a quarter. Yum, yum and a half. Yum, yum and three quarters. Yum, yum, yum! Maybe if the rats had come back any sooner, Ginger would have been discovered and her plans would have been blown. But, fortunately for her, she was a fast eater and was already licking her lips clean before she heard squeaks coming back up the path.

'Oops,' she said to herself, somewhat unconvincingly.

She ran to a nearby chestnut tree, climbed it at speed and crawled along a branch so she had a good view of the ground below her. Within a minute, Bumfluff McGuff and Fleabomb McGee appeared on the path, followed by two of the ugliest rats Ginger had ever seen. She could tell at a glance they weren't native to the forest. Oh vile vermin, no! These were stinky city sewer rats, pale grey from the tips of their twitchy noses to the ragged ends of their thick tails. They were wearing thick black leather jackets which, Ginger saw as they passed below her, had *Riff Raff* written across the back in thick grimy studs.

'What d'you blooming well think we are? Baggage handlers?' said the first of them in a thick city accent. He turned to his equally evil-looking colleague. 'Can you believe the cheek of them, Vicious Lee?'

'It's just with it being so heavy, so,' said Bumfluff. 'And us after pushing it all day.'

'And after pulling it all through the night,' said Fleabomb, who really was the most atrocious liar. Or quite a good one, depending on your point of view.

'Yeah, well,' said the second sewer rat, whose fur was covered in scabs and scratches. 'We and the lads had to shift all the others. Didn't we, Dubious? Don't see us making a fuss about it, do you?'

'But there's dozens of ye, and ye're big and strong,' said Fleabomb with a tremor in his voice. 'And only two of us wee ones. Anyways, it's over here, like. Oh!'

Ginger watched silently from the chestnut tree, the late afternoon light fading by the minute, as the four rats below her looked at the torn and empty bag.

'What's your game?' said the first sewer rat, the one called Dubious. 'You having a laugh?'

But neither Bumfluff nor Fleabomb said a word. At least, not a useful one.

'But…but…it…but…I don't…' said Bumfluff.

'What the…It was…How…?' said Fleabomb.

And they scurried round and round the bag as if that might help them find the missing food. Then they stopped scurrying and turned to the two sewer rats.

'Well,' said Bumfluff, finding some composure. 'Something has obviously happened to this bag, so it has. But this is just one of hundreds. We should still get our payment in full.'

'Er…what he said!' said Fleabomb, making sure Bumfluff was between him and the larger rats.

Before the two grey rats could respond, they all turned at the noise of something approaching along the path. When it appeared, Ginger, high in the chestnut tree above, had to put a paw over her mouth to stop herself gasping.

She had lived in cities all over the world, travelled on great ships, ventured into sewers and lived under piers. But never in her life had she seen such a huge rat. Even in the half-light of the evening, Ginger could see her clearly. Like Dubious and Vicious Lee, she was grey all over, but she was much bigger than either of them. She was as long as a table is wide, as broad as a book is long and her tail was on top of that. She had two huge front teeth and a deep, rasping voice.

'What's all this about, Sergeant Scard?' she said to the rat called Vicious Lee.

'These peasants have lost a bag of loot, Corporal Punishment, ma'am,' he replied. 'But they want their payment in full. Isn't that right, Private Staines?'

'Yes, sir,' said the rat called Dubious. 'Absolutely correct, sir.'

'Really?' said the Corporal. 'Is that so?'

Like the other two city rats she was wearing a black leather jacket which now creaked as she walked over to Bumfluff and Fleabomb.

'Payment?' she said. 'You want payment? Whatever gave you that idea?'

'Yer did,' said Bumfluff. 'Twenty-five num-nums per bag.'

Corporal Punishment laughed a hideously rasping laugh.

'Well, you can forget that now!'

'But yer said—' said Bumfluff.

'I DON'T CARE WHAT I SAID,' squeaked the Corporal in huge capital letters. She stood on her two back legs, her full height rearing above the others. 'To serve his Majesty is payment enough. Be off with you. BE OFF!'

Well, Fleabomb and Bumfluff didn't need telling a third time. They turned on their heels (rats do have heels, you know) and scurried into the undergrowth so fast they were little more than a brown and black blur. Corporal Punishment chuckled nastily, bumped her front paws back down to the ground and led the other Riff Raff rats back down the path and out of sight.

High in the tree above, Ginger thought, '*His Majesty?*' Then she thought, '*The King?!*'

The idea that King Rat really did exist made her tremble all over. It made her remember night was falling and she was deep in the Great Dark Forest. All her life she had heard stories of how evil King Rat was, and how he controlled all the rats in the world through fear. How terrible his torturous deeds were. If there really was a King Rat, and these rats really were working for him, then she'd be crazy to continue. But then she looked down at the forest floor below her and saw the empty food bag lying flat and forlorn. She remembered these rats had taken all the food she'd worked so hard to store and smoke and save for winter. And she thought of Tuck and Minnie, helpless on the farm.

'King Rat?' she said out loud to herself. 'Bring it on.'

WHAT A STATE!

Miaownwhile, on the road towards the city, Minnie was struggling to keep her composure. Oh, how her paws hurt. Ooh, how her legs ached. Ooof, how her belly rumbled. But worse than all that was the knowledge of what a dreadful sight she must look. As she had walked, her fur had dried into clotted clumps until her tail felt like a well-used lavatory-brush and her body like a dirty discarded duster.

'Oh well, Minnie,' she said, pretending she felt better than she did. 'At least it's dark now and no one can see you. And, anyways, you was born under a house and … *sniff* … despite that, you made yourself into the epitome of glamorous beauty. If you done it once, you can do it again. And besides, you're so blooming grotty now, you won't mind sleeping outside, will you?'

It really was properly dark now, and Minnie knew she was going to have to spend the night under a hedge or in a tree. She was looking around, peering into the dark to find something suitable, when she saw a tiny red light away from the road in a small bunch of trees.

'Ooh, ooh,' she thought. 'Civilisation! And a break from this blooming tarmac!'

A little further on, she found a small track that ran off the road and across a field towards the light. Without thinking twice (which, as we know, is normally a good idea), Minnie picked up her pace and followed the track. As she got closer to the light, she could see it was made up of flashing neon letters and, as she got closer still, she could see it hung above a cat flap in the side of a ramshackle old building hidden in the trees. *The Scratching Post* said the sign. Then it said nothing as it flashed off. Then it said: *The cratching Po t'*, until the S's flickered into life, and it said: *The Scratching Post* again. Below the red neon letters, on the rusty old cat flap, was a large paw-printed sign which said '*We Don't Serve Dogs, No Matter How Small.*' Through the door came the sound of miaows and mellow music. Minnie was about to press her nose against the flap when it opened from the inside and two well-groomed tabbies followed each other out. Each of them wore a collar with a little medallion. The tabbies hesitated when they saw Minnie, then they looked at each other and strolled off giggling.

'Gosh, what a state to let yourself get into!' Minnie heard one of them say. 'I'd rather be neutered.'

Well, as you can imagine, Minnie wouldn't normally take any cheek like that. 'Better than being domesticated!' she wanted to shout after them. But she knew they were off to a warm house and some dumb humans who'd probably give them food and tickle their tummies and let them watch telly, and it took all her energy not to breakdown in tears of jealousy. Besides, looking down at her mud-mottled and mangy mane, she couldn't disagree with them. She was in a right state. If she went in looking like this, she wouldn't even get served.

Minnie sat there, the red neon flashing on and off above her, and wondered what to do. Then she heard a bunch of young toms approaching and decided she didn't even want to be *seen* by them. She was about to slink into the shadows when something beside the cat flap caught her attention. It was another paw-printed sign, below the *No Milk Served To Under-One-Year-Olds* poster and above the *Please Be Respectful To Our Neighbours, No Caterwauling Upon Departure* sign. As the voices of the young toms grew louder, Minnie stepped forward and squinted at what she'd seen until the red neon lights above the door flicked off and left her in total darkness. But when the lights came on again, the two S's crackling with the effort, a huge smile had spread across her dirty face.

WHAT A NIGHTMARE!

Tuck lay curled in as tight a ball as he could manage. His eyes were closed tight, his ears were laid back tightly against his head and his tail was wrapped tightly over his nose. If only he could sleep, he thought, then maybe he could wake up again and this nightmare would be over. Or, if only he could wish himself into something else, into a bird maybe, so he could fly high above and look down on the horrible prison where he now found himself. Or, into a clever cat who knew what to do: whether to run away or to stay where he was. But he had no insight to whether fight or flight might be bright or right. Lying there tight, he felt only fright—more than light or slight in that terrible night—and the sight of his spitefully-blighted plight, even from the height of a kite, started to bite until he felt quite white. Because every time he stopped wishing or trying to sleep, he remembered he was still there, locked in the back of a lorry rumbling along a road.

'Oh miaow,' Tuck cried. 'Oh help!'

After a while the lorry slowed its rumbling and then stopped altogether. The engine was turned off, and Tuck heard the humans get out of the cabin, slam the doors and walk away. Then, with his eyes still squeezed tightly shut, he began to hear other noises. Closer noises. Noises of things locked in the back of the lorry with him. He could hear a scratching which could be a cat in a litter tray, or could be a vicious dragon tearing out the belly of one of its victims. He heard a light lapping, which could be a cat having a drink, or a wolf licking blood from something it had killed. He heard a thud-thud-thud, which could be the elbow of a cat on the floor as it scratched behind its ear, or a mad axeman beating down the door.

'Oh, please let it be cats!' he miaowed aloud. 'Oh, please let it not be Dragons or Wolves or a Mad Axeman!'

Then he heard a giggle. Well! That didn't sound like a D or a W or an MA. Tuck carefully twisted an ear in the direction of the giggle.

'What-a is a wrong-a with 'im-a?' he heard a voice ask.

'He's just frightened,' said another voice, so close that it would have made Tuck jump had it not been very soft and gentle.

'Looks like a bit of a pussycat,' said a third voice.

'Leave him alone,' said the gentle voice. 'You remember what it was like when you were first thrown in here.'

Well, it would have taken a far less curious cat that Tuck not to open his eyes at that point. After all, whilst listening to all of the above, he'd had a good sniff of the air around him and that sniff had confirmed what he'd suspected outside. The trailer of the lorry smelled of cats and not, as far as he could tell, of dragons or wolves or mad axemen. So he opened first one eye, then the other. At first, all he could see were criss-cross lines. Then he realised he was shut in a small wire cage, which also contained a small cushioned bed, a litter tray, and a small bowl of water.

Then, as Tuck looked further afield, he saw this was just one of rows and rows of cages which stretched from the floor of the trailer to the narrow windows which ran around the top of its walls. Some of the cages were empty, but as Tuck's eyes grew accustomed to the dim light from the window, he saw that most of them were very much occupied.

'*Buongiorno*,' said a sleek black cat in a cage on the opposite wall. ''Ow you-a doing?'

Tuck said nothing.

'You alright there, mate?' said a sturdy black cat two cages down from the first one who'd spoken.

Still Tuck said nothing.

'Don't worry,' said the petite black cat in the cage next to his own. This was the cat with the soft and gentle voice. He had a quiet American accent and was separated from Tuck by no more than a single layer of mesh.

'You'll get used to it,' said the American. 'You look strong, you'll be fine.'

'Mummy!' wailed Tuck. 'I want my mummy!'

The sleek black cat in the cage opposite giggled, while her sturdy neighbour sighed and turned away. But the American stayed where he was, smiling gently in a way which belied his huge yellow eyes. These were so big and wide that he looked terrified, at the same time as his soothing voice was calming Tuck down.

'Take your time,' he said. 'You've had a shock, but everything will be OK.'

There were more than three dozen cats in the lorry, each of them in a separate cage, each of them pure black. Those in the cages near Tuck gave him an hour to calm himself down and to stop crying, then they gave up and started to introduce themselves despite his tears.

'My-a name-a,' said the sleek cat across the way, 'is the Principessa Passagiata Pawprints. I'm-a from-a the posh-a part-a of Palermo. You can-a call me "Principessa".'

But she was wrong. Tuck couldn't get past 'Prin'.

'I'm Butch,' said her sturdy neighbour, who wasn't quite as butch as he thought he was. He spoke with a light and lilting voice with the tiniest hint of a lisp and wore a diamond-encrusted collar with a little gold medallion hanging from its buckle.

To Tuck's left was a fat old black cat called Matt. He was very quiet and rather grumpy and simply said 'Matt' when Tuck said hello. The cat to Tuck's right, the cat with the quiet American accent and the huge yellow eyes, introduced himself as Bunk.

'Why have they kidnapped me?' Tuck asked Bunk quietly. 'What did I do wrong?'

'Cat, you did nothing wrong,' said Bunk. 'And don't worry, we'll get you out of here. You'll see. But first, you need to sleep. We'll talk in the morning.'

But poor Tuck hardly slept at all that night. He was, after all, a night cat. But, whereas normally it was hunting and exploring that kept him awake through the dark hours, that night it was misery and confusion. Eventually, after hours of crying quietly he managed to fall asleep. He slept long and deeply, dreaming he was back in the attic with Minnie in their chest of drawers. But, the next morning, when the dirty daylight in the high narrow windows above the cages woke him, he realised his dream had been just a dream, whereas this nightmare was reality. Then, as if things weren't bad enough, the door to the trailer began to rattle loudly to the sound of a key in its lock until, suddenly, it was pulled open.

WHAT A DISASTER!

Ginger woke early too that morning. For the second night in a row she'd slept in a tree: this time in the gnarly old chestnut from which she'd watched the Riff Raff sewer rats chase away Fleabomb and Bumfluff. But, unlike the previous night, she hadn't slept well. For one thing, it had suddenly grown a lot colder. Thick clouds had formed and there was the distinct smell of snow on the way. Without her winter coat yet grown, Ginger had shivered and quivered right down to her liver. But that wasn't what had stopped her sleeping. Oh chilly chestnuts, no! Ginger had slept badly because she was worried the sewer rats would leave in the night and she would lose their trail. She had no doubt they would move much faster and much more quietly than Fleabomb and Bumfluff had done. So every half an hour she'd woken herself up, listening intently to be sure that, above the constant rushing noise that came through the undergrowth, she could hear the snuffling snores of three large rats.

Now, as the first light of dawn came weakly through the thick trees around her, Ginger listened carefully once more. But where she could hear the rushing noise still, she couldn't hear any ratty snores. Oh no! What if the rats had escaped?! She jumped quickly down from the tree, wincing as her six bellies each hit the ground at a different time, kerplunkerty flab plunk, flab flab plunk! Ginger froze, but there was no sign anyone had heard her, so she crouched very close to the ground and crept slowly down the path.

She had gone no more than a couple of metres before she saw at last, through a thick patch of greenery, the source of the rushing sound. It was a fast-flowing stream washing and wishing and whooshing and rushing along the forest floor. Well, maybe it was a bit bigger than a stream. More of a brook, perhaps? Almost a creek, but not quite. A crook? A cream? A strook or a streak? Whatever it was, Ginger worried the rats had crossed it while she slept. Maybe all her food was gone forever? She crept closer and closer to the water until, at last, she saw the babbling stream cut right across the path itself. She had no idea if this was good or bad news and so she crept closer and closer to it, until, to her huge relief, she heard the voices of the Riff Raff rats.

'Just a few more,' Corporal Punishment was saying, her voice rasping even more than normal as she lifted something heavy. 'Here, Scard, catch this.'

Ginger's view was blocked by a bunch of tall brown flowers, growing so thickly they cast a dark shade beneath them. She crawled over to them, dragging her six bellies along the dusty path until she cowered in the bower of the towering dour flowers. There she glowered, powerless, and scoured the scene beside the stream. The rats were no more than a metre from her by the edge of the fast-running water. At least, Corporal Punishment was. Private Dubious Staines and Sergeant Vicious Lee Scard were perched in a flat-bottomed boat that was connected to the shore by a thick rope. Between Staines and Scard were four bags just like the one Ginger had watched Fleabomb and Bumfluff struggle with the previous day. But, unlike that bag, which now lay empty on the forest floor up the path behind her, these bags were full. As were five more bags which lay on the ground beside Corporal Punishment.

'Yummy, yummy, they should be in my tummy,' thought Ginger.

'Rork!'

Above the river, bent over in a hole in an old oak tree, was a large black rook. 'Rork!' he called again, pointing his hooked beak at Ginger, as if trying to alert the rats. 'Rork!'

Well, it was a good thing Ginger had eaten the day before or she might not have resisted running down and gobbling up the rats, and then running up the oak to eat the rook too.

'What's that bird on about, Corporal P, ma'am?' said Private Staines. 'I reckon he's trying to tell us something.'

The Corporal ignored him. 'Here's another one,' she said, and for a second she was lost to Ginger's view as she bent down to pick a bag up in her teeth. 'Coming atcha. Catch this, Staines!'

Ginger watched the bag fly through the air, then knock Dubious Staines clean off his feet so that he fell backwards squealing into the boat. Scabby Sergeant Scard turned and laughed at him until—doof!—the Corporal's next bag hit him square in the back and sent him sprawling too.

'Rork!' screeched the big black bird.

Ginger looked above the brook and chucked the hooked rook, crooked in its nook, the gingeriest look in this entire book. Such a look that it stuck, and the rook forsook ever to look at a cat again and took to the air instead.

'Rork! Rork! Rork!' he cawed as he flew away, and, below him—doof, doof, doof—the next three bags flew through the air from Corporal Punishment towards Sergeant Scard and Private Staines so that they had to duck and dive, dish and dash, dodge and weave to stop them landing on their heads. Ginger was impressed, and not a little intimidated, by the Corporal's obvious strength.

'That's the lot,' said the Corporal when she'd finished. 'The last boat of nine bags. One hundred and ninety-nine bags in total, not bad. Except if you two hadn't lost the other one it would have been a round two hundred.'

Ginger watched Scard and Staines look at their paws in shame, but the Corporal ignored them. She was busy unhooking the rope from the stick which had held it to the ground. Then, as Ginger watched helplessly, the Corporal threw herself into the water and pushed the boat out into the fast-running stream before leaping aboard herself.

Ginger sat upright and stared forlornly after the boat. As you probably know, cats HATE water. They might drink it occasionally, but only when they have to. The only thing water is good for—as far as cats are concerned—is providing fish, and even those are better when they're out of it. Ginger felt a tingle on the end of her nose. Looking around her, she realised it was snowing. Winter had arrived.

'Great,' she said. 'Just what I need …'

But, like Minnie, Ginger was not a cat to give up easily. As the three rats and the last of the stolen food drifted away, she walked along the bank of the stream in the same direction. Here, in the soft ground, she found the paw prints of many, many rats and the heart-breaking smell of dozens and dozens of bags of food. As she watched the tracks slowly disappear under the falling snow, it occurred to her for the first time what a huge operation this must have been. She had seen how Bumfluff and Fleabomb had struggled with one bag. If two hundred bags had been stolen in total, that was four hundred rats! The thought of so many sewer rodents was more than a little frightening, but Ginger was nothing if not determined, and nothing ever made her more determined than food.

WHAT THE WHAT?

Tuck cringed against the wall as the morning air rushed into the trailer. He closed his eyes tight and tried not to think of what awful thing might be about to happen to him. Then he realised the air coming through the newly-opened door brought with it lots of familiar smells: like a stables and a smokehouse and a very familiar farmhouse. His heart gave a leap as he thought maybe he'd misunderstood; maybe these people were just giving him a lift home after all. He was saved! He didn't even tremble when the metal steps, which lay folded on the trailer floor, were dragged loudly down to the ground outside. Nor when, seconds later, the male human's straggly silhouette appeared in the doorway.

'Oh, thanks so much for having me!' he miaowed. 'And for the lift, but oh, it's so good to be back home!'

Then he saw what the man was carrying in his rubber-gloved hands. It wasn't a key to open a cage: it was a large tray, full of cat-food dishes. Nutritious nutty num-nums, it smelled good! Tuck suddenly realised how hungry he was.

'Oh well,' he thought. 'I might as well have a little snack before I say goodbye.'

'Don't eat this food,' said Bunk in his quiet American accent from the cage beside him, as if he could read Tuck's thoughts. 'Don't eat anything until you hear the gong.'

'Hear the what?'

Bunk motioned with his head to the far end of the trailer where a bronze gong hung from the back wall, faintly glowing in the light from the open trailer door. Tuck watched with wide eyes as the male human walked slowly down the aisle between the cages, reaching tentatively into each one through an inwards-opening flap. He had an expression on his face like he'd just trodden in some dog-do, and he left his heavily-gloved hand in each cage for the least possible time before leaving a dish of the yummy-smelling food inside.

'Don't eat it,' said Bunk again. 'You're going to be in here for a long time, so you need to keep healthy.'

Tuck turned to see his neighbour leaning against the mesh which separated them, staring at him closely. He had a strange underbite which Tuck hadn't noticed before, and a rather small head, especially for a cat with such huge circular eyes.

'But I want to go home,' said Tuck.

'We all want to go home.' The American shrugged his shoulders sadly and looked away.

Tuck ran to the very back of his cage as the man approached.

'Eugh, disgusting animals,' said the man as he dropped a dish of food into Tuck's cage. The dish landed with a loud clatter, and Tuck thought his heart would burst with fear. Only when the man had once again left the trailer did Tuck dare to approach the food. Mm, it smelled so good! It smelled of rodent-water and vole-fluff and … oh, something not quite right. Tuck sniffed the dish more closely still. There was something metallic in there.

Looking around the harshly-lit trailer, he saw the other cats sniffing at their dishes, none of them wanting to eat. Fat-cat Matt and Bunk, he noticed, didn't even bother smelling the food.

Tuck closed his eyes, and thought he'd never been so unhappy. The smell of the farm had raised his hopes, and the sight of a farewell snack had raised them even higher. But now his hopes were crashed and smashed and dashed and bashed.

'Yo, cat,' said Bunk quietly. 'You're about to start crying again.'

'Thanks,' sniffed Tuck, closing his mouth tight so that he couldn't wail. But no matter how tightly he closed his eyes, tears still rolled down his cheeks.

It was a little over an hour later when the trailer door rattled again to the sound of keys in its lock. Startled, Tuck ran to the back of his cage. Then he watched with wide eyes as the dumpy female human, with her pretty green eyes and even prettier freckles, entered the trailer wearing a sleeveless wrap-around dress. She was dragging behind her a large black rubbish bag and, under her arm, she carried a huge pair of barbecue tongs. Just like her husband had done, she visited each cage in turn. But Mrs Pong wasn't delivering food—oh vacillating visitors, no! Instead, she used the long tongs to reach into each cage in turn, grab the strange-smelling food, lift it out and throw it into the black plastic rubbish bag. As she moved from cage to cage, she sang in a rather lovely voice, her yellow teeth visible in the dim light.

'Dong-ding, ding-dong,
This first breakfast tastes so wrong.
Ding-dong, dong-ding,
Let's throw it in the bin.
Dong-ding, ding-dong,
Second breakfast won't be long,
Dong-ding, ding-dong,
Though the gong sounds so wrong.

'Ding-dong, dong-ding,
Dong-ding, ding-dong,
The tinned din-dins dinner gong
Always sounds so wrong!'

When she had taken the food from the very last cage at the end of the trailer, Mrs Pong, the ning-nong, singing her song in her sarong, hit the bronze gong with a prong of her long tongs, making a strong bonging dong which, indeed, sounded wrong. Then she left the trailer. A second later she was back, carrying a brand new tray of food dishes. Again, she visited each cage, this time leaving a dish of food inside it. Then she left once more, this time carefully locking the trailer door behind her. Before Tuck's eyes had had a chance to grow accustomed to the dimmer light, he could hear the unmistakeable sound of a truckload of cats eating. He approached the bowl in his own cage and sniffed at it carefully.

'You can eat it,' said an American accent in the dark beside him.

'It's not fresh,' said Tuck.

'No, it's from a tin. But it's good, you can eat it.'

Well, Tuck didn't need telling twice. He ate the food quickly and then sat licking his lips. As he did so, he listened to the other cats around him washing themselves and yawning before curling themselves up in their beds. Soon it grew quiet and Tuck thought he was the only cat in the entire trailer who was still awake. It was very still and the light was quite dull, the shadows of the trees outside moving across the windows high in the opposite wall. Tuck turned to his right and saw a huge pair of round yellow eyes looking back at him.

'Don't want to sleep?'

'No,' said Tuck sadly. 'I want to go home.'

'Good,' said Bunk. 'That's very good. Your name's Tuck, right? And you say you come from this place where we've stopped.'

Tuck nodded, but said nothing.

'Don't feel like talking?'

Tuck shook his head.

'I get that,' said the American. 'And normally I'd respect it. But I have some things I need to tell you. Firstly, I'm an undercover agent with the Cat Intelligence Agency. Secondly, I'm going to get us out of here. And thirdly, you're going to help.

WHAT A PUNK!

Ginger followed the ground beside the stream, blinking away the snowflakes and trying her best to keep the rats in sight. But as their boat had floated into the middle of the stream, it had picked up speed and soon Ginger had to break into a run to keep up. Just as she was building up to her maximum speed (which, as we know, wasn't that fast), she started feeling the strangest sensation. It wasn't the feeling of snow falling on her head and back; it wasn't the feeling of cold air rushing past her nose. Oh secret spies, no. It was the feeling of being watched. Ginger squinted through the snow to the boat full of rats to see if they could be watching her. As she did so, she realised how much further away they had drifted. With all the snow in the air she could barely see them. Ignoring her other feeling, she ran on a little bit further, determined to keep the rats in sight. But then the stream turned a sudden bend, and the rats were completely lost to view.

'Hu, ahu, ahu, ahu,' Ginger panted. 'Flipperty flabby-bits, I'm not as fit as I used to be. Must. Carry. On.'

She was about to make herself run again when once more she noticed the feeling of being watched. Well, it definitely wasn't the rats on the boat watching her now. She looked behind her along the bank, then out to the stream again. Then she looked left, up into the grass which grew thickly above the bank. There she saw a jet-black animal a little larger than herself with two thick white stripes down his back, a safety pin through one of his nostrils, and a tartan baseball cap worn backwards on his head. It was a punk skunk.

'What you doing, missus?' the skunk called out to her. 'You missed da bus or something? He, he, he, heee.'

'I was trying to follow those rats,' said Ginger, still panting. 'They stole all my food. Have you any idea where this stream goes?'

'Downstream I reckon, he, he, he, heeee,' said the skunk, before sniffing loudly and spitting into the grass. 'No dins-dins for ginge-ginge, he, he, he, heee.'

'Well, what are you doing here?' said Ginger.

But she knew the answer for she had seen what the skunk was holding between his front paws. It was a wooden skateboard with 'SKUNK' scratched on it in angular letters.

'What does it look like, ginger nut?' said the skanky-skate punk-skunk, waving his skateboard at her in a rather aggressive way. 'Practising, durrh!'

Now, you might think Ginger was annoyed at this tartan-wearing skunk being so rude to her. But she was glad, not sad, the plaid-clad rad-lad was mad and bad, for she had to be a cad and this made her feel less bad about it.

'Yes, well, you probably need to practise in the snow,' said Ginger, as if she'd forgotten all about the rats. 'You probably fall off a lot and need a soft landing. But I bet you can't jump as far on that thing as I can.'

'Tja!' said the skanky skunk scornfully. 'You? Jump? What, you got an anti-gravity suit or something? Watch this!'

And he disappeared into the grass behind him. Then, without warning, he came flying out on top of the skateboard, his thick black-and-white tail flowing in the snowy air behind him. He had flicked up his heels so now his skateboard twirled beneath him, until—after a wee wibbly wobble—he landed next to Ginger.

'I bet you fifty doodahs you can't jump further than that,' he said.

'You're on, rude-boy,' said Ginger putting out her hand for the skateboard. 'Watch this.'

Well, I'm guessing you know what happened next. Ginger took the board and—two feet on and two feet off—skated it up into the bushes above. Then she skated it a bit further, pushing past grasses and cobwebs and low hanging branches, all of it lightly dusted with snow; and then a little bit further still, although a lot more to the right this time, until she came back out onto the flat ground beside the stream. She was about twenty metres away from the skate-punk skunk, and halfway to the water before he spotted her.

'Oi, dumb-bell! What you doing?' he yelled at her. 'You're supposed to jump!'

But Ginger ignored him. Instead, she kept on skating, building up more and more speed, faster and faster, using all her muscles (not much) and weight (very much) to get the board going as fast as it could until— SPLASH! —it hit the water. Then, and only then, did she lift all four paws onto the surface of the board.

'Come back,' screamed the skunk. 'That's my wood!'

'Serves you right for being so cheeky,' said Ginger as she and the board floated downstream through the falling snow. The scornful and scoffing skanky skunk sank on the dank bank looking blank at the frankly rank prank to steal his plank. Looking back at him, Ginger felt a bit guilty, and she shouted out to him.

'I'll leave your skateboard on your side of the water. Just follow the bank until you find it!'

But the water was running so fast, and she was already so far away, and the snow was growing so thick, that she couldn't tell if he'd heard her or not. She turned to see which way she was going, and gasped to see she was no longer on a stream at all. For as the water had turned the bend in the direction the rats had travelled, it had joined a wide river, the opposite bank barely visible through the thickening snow.

WHAT AN OFFER!

It was snowing where Minnie was too, not that she'd noticed. Oh busy brushes, no. For Minnie had got up bright and early and was now working hard.

What?! Minnie up bright and early?

And 'what' squared to the power of 'you're kidding'— working hard??

You probably think I'm talking about the wrong cat. Or maybe you think I've applied a less than feasible character-change to get the story moving along. Well, if that is what you think, then you're as wrong as a Pong (and you are soon to find out quite how wrong a Pong can be). Because no sooner was the sun up the next day than Minnie was working hard at cleaning.

'Aha!' you're thinking. 'Minnie was working hard at cleaning herself. Well, that makes more sense. No doubt she was primping and preening, crimping and cleaning, braiding and plaiting, brushing and combing.'

Well, wrong again! Minnie was cleaning the floor of The Scratching Post. For the sign that she had read the night before had said:

Now hiring.
Cleaning staff required.
No experience necessary.

'Oh!' Minnie had thought, 'I'm purrfectly qualified!'

And she was right, for what could be more perfect for a cat like Minnie than a job which needed absolutely no experience of cleaning or housework whatsoever? The answer is: nothing. And so, the previous night, before the group of toms could get any closer, Minnie had torn down the sign with her teeth and run into the trees. There she had found an old thistle and used it as a comb to tease out all the knots from her fur. Then she'd rolled in some dust before climbing up to the roof of The Scratching Post to let the night breezes blow it all out again. Then she'd licked and licked and licked and licked herself back into shape. After that she'd applied a little of the salvaged paw-paw lotion around her eyes and then—and only then—had she hot-tailed it round to the backdoor of the milk bar. There she had used her not insignificant charms to persuade the manager to hire her on the spot.

'I might look grubby,' she'd said humbly, 'but it's only 'cos I spend all my time cleaning other things. Floors, tables, glasses and saucers are my speciality, but I reckon there's not nuffink what I'm not good at cleaning.'

Well, the milk bar manager clearly cared more about cleanliness than he did about grammar because he hired Minnie immediately. His name was Mr Soffalot and he was an ocelot, which—in case you don't know—is a rather beautiful type of wild cat found in the Caribbean. Mr Soffalot, like many ocelots, had amazing brown eyes and a beautiful yellow-and-orange coat with thick black stripes. He came from Trinidad and how he came to manage The

Scratching Post is itself a fantastic story, but, sadly, not one for which you have paid.

'Saucer of milk, leftovers from the kitchen, and a room over the café is what you get,' he told Minnie in his deep Trinidadian accent. 'I run a clean milk bar, and no funny business. Any trouble and you be out.'

'Trouble?' said Minnie, in one of her less convincing lies. 'I dunno what the word even means, darl.'

Now, I'll admit it, I was somewhat surprised when Minnie told me about this part of the story because—between you and me—I've always thought Minnie was a bit too in love with herself to do a job like cleaning a milk bar. But then, you see, I'd forgotten how ambitious a cat Minnie has always been. If a cleaning job would help get her to her audition, then a cleaning job she would do. And good old Minnie, did she whinge and whine and complain about it? Well, bells yeah, of course she did! But once she'd done that, she decided she may as well enjoy it.

'It can't be a rag-to-riches story without a rag in it, can it now?' she said to herself, washing out a dirty cloth as she prepared to clean the floor that morning.

'I can't be Cinderella without a few cinders on me face, can I?' she said as she cleared out the fireplace.

'And there's no use crying over spilled milk, is there?' she said, as she cleaned up all the splashes of milk from around the saucers on the floor. In fact, she got so into the spirit of things that she started singing as she worked.

'Oh, polish and spit, I don't mind a bit,
Cleaning and dusting in a bar!

For one day soon, I'll sing my happy tune,
And I'll be a superstar.'

As she sang she started to dance a little bit, wiggling her bum, and using her very fluffy tail to dust along the top of the bar as she mopped the floor.

'Oh, Minnie, they'll say, it's your lucky day,
You've got your own telly show.
They'll tell me I'm a cutie; they'll say I'm a beauty,
And I'll say "Yes, I know!"'

And then, because Minnie was feeling better than she had felt in days, and because there was no one else around, and because she was Minnie, she got up on the stage which took up one whole end of the room and started clawing at the tall scratching post which stood there and gave the bar its name.

'Oh, scritchy, scritchy, scratch,
I'm such a catch,
I am unique and not one of a batch.
Scratchy, scratchy, scritch,
There just one little hitch,
I can be—'

Minnie suddenly stopped singing. She wasn't alone in the bar at all! The front door was locked so no customers could come in, but the door to the kitchen was open and, without her noticing, the manager had come into the room and now stood watching her.

'Oh! I'm so sorry, Mr Soffalot,' she said, quickly retracting her claws from the scratching post and jumping back down to the floor. 'I'm so sorry, I was just mucking about a bit, innit? Fixing my paws so I can work harder.'

Minnie produced the tube of paw-paw ointment and started rubbing it into her pads to give credence to the lie. Because, for once, she was desperate to keep out of trouble. She had promised herself she would hang onto to this job until she'd got back on her paws, saved up some doodahs and/ or met someone who would give her a lift to the city. But, to her dismay, when she looked up from putting the ointment on her paws, Mr Soffalot, the ocelot, was still standing there. And still looking at her.

'You sing?' he said.

'Ooh, yes, love singing,' said Minnie.

'And you dance.'

'Bit of a wiggle and a giggle from time to time, doesn't hurt, does it, darl? Listen, Mr Soffalot, I'm really sorry for mucking about. It'll be the last time, I promise. I really need this job just now, so, like you said, no trouble. Never again, all right?'

'No,' said Mr Soffalot.

'No?' squawked Minnie. 'Really?'

'Really. Because you sing too well, Miss Minnie, and you dance too well too. I think you mopping my floors like this is not enough. Not the best use of my resources. I think perhaps we should see you up on the stage tonight. What do you think?'

Minnie paused from pouring the paw-paw on her poor paws, then pretended to ponder and peruse the proposal. What did she think?! Have you met her? She'd love to do it!

'Well, I guess I could give it a go,' she said, as if she wasn't sure. 'Just to be polite; only if you insist.' She pulled off the rag she'd used to tie back her hair and, with a shake of her whole body, let her luscious locks flow in slow motion around her. 'Of course, I'll need my own dressing room, fresh flowers every day and ten per cent of takings.'

Mr Soffalot laughed, his own beautiful stripes oscillating along his body as he did so. 'Let's see how you go on Friday, and then we'll see if we give it a second go. In the meantime, the ladies' litter tray needs emptying.'

'But …'

'Now.'

Minnie stared at Mr Soffalot furiously, and Mr Soffalot stared back at her. Like she needed any more motivation to make sure that night's performance would be the best of her entire life.

WHAT A DILEMMA!

As Minnie was being made her exciting offer, Tuck found himself facing a dreadful dilemma. To explain what it was, it's time for another flashback, so hold onto your hats and let's return to where we last left Tuck and Bunk: whispering in the dark as all the other cats slept around them.

'Look up at the windows near the ceiling,' Bunk had said in his quiet American voice. 'They all have mesh across them. All except for that one up there, above the cages opposite. I've spent the last few nights pulling it away and the Pongs haven't noticed. Now I just need some help opening the window. You see there's an 'O' shape in the handle?'

'Who are the Pongs?' said Tuck.

'The humans, the man and the woman.'

'Humans have names too!' said Tuck. 'Who knew?'

Bunk looked at Tuck strangely with his massive yellow eyes, but said nothing. Instead, he used his back leg to scratch extra hard at the collar he was wearing until it came apart. As it did so, two little pins fell from it to the floor of his cage.

'Take this,' he said, picking one up in his mouth and passing it through the wire mesh between him and Tuck. Tuck took the pin into his own mouth.

'Tomorrow night you must use that pin to pick the

104

lock on your cage. The procedure can take a while, so you'll need to familiarise yourself with it. Use tonight to practise.'

Tuck gasped.

'It's just like a spy movie, gurgle, gargle, ach, ach!' he said.

Bunk gave him another strange look. 'You all right, cat?'

Tuck smiled and nodded. But in reality he wasn't all right because, as he'd gasped with excitement, he'd swallowed the pin Bunk had just given him. Now he could feel it working its way down his throat and into his tummy.

'Good,' said Bunk. 'I've done this several times before, so tomorrow night I'll probably be out of my cage before you. As soon as I am, I'll start climbing up to the window. Once there, I'll thread my collar through the 'O' shape in the handle. By the time I've done that, you shouldn't be far behind me. Then we each tug on one end of the collar with our teeth and the window should open. Affirmative?'

'A furry motive,' said Tuck sadly. He couldn't bring himself to tell his new friend that he'd already ruined his plans. 'But maybe you should pick someone else?'

'Negative. I have sought assistance from the other felines and none has been willing to assist. I tried approaching them individually, no dice. I even tried getting them to work together, to create a prison riot by chanting "What do we want? We want din-dins! When do we want them? Miaow!" None of it worked, so I need you.'

'Ooh, that's good,' said Tuck. 'I like that. What do we

want? We want din-dins! When do we want them? Miaow!'

'But—'

'What do we want? We want din-dins! When do we want them? Miaow! It's fun! What do we want …'

'Tuck—'

'We want din-dins! When do we want them? Miaow!'

'Enough!' Bunk frowned and stuck his underbite out even further. 'The point is, I am relying on you and you alone. But we should have no contact tomorrow to avoid any suspicion. Keep yourself to yourself.'

Tuck nodded again, suddenly remembering he'd swallowed the secret weapon Bunk had passed to him. He had no idea how to keep himself to anyone but himself, having been given away as a kitten. He suspected keeping himself to himself was going to be as difficult as being in two places at the same time, which he'd tried on several occasions with no success. Not that any of this mattered, for he doubted that the next day he'd be in a mood for talking anyway.

How right he was. For the first half of the next morning—as Ginger was purloining a skateboard and Minnie was cleaning a milk bar—Tuck lay sadly on his little cat bed thinking how unfair life was and what a huge disadvantage it was being intellectually challenged. Except, he didn't use long words like 'intellectually' or 'challenged'. He just used the word 'me'. Poor Tuck. He had spent many a sad and sorrowful day before now (well, five to be precise), but this was sadder and more sorrowful than any of them. He was going to be stuck in this smelly little cage refusing half his meals whilst Bunk was going to be an international adventure spy and go to the CIA Headquarters and probably get a bowl of milk on the way. For the first time in his entire life, Tuck was so sad he couldn't even cry.

But then, just before lunch time, he felt a familiar gurgling sensation in his tummy. Soon, he was uncomfortable and very soon after that he realised he had to go to the litter tray. Tuck hated doing the do in front of other cats, but there were no two ways about it. Or rather, no number-two ways about it. He had to go.

On the litter tray, he closed his eyes and pretended he was behind the old stables, amongst the gravel, where he normally liked to do his business, listening to the birds tweeting their tweets. In fact, he pretended so hard that, when he opened his eyes, he was surprised to find himself on a litter-tray locked in a cage in the back of a lorry.

'Oogy,' he said. 'How disappointing.'

Then he turned around to bury his poo, but as he put his one paw forward to do so what did he see? Can you guess? Yes, cat poo, thank you, we all got that bit. But what was *in* the cat poo? That's right! It was the pin he'd swallowed the previous evening. He was saved! All he had to do was ... eugh! Bunk had told him he'd have to hold the pin between his teeth to get it into the lock on his cage. Now he wasn't certain he wanted to do that.

'Oogy,' he said. 'What a problem.' Because 'dilemma' was outside his vocabulary. In fact, let's face it, 'vocabulary' is outside Tuck's vocabulary.

'Oh, pin-in-a-poo, I don't know what to do,' he said,

but he was interrupted from his dilemma by a whisper behind him.

'Psst, cat.'

It was Bunk, who had sidled up to the wire which divided their cages and was talking out of the side of his mouth.

'You said no contact,' said Tuck as quietly as he knew how, which, as anyone who has ever met him will tell you, was not very quietly AT ALL.

Oh, sorry, now he's got me shouting too.

'Ssh!' said Bunk (to Tuck, not to me, although if he had heard me just then, he'd probably have said it to me too). He looked around nervously in case any of the other cats had noticed them talking. 'You still got your pin?'

'Er ... sort of,' said Tuck.

'Sort of?'

'I mean, yes. Why?'

Bunk looked a bit bashful. 'The two pins are different sizes,' he said. 'Only one of them fits my lock, and I gave you the wrong one. Here.'

Bunk motioned with his nose towards one of his paws. He was using it to push a pin along the floor of his cage and through the wire mesh into Tuck's.

'Go and get the other pin and push it through to me.'

'Do I have to? said Tuck. 'Can't we both use this one?'

'Didn't you hear me, cat?

'Oh ... eh ... ah ... OK,' said Tuck. 'Meet you back here in a minute.'

Bunk nodded almost imperceptibly and wandered off, as if he'd just been rubbing his side-fur against the wire. Tuck walked back to his litter tray.

'Oh, eugh,' he said. Then 'Pwoar'. Then 'Ooh, oogy!'

He put out a paw, extended his longest claw, and carefully pulled the pin out of his poo.

'Icky sticky!' he said, and he was quite right, for the poo had stuck the pin to his paw. Not waiting for it to become unstuck, Tuck quickly hobbled with three legs back to the wall of wire he shared with Bunk. There, he tapped his paw against the mesh until the pin—and a few little brown flakes—fell to the ground on Bunk's side of the wire.

'There's something you should kno—' he said as Bunk walked over.

'Sssh, cat, keep it down. I'll see you later, up near the window.'

And so Tuck, who did like to do what he was told, wandered silently away.

Picking the lock that night was far easier than Tuck had imagined. For a physically-intelligent animal like him, anything which involved using his various body parts to do different things at the same time comes very easily. That is why I will never have it said that Tuck is stupid. Intellectually-challenged, perhaps; academically lacking, definitely; but stupid, no. Because, physically, Tuck was a genius. Do remember, dear reader, everyone's good at something, and just because it's not the same thing as you, doesn't mean that they're smarter or dumber than you are.

Truly stupid beings are as rare as truly ugly ones, and can normally be identified by the fact they use words like 'stupid,' or 'ugly' to describe anyone.

Bendypoos, Tuck found picking the lock very easy and, once out of his cage, he naturally found it super-duper, easier than a trooper, to climb up the cages opposite his own. He could even have jumped from the floor of the trailer to the top of the uppermost cage if he'd wanted to, but Bunk had made it very clear he shouldn't do that in case he woke up the cat who lived there.

'You made it,' said Bunk when Tuck arrived at the narrow row of windows above the cages. 'That was fast, cat. Look, I've nearly finished threading my collar through the hook on this handle. Good work on lubricating that pin by the way, it turned in the lock smoother than ever. What did you use?'

Agh! Another dilemma, no more than twelve hours after the last one! Tuck, you see, was a very honest cat and had been brought up to believe you should never tell lies. But just now he wasn't sure he saw the value in sharing the truth about the pin which Bunk had so recently had in his mouth.

'Gut instinct,' he said, thinking this had a good ring about it.

But Bunk didn't seem very interested anyway. He was still fiddling with his collar, pushing it through the O-shaped hole in the handle of the window.

'Got it!' he said at last. 'Now, you bite on one end and I'll bite on the other. We both pull on three.'

'Three?'

'Yes, I'll count to three, and then we both pull.'

'The thing is,' Tuck whispered nervously. 'I'm not very good at counting. Can't we pull on two?'

All Tuck could see of Bunk was his wide yellow eyes looking at him strangely.

'Fine, we pull on two. You ready? One, two!'

Well, poor trim Bunk had underestimated Tuck's strength. As soon as he said 'two', Tuck pulled with all his might, and Bunk was dragged by his teeth towards the O-shaped window-handle until his nose collided with it.

'No,' he hissed. 'Pull away from the window, not away from me!'

'Ooh, so sorry,' said Tuck. 'But why don't I just put both ends of the collar in my mouth and pull the handle open myself?'

Bunk looked at him strangely. 'You that strong?'

'No verb!' said Tuck, who did like people to talk properly and had once even got two out of ten in a grammar test. This had been the highpoint of his education and he had never again forgotten what a verb was.

'"You that strong?" has got no doing-word in it,' he explained. 'You should say, "Are you that strong?" And, yes, I think I am.'

And with that, Tuck reached down and took one end of the collar, then the other, and with a quick flick of his head pulled on the handle until the window creaked wide open.

'Ooh,' he said. 'It's been snowing!'

'Nice work, cat,' said Bunk. 'I'll see you get mentioned in the debrief. Stay here and keep the others calm.'

'Stay here?' said Tuck. 'But they'll put me back in the cage!'

'Ssh! Keep your voice down. That was the plan. You help me escape and I'll get help. You stay here.'

'But I want to come with you to the CAI,' said Tuck, who really couldn't spell at all. 'I want to be free too!'

And with that he started crying.

'Boohoo, weewah. What if you fail, and I'm stuck in jail?'

'Ssh!' said Bunk, looking nervously at the cages below him. 'Keep it down! Do I need to remind you we're on a covert mission?'

'I already kept it down and it came out my bum,' said Tuck. 'I did everything you said. Oh, boohoo …'

'OK, OK, OK,' whispered Bunk hurriedly. 'You can come with me. But you have to keep quiet and do exactly as I say, you clear?'

'No verb!' said Tuck. 'But, yes, hoorah! Oh me, oh my, I'm going to be a spy!'

And with that he climbed through the window, jumped down to the ground and waited for Bunk to join him in the snow.

WHAT A SPLASH!

Oh, the seesaw of life. Just when things start looking up for one of our furry feline friends, they get significantly worse for another. At the very moment that Tuck started breathing the sweet air of freedom, poor Ginger was battling for any breath at all. It was dark and cold, and she was wet and frightened and didn't know how much longer she had to live.

For just as the punk-skunk stream had widened into a fast-flowing river, so the fast-flowing river had accelerated and widened further into a ... what's faster and wider than a river? A great **big** river, that's what. A river so big that both banks looked a long way away, even when it stopped snowing, and Ginger could see them speeding past. A river so big it had waves: freezing little whitecaps which splashed over the skateboard and made its wooden surface very slippery, not to mention very cold. Ginger had tried steering the board by leaning more of her six bellies to one side than the other. But the eddies and currents and slips and slews of the grey water had other ideas, and she soon had to accept that she had no control whatsoever over which way she drifted.

Worse than that, Ginger had once again lost sight of the rats and the last bags of her winter store. A little after setting herself afloat on the stolen skateboard, she'd spotted them cruising downstream in the slower water near the opposite bank. She had soon caught up with them, and was even worried one of them might turn around and notice her.

Speed was one thing, though, and direction was another. Whenever the rats wanted to steer, one or two of them would jump into the water beside their little boat and push it left or right. But Ginger, being a cat, would do anything rather than get into the water. When the river first widened, and the rats steered hard right away from current, there was little she could do but float on in a straight line. Then, when the cold grey water forked around wooded land, and the rats steered right again, all Ginger could do was follow the main current down to the left.

That had been in the middle of the afternoon, when the sun, though pale behind the snow clouds, was still up in the sky. Ginger had hoped she could drift towards the shore before it got too dark, and then, perhaps, run across the land which had forked the river and follow the rats from there. But now that hope was gone. On and on she floated with no way of doing anything about it.

The river had long before left the Great Dark Forest, tracing its way at first through frosted fields and meadows, then winding through increasingly built-up suburbs. Soon Ginger saw great factories and huge high-rise blocks, and she realised she was passing through the city. This made her very nervous indeed, because if she carried on floating at this rate soon the river would reach the ocean, and there she was certainly done for. By staying awake and balancing carefully, she could just about stay afloat on the river. But in the shifting ocean, with its treacherous waves, she wouldn't last a minute.

As if all of that wasn't scary enough, now night had fallen and Ginger couldn't even see where she was going. Her only consolation was that the river had grown slightly narrower as it entered the city. She could see this by the lights which shone through the black air from the shore on either side of her. Shopfronts and apartment windows, office blocks and streetlamps, all twinkled in the dark, their lights reflected on the wobbly surface of the black river. It was a strangely comforting sight, and Ginger was able for seconds at a time to forget the damp and the cold, her hunger and the perilous slippiness of the skateboard, and remember her old city days as a street fighter, running through alleyways and hiding under cars. She remembered how she'd first met her true love Major on a winter's night such as this. How he'd turned to her and said—SPLASH!!!

'Miaowwwww!!! Yeweeeee!!!!'

What? Major had said what? Why did he say 'splash?' Oh! Major didn't say 'splash' at all! Poor Ginger had fallen asleep on her skateboard, exhausted by the day's events and the nerves of staying afloat. The splash had been the noise of her falling into the freezing black river water. And it was she that now screamed as she sunk her front claws into the wooden skateboard. She kicked and pummelled and splashed with her back legs and pulled with all her might on her front legs, but there was no way she could get back up on the board. She tried again and again, the water dragging down on her fur and the cold of it seeming to enter her very bones. Again she pulled on her front claws, just managing to keep her face out of the bitter water. Never in her life had she been so frightened, and she

screeded   in   a   most   pitiful   way.
MMYEEEANGGGGOWWWW!!! Who knew what
lived in the river that would like a nice big cat for dinner?

Ginger was about to screech again, but then—phew!
—she remembered she was a sensible cat. She also
remembered this: in a dangerous situation, fear is the thing
mostly likely to kill you. She took a deep breath and told
herself to CALM DOWN!!!! Try again. She took another
deep breath and told herself again to calm down, because
shouting wasn't going to help.

'I've still got the skateboard,' she told herself. 'I just
need to hang on. Maybe by kicking I can move myself
towards the shore.'

So she tried kicking her back legs again. Not to get
back onto the skateboard, but to try and steer towards the
shore, the way she'd seen the rats do. But the more she
kicked, the more tired she grew. Soon she was struggling to
hold her mouth above the level of the dark and dirty water.
Three times she swallowed a huge mouthful of the river
and choked, spluttered and coughed. Each time, she
calmed herself down until she was ready to kick some
more, on and on until at last she just couldn't continue. She
had stared death in the face before and decided it wasn't
the worst thing in the world. Now it was time to look at it
that way once more. Major, her late husband, the love of
her life, was waiting for her in Purrvana. As Ginger
thought of him she closed her eyes, and a single tear rolled
down her face into the freezing black river.

WHAT A SECRET!

The farm smelled different. When Tuck had left it the previous morning, it had still had a lingering odour of smoke from the smokehouse, of the food stores which had disappeared, of Ginger, of Minnie, and of Tuck himself. Now it smelled of strange vehicles and their horrible exhaust fumes, not to mention the damp milky smell of humans.

'Come on,' Tuck said to Bunk as soon as he'd landed beside him in the snow. 'The quickest way out is up the driveway.'

But Bunk shook his head slowly.

'Not yet,' he said. 'I need to gather some intel for the mission.'

'Ooh,' said Tuck. 'What *is* the mission? Is it impossible?'

Bunk didn't answer. He simply looked around him. Tuck looked around too and spotted a little caravan that had been parked by the farmhouse.

'Ooh,' he said. 'What's that?'

Again, Bunk didn't answer. Instead, he walked slowly towards the caravan. Tuck followed him and watched with amazement as Bunk managed to open its door with his nose. Immediately, the fusty smell of sleeping humans drifted out into the night air.

'Be careful!' said Tuck loudly. 'That must be where the Pong people are!'

Bunk turned to him, his yellow eyes narrowed. 'Which is why we must be so silent. Not a word, you understand?'

Tuck did understand. He sat mutely and watched as Bunk climbed up the steps into the caravan and disappeared inside. **Eek**! What to do? He didn't want to get any closer to the humans, but he was too scared to be out here alone with everything that had happened. What if there were more humans hiding nearby? He forced himself forwards, as close as he could bear, to the caravan door.

'**Zzzzzzz.**'

Through the doorway, he could see the corner of a bed, with one of Mr Pong's smelly feet sticking out of it.

'**Zz zz zzzzz.**'

Tuck was too scared to go any further, but from where he sat, he could see a huge picture on the wall of the caravan opposite the open door. It was a picture of a black fur coat, made up of lots of strange, but similar, shapes sewn together. Then he gasped as he realised those shapes were animal skins, each one the size and shape of a flattened black cat. Next to the diagram of the coat was a poster with garish writing, colourful pictures of cat food and lots of crossings-out on it.

'**Zzzz**! *Snuffle, snuffle* … Move over, Willy.'

Mrs Pong's deep and throaty voice mumbled inside the caravan, and Mr Pong's foot disappeared from view. Well, that was too much for Tuck. He wasn't going to hang around to see if the humans were waking up. He turned on his tail and fled to the other side of the farmyard. From there, he watched as Bunk came slowly out of the caravan, then used his nose to push the door closed again.

'She wants to turn us into a coat!' Tuck said to Bunk when the American arrived beside him. 'And what was that poster? What did it say?'

Bunk spoke slowly, as if trying to work something out.

'It said: *Free cat food for everyone. Coming soon.* It had a date on it that had been changed several times. It's like they're waiting ... Oh, cat! They must be waiting to develop a poisonous food that cats will eat! I found lots of recipes in there, all of them containing toxins. That's why the man keeps bringing us toxic food every night. They're trying to get it right and then ... then they're going to give it away for free.'

'Ooh, how awful,' said Tuck. 'Was that why you were sent to spy on them? Was that your secret mission?'

Bunk didn't answer. He walked past Tuck towards the smokehouse, gesturing for him to follow. Above them, the thick clouds which had brought the snow were breaking up, the infinite black sky showing through in ragged patches.

'What's this?' said Bunk, pointing with his nose at the smokehouse.

'What's the mission?' said Tuck. 'I asked first.'

'It's top secret,' said Bunk. 'I can't share it. Tell me about this building.'

'You tell me about the mission,' said Tuck. 'The Pongs are so ghastly and gruesome; I want to hear what you're going to do about them. And I've never met anyone from the Feline Bureau of Investigation before.'

'I'm not from the Feline Bureau of Investigation!' Bunk's underbite was even more pronounced than normal. 'They only look after domesticated affairs. The Cat Intelligence Agency has a much broader mandate. We tackle interspecies issues.'

'Ooh, so sorry,' said Tuck, who had no idea what any of these long words meant. 'Tell me about the Pongs anyway.'

'No. This building smells strongly of food, but now it's empty. What happened here?'

'Not telling!' said Tuck. 'Not until you tell the story. You said we were going on a covered mission and now you won't tell me what it is. It's not fair. So if you won't tell me anything, I won't tell you anything either. So there.'

And, with that, Tuck sat down in the snow and curled his tail over his front paws to show he meant business. Bunk stared at him for a second or two, then closed his eyes and sighed.

'I was recruited into the Agency last year, straight out of college. It was a huge honour.'

'A collage!' whispered Tuck. 'Like with bits of paper?'

Bunk gave him a wide-eyed look before continuing.

'They approached me in my final year,' he said. 'The vetting process was so well-disguised I didn't even know it was happening.'

'Ooh, that's good,' said Tuck. 'I went to the vet once and I hated it. She was disguised too, in a white coat and a mask, but it didn't help at all.'

'Cat, you going to let me tell this story or not? You

need to stop interrupting. Where was I? Oh yes. Training was intense. We had to dive through burning cat flaps; sit for days on end under a sofa; resist bits of string pulled along the floor. We had to learn bird languages and how to transmit messages to humans. Sometimes we were placed in homes with them, had to live alongside them without them noticing. At other times,' Bunk's voice quavered at the memory, 'we had to let them pick us up and tickle our tummies. Then there were the other cats. We had to let them attack us without responding. It was tough, but it was meant to be tough. I'd wanted to get into the Human Manipulation Program, but I wasn't fluffy enough, so I trained for Black Ops, the elite night division. A month ago, I was called in to receive my first brief.'

'Brief what?'

Bunk turned and looked at Tuck in the dark night. His head seemed even smaller now they were outdoors.

'Ooh, sorry,' said Tuck. 'Do go on.'

'I was to be dropped into the garden of a suspected super-baddy,' said Bunk. 'I was to enter the house … I was to …'

'Go on,' said Tuck. 'This is so exciting!'

Bunk looked away. 'It doesn't matter,' he said at last. 'Maybe you're right, maybe we should get out of here as fast as we can.'

'Oh, but I want to hear about the story. What were you supposed to do when you got into the super-daddy's house?'

Bunk ignored the question and walked towards the smokehouse.

'There was food in here, wasn't there?'

'Not telling until you finish the story,' said Tuck.

Bunk stopped walking, put his head down, and sighed.

'A fly got into the room,' he said, 'during my briefing. The Director of Black Ops started telling me what I was supposed to do. The agency had discovered the Pongs were up to something, and they thought King Rat might be involved to.'

Tuck gasped. 'King Rat!'

'They were going to drop me into the garden of the Pongs. As a pure black cat, they knew I'd be taken. Now we know why. The Director started to explain the rest, but then a fly got into the room, and I couldn't stop watching it. It buzzed and buzzed and buzzed, like it was about to land where I could catch it. It was big and thick and slow, but eventually it just flew out of the window again. By that time the Director had finished talking. "All clear?" he said, and I was too embarrassed to admit I hadn't listened to a word. It was all about the Pongs and what I was supposed to do, but I've no idea what he said. The agency dropped me off that evening, and I still don't know what I was supposed to be doing.'

'Ooh,' said Tuck. 'That is embarrassing.'

He and Bunk stood looking at each other across the snow.

'Still, though,' Tuck continued cheerily. 'I wouldn't worry about it too much. I once vomited up half a crow and forgot to tidy it up. I left it lying there for days until Ginger told me to do something about it. It was *SOOOOO* embarrassing. Doesn't that make you feel better?'

'Much,' said Bunk. 'Thanks so much for sharing.'

'And that's the smokehouse,' said Tuck. 'Or at least it used to be. It's where we kept all the winter stores, but they were stolen at the same time Ginger disappeared; but she didn't do it, because she's not like that; although, as Minnie said, you do have to admit it is a bit of a go-in-sea-dance.'

Bunk looked at Tuck, his yellow eyes wide.

'You had food stolen? This cat who disappeared, Ginger, is she black?'

'No, she's ginger,' said Tuck, who thought it was a bit of a stupid question, but was far too polite to say so.

Bunk walked over to the smokehouse and blinked at it hard. Then he walked inside it, which Tuck thought was almost as brave as going inside the caravan. Again, Bunk blinked in every direction. Then he walked blinking all around its outside, before disappearing behind it once again, this time sniffing carefully at the ground. Finding himself alone, Tuck looked back at the caravan. As he did so, he thought he saw it rock gently back and forth on its wheels.

'Can we go now?' Tuck whispered. 'What if the humans wake up and find us and decide to skin us now? Bunk?'

When there was no answer from behind the smokehouse, Tuck called again.

'Bunk? BUNK?!!'

He ran around the back of the smokehouse, following Bunk's tracks through the thin layer of snow, to find the

American staring at him furiously.

'Cat!' hissed Bunk. 'If you are to join me on this mission you must remain quiet and calm at all times. I will allow you to accompany me only under these circumstances. You clear?'

Tuck stuck out his bottom lip and nodded sadly. He wanted to say 'No verb,' but he didn't dare.

'Good,' said Bunk. 'Now follow me, the trail leads this way.'

And he led Tuck across the grass, through the tunnel under the ruins of the milking shed and into the overgrown field.

WHAT A GANG!

MIAOWNTIME, down in the city, Ginger was waking up. Oh, come on, you didn't think she was going to go down that easily, did you? She might have given up one of her nine lives, but being middle-aged she had another three or four left. So once she'd had a little break, she carried on kicking until, at last, her back legs kicked into something. She gasped, kicked again, and found the something was still there. Oh curdled cod-breath, she'd only kicked herself all the way to the river bank! With a surge of energy—which a minute before she would have thought impossible—she pushed against the ground below her, harder and harder, until first her tail, then her bum ran aground. Then, and only then, did she retract her claws from the skateboard, letting the far end of it fall—splat!—into the shallow water.

Ginger turned onto her paws and dragged her raggedly bedraggled bellies out of the dark water and onto the mud beside the river. She lay there for a while, panting heavily, the shallow water still lapping at her tail. Then she forced herself to her feet and looked into the night air around her. There weren't many lights here, just a few weak streetlamps that barely lit the old warehouses around them or the ancient wooden ramps which ran down from the warehouses into the river. Here and there, shadowy rotten staircases with half their steps missing ran up from the mud to deserted piers, but, otherwise, there was little but litter in sight. Ginger wanted to lie down again, right where she was, and sleep in the dark, but she knew many rivers are tidal and this mud might not stay above water for long. So she forced herself up one of the rotten sets of stairs, using the last of her energy to jump over the missing steps. She was exhausted, hungry and cold, but she was alive. Thanking her stars for that, as soon as she got to the top of the steps she lay down on the wharf and slept.

Several hours later, still damp and cold and desperately tired, she awoke to the sound of voices.

'She's dead,' said the first voice, a smoky, croaky, hokey-cokey kind of voice. 'Let's throw her into the mud and let the tide take her.'

'Nah, she's breathing,' said another voice. 'Look, that belly there is moving.'

'Let's chuck her in the mud anyway,' said a third voice. 'That'll teach her not to stray into our patch.'

Ginger opened one eye as narrowly as possible, so narrowly that, at first, all she could see was her own ginger eyelashes in the pale light of a streetlamp. Soon enough, though, other things became clear, and none of them were pretty. Three very rough cats were standing around her. One was a dirty tortoiseshell with a torn ear; one was a tabby with a pink-and-black splodgy nose, and one was an evil-looking white cat.

'She moved!' said the tabby, the owner of the smoky, croaky, hokey-cokey voice. 'I told you she was alive. Let's kill her.'

Then a fourth cat, a stumpy little thing, whose fur

could best be described as poo-brown and vomit-orange, came into view and gave Ginger a rather unpleasant kick in the ribs. Still Ginger didn't react. Not because she was too tired, and certainly not because it didn't hurt, but because she was waiting for the right moment.

'Dead,' said the stumpy one who'd kicked her. 'Chuck her in. Let's go.'

Ginger waited until all four cats were out of her sight and had their noses underneath her back, nudging her towards the edge of the wharf. Then she sprang into action.

'Skkeeeeowwwll!'

She jumped up onto three paws to face east so that as she slashed out with the fourth it was an unexpected southpaw. Without waiting to check if she'd made contact, she immediately slashed in the opposite direction with her other front paw. Then she arched her back, spiked her hair to make herself look huge, and checked on the situation. The tabby, the white cat, and the orange-and-brown stumpy one all had paws up to their faces. The tortoiseshell stood and stared and only then seemed to notice she now had rips in *both* ears. There was a split second before, as one, they all bared their teeth and yelled 'Get her!'

Ginger turned on her tail and ran with all her might, but she only made it a few metres before realising her error. By turning east when she'd first jumped up, she'd put the pier behind her, so that now she was running along it. But the pier stuck out over the mud and the river for only a few dozen metres before it came to a sudden end. Ginger stopped and turned to look at the four furious female felines between her and the shore.

'You maleficent moggy,' said the tallest of them, the evil-looking white cat.

'You're going to regret that,' said the tabby with the splodgy nose and the smoky, croaky, hokey-cokey voice.

'You're for it!' said the tortoiseshell with two ripped ears.

The fourth one, the stumpy little poo-brown-and-vomit-orange cat, didn't say anything. She just scowled at Ginger, bared her teeth, bristled her tail and ran full pelt at her. Ginger waited until the last minute and then ducked out of the way, giving the brown cat a sidekick in the ribs that almost sent her off the side of the pier. But no sooner had she done so than the white cat was on her, biting the back of her neck until Ginger felt her skin pierced. Then she felt the others on her too, felt them scratch her legs, back and tail, all of them screaming and yowling as Ginger scratched and kicked and bit back. But then—louder than any of the noise they were making—a sharp caterwaul broke the night air. Ginger felt the other cats instantly retract their claws and teeth. Instinctively, she jumped up and saw, to her surprise, all four of them standing calmly around her. Then the white cat and the tabby stepped aside to let a fifth cat through. An old grey-and-white mottled cat with faded green eyes and no more than three or four whiskers that drooped towards the ground.

'Stranger on our territory, Sue,' the white cat said to her. 'Attacked us without provocation. We were just seeing her off.'

'So I saw,' said the old grey-and-white cat. 'Although I wouldn't say trying to push her into the mud wasn't a provocation. And I wouldn't say you were seeing her off. Wipe the blood off your face, Killa, you look a sight. And you, Ivana, fix your ears before I rip you a new one.'

The white cat and the stumpy tabby did as they were told.

'You,' she said to Ginger. 'What's your game?'

Ginger looked at the old grey-and-white cat called Sue, then at the other four cats, and considered her options. The truth felt like the best idea.

'Came down the river on that,' she said, pointing over the side of the pier at the skateboard stuck in the mud below them. 'Nearly drowned. Didn't know this was a territory. I'll be off, if you don't mind, don't want any trouble.'

'Not so fast.' Sue held up a grey paw. 'You can fight. You wouldn't be from Citrus Street, would you? No, don't worry, I can see you're not. Still, you can fight. What's your name?'

'Ginger Jenkins,' said Ginger, waiting for the normal reaction. 'Not *the* Ginger Jenkins?!' or 'Ginger Jenkins, it can't be!' But none of the cats on the pier showed any reaction at all.

'So, Ginger, you think you can wander into the Gertrude Street wharves, pick a fight and just saunter on out, do you?'

'Like I said, I didn't know it was your territory,' said Ginger. 'And, like you said, it wasn't me picking the fight.'

Sue looked at Ginger and Ginger looked at Sue and what neither cat saw in the other was fear. It was Sue

Narmi, leader of the Gertrude Street Fur Girls, who spoke first.

'Well then, Ginger, I'll do you a deal. Me and the girls will let you go on your way, but first you have to do us a little favour. Sound fair enough?'

'I don't know,' said Ginger, careful to keep her nervousness from her voice. 'Why don't you tell me what the favour is and then I can decide.'

WHAT A SHOW!

Ginger wasn't the only one feeling nervous just then. Minnie, getting ready for her late-night debut at The Scratching Post, also had the jitters. Now, it probably won't surprise you to learn that Minnie didn't often feel this way. Don't you just hate that about some people? The way they can do anything with confidence? If not, then it's probably because you're a confident person yourself, and if *that's* the case, then I hope you're very grateful. Because most people **absolooooootely** hate the idea of standing up and giving a speech or being in any way the centre of attention. And some cats are the same way. Needless to say (but I'm going to say it anyway), Minnie wasn't one of them. Normally, she **lurrrrrved** being the centre of attention. And yet, that night, as she peeked through the curtain from behind the stage and watched the milk bar get busier and busier, she found she had butterflies in her stomach. This was probably because she'd caught and eaten several butterflies that afternoon. But, on top of that, she was also a little bit nervous.

Minnie had thought a cold winter's evening would find The Scratching Post fairly empty, only a few friendly locals and friends of Mr Soffalot's showing up. But now, as she peeked through the curtain, she saw almost every stool at the bar held a very rough-looking tom, whilst the booths were full of equally rough-looking groups of toms and females.

'Why's it so full?' she squealed at Mr Soffalot when he passed her on the way to fetch some extra saucers.

'I put word out we had big star in town. "Minnie, The Toilet Brush", I called you on the posters. That alright, girly?'

Mr Soffalot laughed so hard that the black lines in his fur wiggled all along his sides. Somewhat unsurprisingly, Minnie didn't like the oscillating ocelot Mr Soffalot's scoff a lot. She gave him a withering glare and stuck her chin up in the air.

'I *am* a star,' she said. 'I'm just working here undercover so I can get back to my roots and remember what slumming it feels like.'

And with that she pulled the curtains apart and strode out onto the stage.

Now, as you can imagine, Minnie had spent an awful lot of time that afternoon—when not cleaning, eating butterflies and practising her songs and dances—on her appearance. She'd given herself a full caticure: polishing and painting every one of her eighteen claws. She'd also polished her teeth with a rag from the cleaning cupboard and backcombed her tail in a way that even Ginger had once said looked pretty. She'd put sugar water in her whiskers to make them springy, and a dash of glitter in her fur to give herself extra sparkle. Of course, at the end of all this she thought she looked absolutely **gooooooooorgeous**, and therefore she expected everyone in The Scratching Post to think so too.

'Ta-da!' she sang as she walked out onto the stage, flicking her tail back and forth like it was a furry snake doing a dance. 'It's me, Minnie!'

There was a second's silence as every cat in the place turned to look at her, then the previous hubbub of chatter and mewling and even some rather loud bum sniffing started up just like before. Minnie didn't know what to do. She'd thought everyone would clap and cheer, shout and rear up on their back legs, pummelling their paws in the air.

'I'm Minnie!' she miaowed again.

Again, no one reacted apart from a crotchety old bagpuss seated at the bar who yelled 'Get on with it, or get off!'

Minnie swallowed hard and walked over to the stereo. There she started up the backing track she'd chosen for her first number, a bass-heavy break beat with a jazzy melody over the top. She coughed nervously and started singing in a timid little voice.

'I can't help that I'm so pretty,
But I come from the big city,
So just you listen to my ditty,
Even though you're feeling gritty.'

'Rubbish!' shouted the old bagpuss at the bar. 'Get her off!'

'Yeah, terrible,' shouted someone else, who Minnie couldn't see. 'Boo!'

Minnie tried another verse, her voice trembling with nerves.

> *'It's awful being me,*
> *I'm such a great beauty,*
> *But, oh, why can't you see,*
> *Your love could set me free?'*

But this verse didn't help at all. A few other cats in the bar started booing and the grumpy old bagpuss on the stool threw a milk-bottle top which whistled through the air and hit Minnie on the nose. Well, Minnie wasn't standing for that! She jumped from the stage right onto the bar, ran along it, knocking saucers of milk and bowls of nuts to the ground as she did so, until she was standing above the old bagpuss and could scream down at him.

'Shut ya gob, you whiskerless old moron! You wouldn't know a good tune if it came out of ya bum!'

The old bagpuss below her sat staring at Minnie as if he were turned to stone, but all the cats around him laughed.

'Yeah,' shouted one of them, a severely shorn female. 'You go, girl!'

Well, Minnie didn't need telling twice. She jumped down to the floor and, trailing her fluffy tail across the faces of the most handsome toms, launched into a much more upbeat gangsta-rap version of the same song:

> *'Don't mess with the Min, yo!*
> *Not even from the back row!*

When the Min is miaowing,
You should be bowing,
Or you'll get a scratch on your chin, yo!'

More by luck than by judgement, the backing track now came in with '*Yo, yo, yo, miaow. Yo, yo, yo, miao*w.'

Minnie jumped back up onto the stage and started rapping again.

'My name is Minnie and I bring with me thunder
Heavier than the house which I was born under
I got love you can't tear asunder
Messing 'bout wiv' me would be a big blunder.
I'm not yet thin, but I'm making a din,
Remember my name, cos I am the Min.'

And again, the backing track sang '*Yo, yo, yo, miaow*', except this time half the audience was singing along with it. Minnie went on:

'Don't you ever take a stance with me,
Don't you ever take a chance with me,
Voulez-vous go to France with me?
Well, get up on your paws and dance with me!'

And soon all the cats in the milk bar were doing just that: dancing on the floor, dancing on benches, dancing on tables and even dancing on barstools while Minnie ran between them shaking her fur furiously in all directions.

'I am the Min and I got fur,
Look at me and you got to purr,
Am I the best? Well, durrh!
Come up here and hear my grrr.'

And the audience screamed in response:

'Yo, yo, yo, miaow.
Yo, yo, yo, miaow.'

Minnie followed 'I Am The Min' with a human-house remix of 'Scritchy Scritchy Scratchy' which made the audience do nothing but caterwaul for more. But she left them begging until Mr Soffalot dragged her back onto the stage for an encore. Being a total star she had, of course, left the best for last, bringing the house down with a big-band bombastic blowdown version of 'I'm Too Furry For Your Love.'

Well! The noise from the audience was so loud Mr Soffalot was worried the cat cops would come and shut The Scratching Post down. He told the audience if they wanted more of Minnie they'd have to come back the next night, and they had to leave now or there would be no more performances ever. With that he ushered them all out into the night, pressing himself against the door to keep out a group of underage kittens who'd had too much milk and were still singing, *'Yo, yo, yo, miaow!'* Once that was done, he bolted the door behind him and turned to find himself face-to-face with Minnie. She was twirling her whiskers with a wicked look on her face.

'The price just went up, innit?' she said. 'Two saucers of warm milk a night, my own dressing room, an assistant and twenty per cent of the takings.'

Mr Soffalot stared at her wide-eyed. Minnie's winning grin put him in a spin, but he recognised pulling-power when he saw it. After tonight he'd soon be able to charge entry, maybe even extend The Scratching Post to get more cats in.

'Done,' he said. 'But I want an exclusive twelve-month contract. You perform five nights a week, every week, for a year.'

'Oh no,' said Minnie, aghast. 'I can't do that. There's an audition in the city I've got to get to—'

'Take it or leave it,' coughed the bossy ocelot, who was cross because he knew Minnie would cost a lot, but hadn't made the toss as to whether he'd make a loss or not. 'Either you take a twelve-month contract this minute or you take nothing. You decide.'

WHAT A FRIGHT!

I want to point out, right now, that this story is not a series of 'who-was-facing-the-biggest-dilemma' competitions. If it were, I would suggest that Ginger and Minnie had already won one each. But, worry not, Tuck is about to win one too. Not that it was his wont to want to win one that winter.

'No!' he was saying to Bunk, as Minnie was being heeded in The Scratching Post and the Fur Girls were seeing who needed patching most. 'I can't! You can't make me! I won't go in there!'

For just as Ginger had stared fear in the face that night and had decided to remain calm, so Tuck was now staring fear in the face and deciding to panic and cry.

'Cat,' said Bunk, 'you don't have to go in there. We've been through this twelve times now. I'm going to go in there and you can either stay here, or go back to the lorry, or maybe try and hide on the farm.'

'I can't,' said Tuck. 'You can't make me! You said I could come with you.'

'So come with me.'

'I can't! You can't make me! I won't go in there!'

'Thirteen times,' said Bunk.

Tuck looked at Bunk fearfully, then even more fearfully at the frightening sight behind him, before swallowing hard and bracing himself for the shouting. It was always at this stage in the conversation—when it had gone around more than ten times—that someone started shouting at him. Minnie tended to shout and snarl and walk off, whereas Ginger was more likely to shout and sigh and roll her eyes and walk off. Bunk, however, remained where he was.

'You're not shouting,' said Tuck.

'A raised voice is generally not helpful to a stressful situation,' said Bunk in his quiet American accent. 'I detect you are unable to make a rational decision and will therefore help you determine the best outcome. Are you more scared when you are with another cat or when you are by yourself?'

'By myself,' said Tuck. 'There's no one to shout at me when I'm by myself.'

'Then the choice is made. You will accompany me into the Great Dark Forest.'

'But what if I go fungal in the jungle?'

'I will remain by your side at all times,' said Bunk. 'You clear?'

Tuck nodded, so shocked at what he was agreeing to that he forgot to say 'No verb'. Instead, he stood, his legs trembling beneath him, and walked close by Bunk's side as they left the overgrown field behind them and entered the GDF. He looked up to the sky, where heavy snow clouds were forming once more, and knew this would be the last time he saw it until the forest was behind them. If they ever got that far.

'Do not be afraid,' said Bunk, as if reading his thoughts. 'All we have to do is remain on the path, then we cannot get lost. You clear?'

'But what if we lose the path?'

'As long as we stay on it, we can't lose it. Stay close beside me, and you'll be fine.'

Soon the forest canopy closed above them and the air around them was darker than ever. Tuck was happy to stick close to Bunk's side, not only to stave off fear, but also to stave off the cold. He remembered how, on his previous journey through the forest, he and Ginger had often had to snuggle close together for warmth. Strangely though, Bunk didn't feel warm at all, so being beside him didn't feel as comforting as it should have done.

Now Tuck had—I need not remind you (but I'm going to anyway)—all the physical attributes of being frightening himself. Indeed, if you were a little bird or a rat or anything edible to a cat, he probably was frightening. But, of course, Tuck wasn't self-aware enough to realise this. Like a human who screams at the sight of a spider, he had no idea he was far scarier than the things he was scared of. Like leaves, for example.

'Agggh!' Tuck screamed, as an oak leaf drifted down from the windblown canopy and brushed his right-cheek whiskers.

'Eeek!' he yowled, as another fell and brushed him on the left.

'Oh, someone save me, save me,' he cried as two more leaves dropped. 'Save me from this long and torturous death by a thousand flutters!'

'Stay calm,' said Bunk beside him. 'As long as we stay on the path—'

But just then a strong breeze lifted a whole crowd of leaves from below their feet and swirled them all around them.

'Ooh, ooh, ooh, it's a torn-hay-doe,' shouted Tuck. 'It's a whirly-wind; a Thai-phone; a cycle-own.'

And he ran as fast as he could to escape the flurry of leaves. Well, let's not forget how fast a cat Tuck is at the best of times; and let's not forget, either, how much faster we all are when we are scared. It was two minutes before Bunk caught up with Tuck in the shadowy undergrowth beneath the trees.

'Calm down,' Bunk said again. 'I am here. All is well.'

'All is well,' Tuck repeated. Then he repeated it another ten times, until even he was bored and thought it might be a good idea to say something else. So he said 'Stay calm. All we have to do is stay on the path.'

As he said it, he watched a strange expression appear on Bunk's face. Then he watched Bunk look down at the ground below his paws. Not only were they not on the path, neither of them knew in which direction the path lay. As Bunk looked up at Tuck again, his underbite rather more pronounced than normal, a gust of wind opened the forest canopy and heavy snowflakes began to fall from the sky, landing heavily on the two black cats.

Have you ever seen a blizzard? It's like the heaviest windstorm you'll ever see combined with the heaviest snow you'll ever see. A snowstorm, you could call it. In fact, you could probably replace the word 'blizzard' with the word 'snowstorm' in most situations and no one would ever notice. Unless, of course, you're playing Scrabble, in which case I want to know where the second 'Z' came from in the first place. **Bennyhoo,** for the rest of that night the snow fell so fast and so thick and in such huge great flakes that had Bunk and Tuck not stuck to each other's sides, they would have lost each other for sure. At the same time, the wind howled and blew and blustered. It shook the great dark trees of the Great Dark Forest like they were long-armed monsters, angry with the world and keen to do nothing but shake the snow off their shoulders and onto whoever was below. Tuck and Bunk had to shout to each other over the howling wind and the complaining trees, and they had to blink and shake their heads to keep the snow out of their eyes. Progress was slow, and they had no way of knowing which way they were heading, or indeed if they were heading in a particular way at all rather than going around in circles. After an hour or so, cold and wet and tired, they found a slope with a large rock jutting out, and Tuck begged Bunk to let him rest underneath it.

'I know we have to tell the Agency about the evil Pongs as soon as we can,' said Tuck as they crawled in beneath the rock. 'But I also want to sleep and rest my frozen paws. Ooh, this is all my fault. If I'd only stayed on the path, we'd be in the warm and snuggly Agency headquarters by now.'

At first Bunk said nothing. He looked out at the snow, which was blowing horizontally between the creaking trees. Then he said, 'Negative. The path has the probability of being the fastest way through the forest. But we would not be in the CIA HQ yet.'

When Tuck asked why not, Bunk hesitated again.

'The headquarters moves,' he said at last. 'For security reasons.'

'Ooh,' said Tuck, shaking the snow off his back. 'That's so Mr Reeyus! Where is it now?'

This time Bunk's hesitation was longer still, and Tuck thought maybe he'd said something wrong. He too looked out at the blizzard raging outside until Bunk turned back to him.

'I don't know,' he said quietly. 'It was part of the brief I was given by the Director when I was distracted by that fly. He told me the precise location they were moving to but … I wasn't listening.'

Tuck gasped. 'But who does know?'

Bunk shook his head sadly, then flinched as a brief change in the wind brought some snow in under the rock, dusting his back white again.

'Nobody,' he said. 'There was nobody the Cat Intelligence Agency could trust. We used to have a contact in the forest—an underground digger with a velvety coat—but he turned out to be a mole.'

'But … but … somebody must know!' said Tuck. 'What about Santa? Or the fairies? Or the elves and the mushrooms? What about the wise old owl? Or the magic wishy-washy tree?'

Bunk turned to him again, his yellow eyes suddenly bright in the shadows.

'What did you just say?

'But … but … somebody must know! What about Santa? Or the fairies? Or the elves and the mushrooms? What about the wise old owl? Or the magic wishy-washy tree?'

'Yes, thank you,' said Bunk, 'it was a rhetorical question used as an expression of surprise. There was no actual need to repeat what you said. However, Tuck, I am very grateful you accompanied me on this mission. For now I know exactly where we must go.'

WHAT AN EFFORT!

Downriver, in the mean and gritty streets of the big bad city, Ginger was working hard. But unlike Tuck and his frozen toes and no-doze woes, Ginger wasn't confused. And unlike Minnie and her prohibitively perk-packed contract, she wasn't facing a dilemma. After all, when a vicious street gang offers to let you go, but only if you do them a favour, what choice do you have? (Here's a clue: none!)

And what was the favour? Stop, stop, it was another rhetorical question! Who do you think is writing this story after all? You're just the reader, don't forget. Well, not 'just', I mean, the reader is a pretty big part of a book, I'll give you that. Without you, dear reader, these pages are only nicely-bound litter. Or a convenient bundle of paper for stopping your table from wobbling. Not that Ginger or Minnie care, of course, not as long as you paid full retail price, but Tuck is very sensitive about such things.

Anyhoo, the favour wanted by the Gertrude Street Fur Girls—a gang so fearful that Ginger had heard of them even if they hadn't heard of her—was this. They wanted her to represent them in a duel against their sworn enemies from across the wasteland: the Citrus Street Sourpusses.

Oo-ee, I know! Doesn't the very mention of these two gangs strike fear into your heart?

Doesn't it?

Really?!

Man, you are as hard as nails! Unless of course—and I suspect this is the case—you're not up-to-date with feline street wars. If this *is* the case, then trust me, these two girl gangs are meaner than a cleaner from Argentina. I get nervous just typing their names! For, whereas everyone (apart from you) knows the Gertrude Street Fur Girls—and particularly their leader Sue Narmi—are the most malevolent, malicious and meanest moggies in the metro area, everyone (apart from you) also knows the Citrus Street Sourpusses—and their leader, Anna Fellactic—are more vicious, villainous and vile than vermin. And that's saying something. (Isn't that an annoying expression? I mean, of course it's saying something! Did you think I hummed it?)

Sennyhoo, every year, the Fur Girls— Oh! I should introduce them, I think. Remind me, I'll get back to what happened every year in a minute. First of all, here are the FG's.

The big white cat with the evil face was Killa Heels, one of the well-known cracked Heels, always angry at being downtrodden. The tabby with the splodgy black-and-pink nose and the smoky, croaky, hokey-cokey voice was Shutya Face, as foul-mouthed a feline as ever you might meet (with the exception, of course, of our own darling Minnie). The tortoiseshell, now with *two* ripped ears, was Juliet Balcony, and the stumpy brown-and-orange cat who had kicked Ginger in the ribs was Ivana VeeVee. Ivana VeeVee was a proud ex-fighter herself and often carried around her old boxing gloves. She'd scrawled records of all her old fights on the gloves and had even written on a mitten that she'd bitten a kitten. But the meanest of all the Fur Girls, and the boss of all them, was old grey Sue Narmi.

They were nasty to the bone, the Fur Girls, but above all they were a team. Or, you could say, a gang. Each of them had their own reasons for ending up on the street, but, once they joined the Fur Girls, none of them ever looked back. The gang became the family they'd never had, and they swore to gladly die for each other, or kill each other, depending on the time of the month.

Now, every year (you *were* supposed to remind me) at the start of winter, the Gertrude Street Fur Girls and the Citrus Street Sourpusses would settle their territorial disputes with a duel. This was a battle not only for pride, but also for survival. Whoever won the duel won the greatest territory and therefore had the greatest chance of finding food through the winter months. Scraps in rubbish bins, open windows to enter houses and steal dinners, rats and mice, even humans to beg food from. The gang which lost the annual duel, on the other paw, would go hungry and not all of its members would make it through the winter. Oh yes, folks, it's tough on the streets, and don't you forget it.

So each year the Gertrude Street Fur Girls and the Citrus Street Sourpusses would put forward their best fighter for a one-bout-wins-all catfight. You may have seen one of these? If not, I must warn you before you read on, they are gruesome. The two cats involved stare at each

147

other, ears flattened back on their heads, screaming with their mouths closed until— Oh, oh, I can't bring myself to write it! There are scowls and fouls and howls and yowls with multiple vowels, which would empty your bowels if you heard them.

'You up for it, Ginger?' asked Sue Narmi that day on the wharf, with a lack of verbs Bunk would have been proud of. 'You willing to represent the Fur Girls?'

Well! What choice did Ginger have? Oh, come on, I know you know the answer to this one. And yet, Ginger was torn, for she thought of Tuck and Minnie waiting for her back on the farm. Their chances of making it through the winter if she returned empty-pawed were worse than those of a losing city street gang. On the other paw, if she didn't do this favour for the Fur Girls, maybe she wouldn't return at all.

'Bring it,' she said, pretending it was an easier decision than it really was. 'But first I'll need a training montage.'

Now, for those of you who've never seen a film, I must explain what a training montage is. It's what happens when the main character wants to achieve something **REEEEEEALLY** difficult and they have very little chance of succeeding. What happens next is this: a song starts up in the background and you see a series of scenes where the character is working **REEEEEEALLY** hard to get fit, or work in a team, or learn to dance, or whatever it is. So now I must cut to a scene of Ginger running up and down the biggest flight of steps in the city, carrying a bag of flour on her shoulders, while Sue Narmi yells at her to work harder. Then (don't forget to put on some music while you're reading this bit), let's see her running along the street, the cold winter air fogging her breath as she tries to keep up with tall white Killa Heels. Now here she is, practising her flying hook kicks over Ivana VeeVee's head, while Sue Narmi sits in the corner with a critical look on her face. Dum! Dum-dum-dum! Dum-dum durrh! That's the music fading away as we see Ginger is fitter, firmer and more fluid than ever. The old girl has got her game back. Why, she's even down to two bellies!

But what's this? Sue Narmi and the Fur Girls are not the only one's watching Ginger's progress. As she struggles up and down the stairs, a pair of beady eyes is watching her from the shadows. As she runs alongside Killa, those same eyes observe her from a gutter across the road. And as she practises her hook kicks, they stare at her from a nearby drain. Who could it be? We will have to wait and see, for with the music they too fade away, disappearing into the fade-out of the montage.

Once the music had fully faded, and Ginger's heavy breathing from her latest super-tough workout could be heard, Sue called her over to the corner where she was sitting.

'I've got news.'

'Oh yeah,' said Ginger, wiping the sweat from her face with the towel that was draped around her shoulders. 'What's that?'

'Word on the street is the Sourpusses have a new member. I didn't believe it at first but we've checked it out and it's true. They've brought in a pro. It's … it's Kimberley Diamond-Mine.'

'Not Kim DM, the world champion professional street fighter?' said Ginger.

Actually, she didn't say that at all. What, did you think you were still watching a film? Only in bad films do people really speak like that, and this book might be bad, but it's still not a film. Oh dicey dialogue, no. In reality, Ginger said, 'Never heard of her.'

And Sue said, 'She's the world champion professional street fighter.'

And Ginger said, 'Oh right, thanks.'

At first Ginger didn't think much about the conversation, after all she too had been a champ in her own time. But later that evening, as she and Ivana were walking along the wharves watching the sunset reflect on the dirty river water, the stumpy brown-and-orange cat put a paw on Ginger's shoulder.

'Listen, Ginge, I know we didn't get along well when we first met.'

'You kicked me in the ribs,' said Ginger. 'Over there.'

'Yeah, well, I didn't know you then. But now I do. You've worked hard for this fight and you're one of us. But let's be honest, you're past your best, Ginge. Kim DM's going to tear you to pieces. You've worked hard, but how many lives have you got left? Two, three? Maybe you should clear out while you can. Run away, you know?'

Ginger thought about it for a minute or two. It was a tempting offer. Ivana was right, she wasn't the cat she had once been. But to run away from a fight? She knew the rules of the street. If the Fur Girls failed to put a fighter forward, they would lose all of their territory, not just some of it. Which meant none of them would make it through the winter. She couldn't bring herself to leave them to starve.

'No way,' she said. 'Like you say, I've worked hard and now this fight is mine. I'd rather give it my best shot and lose than not try at all. Whoever this Kim DM is, let's see how good she is.'

Well, Ginger didn't have to wait long to find out. On their training run the next day, she and the Gertrude Street Fur Girls ran to the no cat's land which sat between their territory and the territory of the Citrus Street Sourpusses. It was an overgrown wasteland where weeds grew amongst empty oil barrels and discarded milk crates and the snow lay brown and slushy. The Fur Girls had planned on practising with their num-numchucks, but when they arrived they found they were not alone. The Sourpusses were also there—all of them—over on their side of the wasteland, but still clearly visible. There was a Siamese called Sarong Sorite; a brown cat called Jean Poole and her ginger-mix cousin, Julie Noted. There was an old cat, more yellow with age than white, whom Ginger recognised as Citronella Tealights. She was talking with the leader of the gang, wizened old Anna Fellactic. And, of course, Kimberley Diamond-Mine was there too. It was obvious which one was her. Even from the very first glance, Ginger could see the huge white cat was the fittest, fiercest and most ferociously frightening feline fighter she'd ever seen.

'*Gulp*,' she thought.

And then she saw something that made her feel even worse. It was an old dried-up rat dropping. It reminded her of the Riff Raffs and what they'd done, and why she was so far from home in the first place. Never in her life had she felt so lost.

WHAT A HOOT!

The blizzard never made it as far as the city, but in the Great Dark Forest it raged half the night. Only when the first weak signs of daybreak were appearing in the eastern sky, did the wind stop howling and the air clear of snow. Despite being cold and more than a little damp, Tuck managed to sleep. But when he awoke he saw Bunk hadn't rested at all. The American had been busy all night digging a tunnel through the snow that had piled up around the rock.

'That's brill!' said Tuck. 'Aren't you tired?'

'Negative,' said Bunk. 'Are you rested?'

'I am! Do you want me to go and hunt for some breakfast?'

'Can you hunt for chocolate?'

'Er …' Tuck wasn't sure. 'No?'

'Then, negative. Besides, we have no time to lose, for I fear it will take us a long time to find where we need to go. And there is no time to lose if we are to stop the Pongs before they develop the poison and start distributing it.'

The forest they found outside the rock had been completely transformed. Whereas the night before it had been shaken by a storm, swirling snow and swaying shadows, now it lay—even in the weak light of pre-dawn— in a million shades of white. Every branch was heavy with snow, and the sides of the trunks which had faced into the blizzard were covered in a thick layer of it.

'Ooh,' said Tuck. 'The forest doesn't look great and dark at all now.'

'And yet it is,' said Bunk. 'More so than ever. Let us proceed with caution.'

And so they walked. As they did so, Tuck noticed how eerily quiet the dim landscape around them was. He wanted to ask where they were going, but was scared even his quietest whisper would sound loud amongst the silent trees. His deep paw prints seemed to crunch loudly beneath him. Looking back, he saw he and Bunk had left a very clear trail behind them and he hoped there were no foxes or wolves or dragons out on a pre-dawn hunt. He pressed closer than ever to Bunk's side, and they walked slowly forward, like a two-headed, eight-legged, two-tailed black cat. They continued in this way, neither of them saying a word, until Tuck heard a rapid scuttling noise in a tree to their right. Beside him Bunk flinched and then changed position very quickly. Tuck desperately wanted to scream, but found he couldn't, because Bunk had put a paw over his mouth. He also found he couldn't move as Bunk had him locked in a surprisingly strong shoulder-lock for such a small cat.

'Mmf!' said Tuck. 'Mmfy, mmf mmf!'

Bunk ignored him and called out into the trees, his soft American accent clear across the snow.

'Hullo? I know you're in there. We wish you no harm. We are looking for information and can pay for it in nuts.'

'Mmf,' said Tuck again, but this only resulted in Bunk tightening the paw over his mouth.

Then, as Tuck watched in horror, a large furry red snake appeared above the branch of the nearest tree. It wiggled and waggled and wobbled and Tuck thought he was going to wet himself in fear. He wanted to scream and run away, but, of course, he couldn't do either of these things. Then the furry red snake was followed by a furry red bottom and then a furry back and then a square red head with a pair of furry ears, a sniffy little nose and, last of all, a squinty pair of eyes. It hadn't been a fluffy red snake at all! It was the fluffy tail of a red squirrel who was backing himself out of a hole in the tree.

'Nuts?' squeaked the squinty square-headed squirrel, squatting on the branch. 'What kind of nuts?'

'The question you should be asking,' said Bunk softly, 'is what kind of information?'

The squirrel put his square head on one side.

'What are we talking? Chestnuts or groundnuts?'

'For the right information I will pay you in brazil nuts and cashews, walnuts and almonds,' said Bunk slowly. 'A whole bushel; your choice.'

The squirrel put his head on the other side and rubbed his little front paws together.

'What's wrong with your friend?' he squeaked.

Tuck realised the squirrel was referring to him. Then he felt Bunk let him go, and he stood up quickly.

'I'm not scared of squirrels, you know,' he said rather crossly. But then he saw the look on Bunk's face and remembered that sometimes, in special fluffy-red-snake-like circumstances, he was. To cover his embarrassment, he looked up at the squirrel instead.

'Hello, Mr Squirrel!' he said, waving politely.

'Mr Squirrel!' squeaked the squinty squirrel. 'I don't assume you are all called Mr Cat, do I? For goodness sake, the name's Asquith.'

'Mr Asquith,' Bunk said gently. 'We need to find the Wise Old Owl.'

The squinty squatting squirrel squirmed squiffily.

'The … the Wise …'

'Yes.'

'… Old …'

'Yes.'

'Owl!' said Tuck.

Asquith the squirrel looked from Bunk to Tuck and Tuck to Bunk and back again.

'I don't know,' he said. 'Do you have a referral?'

'Well,' said Bunk. 'The thing is …'

'Sheryl the scarecrow said he could help,' Tuck shouted out excitedly.

Well, that stopped the squatting squirrel squirming and squinting and made him square up his shoulders instead.

'That Sheryl!' he said, fluffing up his tail. 'She refers half her work to this branch. It's ever since she went part-time. "Part-time is fine," I said when it happened, "but who does the other part, that's what I want to know."'

Naturally, Tuck, who hated questions, didn't have an answer for this one, and neither, it seemed, did Bunk. Instead, an awkward silence descended, broken only by Tuck's tummy rumbling.

'Well,' said Mr Asquith at last, 'you better come with me. I'm presuming it's too much to hope for that Sheryl gave you a reference number? No, of course she didn't. Well, come on then, this way.'

And with that the squirrel hopped onto the next tree, and then the next, and then the next after that, the cats running after him along the snowy ground, deeper and deeper into the forest.

The sun had fully risen by the time Asquith finally stopped hopping from tree to tree. He had led the cats to a clearing where six great oaks stood in a circle.

'Mr Asquith,' said Bunk, as he and Tuck trotted up, 'I insist on payment as promised. Will you give me your details so I can ensure a bushel of the best quality nuts is sent to you?'

'Don't be squalid!' squeaked the squinty squirrel squeamishly, looking around in case someone had overheard. 'I can't accept gifts for forest services, not unless I document them on the gift register, and then, oh, the tax implications are enough to make me squiffy! Please, don't mention it again. Oh Gerald, here you are!'

This last sentence was directed to a large rabbit who had appeared on the ground from behind one of the oaks.

'Oh hello, how do you dooo?' said the rabbit to Tuck. 'You must be the larger of the two black cats who are looking to consult the woo.'

'Incredible!' said Asquith on his branch, who clearly knew how fast news travels in the forest. 'Whatever gave it away? Was it is his largeness, his blackness or his catness?'

The rabbit pretended not to have heard the squirrel above him and gave Tuck and Bunk a tight smile.

'Do you have a ticket?'

'Of course they don't,' said Asquith. 'Sheryl sent them. She keeps the tickets for herself, she's saving up for a pair of legs. And don't bother asking for a reference number, either. I honestly don't know why she always gets those "Outstanding In Her Field" awards.'

Again the rabbit ignored him.

'Ticket?' he said to Tuck.

'I want to see the Wise Old Owl,' said Tuck. 'I need some advice.'

'You'll need a ticket,' said the rabbit.

'Oh, for goodness sake, Gerald,' squeaked Asquith the squirrel. 'Go and get the woo. It's not like there's a queue is there?'

Now, at last, the rabbit looked up into the oak. He stared at Asquith, and Asquith stared at him, each seeming to dare the other to look away first, until Tuck said, 'Oh please, let me see him. And maybe ask the woo to find the Wise Old Owl?'

'The woo *is* the Wise Old Owl' said the rabbit, turning back from the squirrel. 'It's an acronym.'

'A what?'

'An acronym,' said Bunk quietly. 'A series of initials made into a word. 'Woo' means Wise Old Owl, just like 'radar' means RAdio Detecting And Ranging and 'sonar' means SOund Navigation And Ranging and 'laser' means Light Amplification by the Stimulated Emission of Radiation.'

The rabbit looked impressed by Bunk's education (and, indeed, you might want to learn the paragraph above

158

off by heart so that one day a rabbit will be impressed by you too) and he relaxed visibly.

'Well, can't the acronym ask the woo to bring the owl with him?' said Tuck.

Asquith the squirrel squeaked a little laugh at this, but the rabbit breathed a frustrated sigh and hopped stompily off to the oak on the other side of the clearing.

'Oh, Wise One!' he shouted to a hole halfway up the tree.

Immediately, a wrinkled old owl wearing a gold crown popped his head out of the hole.

'Hoo, Gerald,' hooted the owl. 'I thought you were never going to get around to it. I'm nearly ready; just fixing my cloak.'

And with that he disappeared into the hole again. The rabbit turned and hopped back to Tuck and Bunk.

'You may enter the inner sanctum,' he said.

The two black cats followed the rabbit into the clearing surrounded by the six great oak trees.

'Terwit, terwoo, you're consulting the woo. Who seeks my advice?' came the voice of the owl from the hole in the tree above them.

'Bunk and me!' said Tuck, before Bunk could stop him, let alone point out his grammatical error.

'And who is "me"?'

'Er … you are,' said Tuck.

There was an embarrassed silence on the forest floor until Bunk whispered, 'What's your name?'

'Tuck,' Tuck whispered back. 'Surely you know that by now?'

Well, this went on for quite a while until, eventually, Bunk gave up and shouted Tuck's name up to the hole in the tree. Only then did the owl appear in all his finery. The gold crown on his head was offset by a beautiful cloak of brown feathers, which blended so seamlessly with his own that the Wise Old Owl appeared to be twice his actual size.

'I am the Wise Old Owl,' he said.

'Hiya!!' said Tuck.

'Hang on, I haven't finished. I am the Wise Old Owl of the Great Dark Forest; the woo of the GDF. The king of the night and the chief of all birds. I am the brownest of brown owls, I am—'

'Oh, do get on with it,' squeaked Asquith from the oak tree opposite. 'It's already light, you know. I think they're lost.'

'Oh, is that all?' said the owl with a frown. 'What a let-down. I feel a right clown after I went to town with the crown and this long brown gown. Where are you trying to get to?'

'We need to know the current location of CIA HQ,' said Bunk.

'Oh marvellous!' said the owl, perking up again. 'Well, you've come to the right place. Terwit, terwoo, I'll tell you what to do. At least, I will if you can give me the password. If not, you will never get the secret from me. Never! So … what is the password?'

'The password is "Password",' said Bunk, in a strange voice that didn't seem like his own.

'Oh yes, yes, it is,' said the owl disappointedly. 'Bother. CIA HQ is currently in Old Bodgkins Car Yard.'

'I don't suppose you have the GPS co-ordinates?' said Bunk. 'Or know where that is?'

'I know where that is!' called out Asquith. 'It's in the pale vale beyond the Dell of Hell.'

'Do you mind!' said the rabbit. 'You're not in the inner sanctum, you can't give advice.'

'To find the yard is not so hard,' said the owl knowingly. 'But first you must pass the Dell of Hell. The Dell of Hell … the Dell of Hell …'

And as he said this, each time more quietly, he withdrew into the hole in the oak, tugging on his cloak until at last it too disappeared.

'Session over,' said the rabbit sniffily. 'Cash or credit?'

WHAT A CUTIE!

Yes, yes, I know you want a bit more Minnie. She's always telling me that anyone reading this book will only care about the chapters with her in them. But fear not, there is more than enough Minnie to go around.

As you'll remember, when we last left her Minnie was facing a terrible choice. Mr Soffalot had offered her a contract, but she could only fulfil it if she gave up her audition for *Kitten's Got Talent*. What would you do in Minnie's shoes? I suspect you'd probably squeal, 'Eek! These shoes are WAY too small for me!' Unless, of course, you have unfeasibly small feet. Or you're a cat. But I didn't actually mean that. I meant, what would you do if you were faced with the choice facing Minnie?

Would you sign a twelve-month contract in a small country milk bar and forfeit your chance of a national audition? Or would you give up a rock-solid offer for a very slim chance of television success? Is a bird in the hand worth two in the bush even if you don't have hands and you live in the bush? No matter how much you like birds? Oh, what a dilemma. Minnie thought about it for a whole ten seconds.

'Deal!' she squealed, quicker than a seal on a banana peel. 'Where do I sign? When do I start? What will I wear?!!'

Well, the answers were: 1) with a big fat paw print on

the bottom of the contract Mr Soffalot produced with a flourish from behind the bar; 2) that very night; and 3) mostly her own fabulous fur, but also a folly of fully frilly frou-frous which she ran up on a sewing machine.

Oh yes, folks, Ginger wasn't the only one slogging her guts out over the following days. Minnie was working it too. Every night she'd put her everything into every song for everyone who saw her. She shimmied and sparkled, strutted and purred, sang and scratched and shook her shoulders in a way the audience couldn't resist. And that was just during the evenings. During the days she worked hard too, not only sewing, but writing songs, practising routines and—most importantly of all—trying to hire an assistant.

'Ah dunt understand it, Mr Soffalot,' she said one day in her dressing room (aka the cleaning cupboard), as she painted her nails. 'I'd of thought there was millions of gals entranced by the glamour of working for me.'

'Why does it have to be a girl?' asked Mr Soffalot, who detested gender-stereotyping in any form. 'And, please, call me by my first name.'

'What is it? Pop? Ah, ah, ah, ah, ah.'

Oh, it was good for Minnie to hear herself laughing again, and for a minute she forgot the difficulties of recruitment.

'My name is Lancelot,' said the ocelot. 'I'm from Trinidad. It's …'

'Mm, interesting' said Minnie. 'Nah, listen. Not one person 'as responded to that advert ah put out. Each day ah wait and wait, but no one comes by.'

But then, as if the narrative had been waiting for this very moment, there came a knock at the door.

'Get that,' said Minnie. 'And, while you're up, my tea's cold.'

What Lancelot Soffalot, the bossy old ocelot, said in response cannot be printed in a book in this country, but he did get up and open the door.

'Oh, my goodness,' Minnie heard him say to whoever was on the other side of it. 'I didn't know she had family! Come on in.'

Minnie only half-heard him, for she had noticed in her make-up mirror (which was surrounded by naked bulbs on all four sides) that one of her whiskers was less than perfect.

''Oo is it?' she said.

When no answer came she turned and, then, she too gasped. In front of her sat a young cat, barely more than a kitten. She had very long fur not only all over her body and her tail, but also protruding from her ears and even between her toes. She was tabby and grey and black and ginger and tortoiseshell and brown and even a little bit white. To put it briefly, she was the spitting image of Minnie.

'Lorky lummocks, you're beautiful!' said Minnie. 'It's like looking in the mirror.'

'Hola,' said the little cat. 'I think my tail is a bit springier than yours? And fluffier? Is no matter. I apply for role as assistant.'

'Oh, do you?' said Minnie. 'Can you type?'

'No.'

'Can you cook?'

'No.'

'Can you wash my hair and make me look pretty.'

The smaller cat looked Minnie slowly up and down, and—what with Minnie's body shape—side to side.

'Si,' she said. 'Is easy for me.'

'Wonderful!' squealed Minnie. 'You're hired! And you look so much like me, it'll be really cute.' She stuck her smallest front left claw in her mouth. 'I shall call you … mini-Minnie!'

'My name Dora,' said the other cat. 'I come from Andorra. Is a small country—'

'Mm, interesting. You can start today. Go and sort out them ribbons and make us a cuppa while you're about it.'

Dora looked at Minnie for a long while.

'Ribbons, no problem,' she said at last and walked off to the ribbon-box, her tail in the air like she'd already been there.

'*Lucky girl!*' thought Minnie watching her go. '*To look like me and to work for me, who could ask for anything more?*'

The next two days were pleasant ones for Minnie, and when she looked back (not easy given her girth) she counted them as amongst the happiest in her life. Maybe this was because they were destined not to last. Dora would lick Minnie into shape before the evening show, then during the performance she would sit at the side of the stage, staring at Minnie's every move. After the show, Dora would take out Minnie's ribbons and hang them up neatly. She'd fold her frilly frou-frous and put them away in a shoebox, and then she'd comb out Minnie's hair. After that, as Minnie miaowed aloud about how she'd wowed the crowd until she'd bowed, Dora would potter around, tidying up the dressing room/ cleaning cupboard. Admittedly, the cup of tea Minnie had asked for on day one never appeared and, no matter how many times Minnie asked, Dora would not massage her paws. But other than that life was sweet, and Minnie felt like she was a real star. With all her singing and dancing she was even losing weight and, therefore, enjoying her reflection more than ever.

It was four days later that the trouble hit.

WHAT A RISK!

As the day of the big fight approached, the Fur Girls noticed a change in Ginger. When Killa Heels went to pick her up for their morning run, Ginger would appear bleary-eyed and yawning, as if she'd hardly slept. When Ivana VeeVee went to spar paw-to-paw with her in the afternoons, she found Ginger strangely distracted. And for three evenings in a row, when Sue Narmi popped by for a motivational chat, Ginger wasn't anywhere to be found.

'*She's nervous,*' thought Killa.

'*She's scared,*' thought Ivana.

'*She's lost her bottle,*' thought Sue.

But they were wrong.

The reason Gingey-pants was tired in the morning was because she had started spending her nights in an Internet café. While the other cats were dreaming of chasing mice, she was clicking on a mouse and reading, reading, reading. Then, during the day, when she was training with the Fur Girls, while they were punching and parrying, she was planning, planning, planning. Now there were only two days to go before the big fight, and it was time for Ginger to put her plans in motion.

The wasteland which formed the border between the Fur Girls' fiefdom and the Sourpusses sovereignty was quiet at the best of times. That's why it was called a wasteland, durrh. But during the last hour before sunset it was always particularly deserted. This was the time when cats with human connections pretended to be friendly so they could beg some num-nums. Others would be resting to get ready for the busy hunting hours ahead, or just staying indoors to watch *So You Think You Can Scratch*. It was in this quiet twilight that Ginger arrived at the wasteland. She sat for a minute or two, sniffing the breeze, wondering whether what she was planning was really worth the danger.

'Come on, Ginger,' she said to herself. 'Let's do this thing.'

And with that she started to walk very carefully, quite quickly and completely belly-to-the-groundly towards the Sourpusses' territory. Ginger had never been to this grubby, grimy and grotty ghetto before, but she had committed to memory the map of its streets. Kumquat Crescent ran through Lime Lane and into Grapefruit Grove. If she needed to beat a hasty retreat, she could peel down Citron Street and out through The Orangery. But the chances of her getting away unscathed were slim indeed. No zesty street gang worthy of its name could afford to let a member of a rival gang come and go through its territory at leisure. If they found her, the Citrus Street Sourpusses would have no choice but to tear Ginger into a fountain of fleshy furry bits.

Once across the wasteland, Ginger crept quietly along the darkening streets, hurrying from beneath one burnt-out car to the next. She was within a hundred yards of the Angry Puma training gym on Satsuma Street when she heard a strangely familiar voice hiss to her from the dark mouth of an alleyway.

'Hello there, yer big ginger cat, yer. You're a long way from home, so you are. What would you be doing on the wrong side of the wasteland?'

Ginger flinched and squinched into the shadows. There she made out two pairs of shiny brown eyes.

'What are you?' she said, trying not to sound scared.

Now, 'what are you?' is probably not the politest thing for us humans to say to each other. Well, at least I don't think it is. Maybe I'm wrong. Maybe next time you see a teacher you don't know at school, you should walk up and say 'What *are* you?' Or try it with one of your parents' friends; I'm sure it'll be most charming. Either way, between animals this is a very normal question. Sometimes they don't even ask, they just give a quick sniff and make up their own minds. But Ginger was in no mood for sniffing.

'Nigh! What are ye doing in this part of town, like?' said a second equally familiar voice from the alleyway. 'Don't be pretending that ye're lost, so.'

'I asked first,' said Ginger. 'What are you?'

She heard a rough snuffling scuffling noise and was amazed to see the country rat, Bumfluff McGuff, step forward from the shadows of the alleyway, with his friend, Fleabomb McGee, following nervously behind. Immediately she felt hungry.

'Don't try it,' said Bumfluff. 'Yer don't want to make a scene around here, do yer?'

'He's right,' said Fleabomb. 'Ever so much.'

'Why shouldn't I?' said Ginger testily. Being interrupted like this was not part of her plan. The less time she spent in Sourpuss territory the better. 'What do you two want?'

'What do we want?' squeaked Bumfluff, sitting up on his back legs and looking at his front claws as if he was considering cleaning them. 'Well, we want the same as yer want, big ginger cat. We want to see King Rat and all them horrible Riff Raff rats get what's coming to them. We want to do a wee deal with yer, so we do.'

Ginger was shocked. She'd never heard of rats even talking to cats before, let alone offering to do a deal with them. She was tempted to eat the two country rats there and then, and let that be a lesson to them (although exactly what they were supposed to do with that lesson when dead wasn't completely clear). On the other paw, the offer was tempting. It wasn't like she'd found any other leads to the Riff Raffs. She was about to say something smart when, at the end of the street, she spotted one of the Citrus Street Sourpusses. It was Jean Poole, an ugly brown cat with dark black whiskers.

'I'm interested,' she said quickly. 'But I can't talk now. Meet me on the other side of the wasteland tomorrow morning.'

'Aye, I'd say those streets were safer for ye,' said Fleabomb nervously. 'We've been watching ye, like. What are ye doing over here, aren't ye scared?'

'Never,' said Ginger, lying through her teeth. (I'd like to know how else you can lie, unless you don't have any teeth.) 'But I must dash, bye.'

And with that she ran across the road, the first streetlights plinking to life above her. She found the alleyway which she knew from her study of online maps ran alongside the Angry Puma gym. She crept along it until she found a row of rubbish bins. There she hid in the shadows and looked behind her. The last thing she wanted was those crazy rats scampering after her. But both the alleyway behind her and the lamplit street she had crossed were empty. She took some deep breaths and settled down to wait and to think about how Fleabomb and Bumfluff had found her and what on earth they could be proposing.

It was close to midnight before Ginger broke from her thoughts and focused once more on what she was here to do. Before then, plenty of cats, a few dogs, and even the odd human had passed across the mouth of the alleyway, each of them silhouetted against the yellow light of a streetlamp which stood directly across the road. One of them had even been Kimberley Diamond-Mine, from this close angle even bigger than she'd looked out on the wasteland. But she'd been with two of the Sourpusses, Jean Poole and Julie Noted, both of them in pink satin bomber jackets, and Ginger had let them pass. It was another two hours before Kimberley returned. This time she was alone. Ginger had planned on hissing to catch Kim DM's attention, but learning from the rats earlier that evening, she spoke in a gentle voice instead.

'Hello Kimberley,' she said. 'You're a long way from home.'

The huge white cat turned and peered into the gloom of the alleyway.

'Who is that? What are you?'

'I'm a cat, just like you,' said Ginger. 'A reluctant fighter, just like you.'

And with that, she stepped forward into the light, half-closing her eyes in a gesture any cat understands as friendly. She wasn't sure if Kim DM would know who she was.

'I don't believe it,' said the white fighter, bristling her fur. 'Ginger Jenkins! What is this, a surprise attack? You got your gang back there with you? Bring them out into the light.'

'I'm alone. I want to talk to you. I have a proposal.'

'Oh, let me guess. You're going to pay me to lose.'

'Oh no,' said Ginger. 'Quite the opposite. I want you to win.'

WHAT A
MAGICAL NIGHT!

On the night Ginger approached her opponent, and while Minnie sang for her supper, Tuck and Bunk walked on and on through the Great Dark Forest. Ever since the two black cats had left the WOO with an IOU for a bag of worms, they had done little other than walk. Every so often, Bunk would insist that they stop to rest, although it was always Tuck who fell asleep first and woke up second. Bunk himself seem unaffected by the journey.

'We must continue,' was all he ever said when Tuck asked if he was tired or hungry or cold. 'There is no time to waste. As soon as the Pongs develop the right recipe, they can use their pet food empire to deliver it to all the cats in the country. We must go on.'

So on and on they walked. Bunk preferred them to travel after dark, and, soon, with an undercover agent close by his side, Tuck learned not to be scared of the forest at night. In fact, on their third night of walking, as the snow clouds at last broke up and the moonlight shone through the canopy overhead, he wondered if he even preferred it. He liked the way the trees let through individual moonbeams that caught the snowy slope of the forest floor. He liked the way the icicles that hung from the trees

173

shimmered in the night air. He also liked the way he could sing songs in his head without any distractions.

'Oh, forest, I thought you were ever so scary,
Thought your trees had eyes that were ever so starey,
I thought you were foxy and wolfy and beary,
Now I think you're as cute as a dairy
Maid.

'Oh, forest, it's true you are great and dark,
But being here's just a walk in the park,
You have no bite that is worse than your bark,
And I'm no longer scared that I'll cark
It.

'Oh, trees, you are big and ever so chunky,
You're ever so branchy and ever so trunky,
If I was like you I'd be more hunky,
Oh, say hello to my good friend Bunky.
Hiya!'

Tuck had just started a fourth verse of this ridiculous song when he heard a huge thump in the trees to his left. He tried to remember he wasn't scared and pressed himself hard against Bunk's side.

'Do not scream or yell,' said Bunk. 'It's nothing.'

'Ooh, ooh, ooh,' said Tuck. 'It sounds like a witch using her magic to escape from her prison cell!'

'It's fine. Please don't scream.'

'It's the sound of a smelly monster oozing thick sticky liquid as he slops towards us!'

'It's the sound of snow falling from branches,' said Bunk. 'It's a normal sound in the forest at this time of year. There is nothing to fear.'

There was something so reassuring about Bunk's calm yellow eyes and his soft American accent that even Tuck struggled to be afraid. He started noticing the patches of moonlight on the snow again and not the dark shadows in between.

'Are we in the Dell of Hell already?' he said. 'Does that mean that we're making good progress.'

'Affirmative.'

'And why do they call it the Dell of Hell?'

'Because of all the wild dogs.'

'Wild dogs!'

A breeze came through the trees, and all around them was the thumping sound of snow hitting the ground. But this time, as it fell pell-mell, Tuck couldn't believe it wasn't a spell from a cell or a smelly hellish gel. He failed to quell his yell, and it rang, well, like a bell, through the Dell of Hell.

'Aggggghhhhhh, mfff—'

Yes, you guessed it. The 'mfff' was because Bunk had his paw over Tuck's mouth again.

'Cat,' he hissed. 'You gotta keep the noise down. We do not want to alert others to our presence.'

'Ooh, sorry,' said Tuck, when Bunk removed his paw again. 'Are we nearly there? Can we go to bed now? Will you read me a story?'

He also asked countless other questions which I really can't be bothered repeating and which Bunk apparently couldn't be bothered answering, for he just walked on silently leading Tuck further down the dell. They had walked for another half an hour or so, the trees growing thicker as the dell grew deeper, when Tuck felt the hairs on the back of his neck stand on end.

'Ooh,' he said. 'Danger.'

Bunk stopped and looked at him. It was very dark under the thick trees and Tuck could barely see his yellow eyes. He could tell, however, that they didn't look as calm as they normally did.

'Danger?' said Bunk. 'Why do you say that?'

'Well, there's no breeze now, but still my hairs have gone up on end. Which normally means danger. Doesn't that happen to you?'

Bunk didn't answer. Instead he turned around—leaving Tuck's side for the first time all night—and stared into the blackness behind them. Tuck looked at him carefully, desperate for a sign of reassurance, and as he did so he thought he saw the strangest thing. It was as if Bunk's eyes had turned red.

'Ooh,' he said. 'Your eyes—'

'Run,' said Bunk. 'RUN!!!'

And with that Bunk turned and ran down the hill into the dell, shouting over his shoulder for Tuck to follow. Well, as we all know, when Tuck runs he is amongst the fastest cats in the whole wide book, and he certainly doesn't need telling twice. Within a few seconds he'd caught up with Bunk and even overtaken him.

'Keep running until you reach the stream,' he heard Bunk shout from behind him. 'Climb a tree there and wait for me.'

Tuck wanted to point out that he wasn't overly fond of climbing trees, but before he could do so, he heard a terrifying noise. It was the noise of dogs barking. And not the sound of distant dogs either, oh carousing canines, no. It was the sound of at least three dogs very close behind him. Tuck ran faster than he'd ever run before, the night blurring on either side of him, until suddenly he saw a stream ahead. There he stopped and was about to climb the nearest tree when he noticed Bunk was no longer behind him.

'Bunk?'

He called Bunk's name over and over, but there was no sight or sound of the little American cat.

WHAT A PROPOSAL!

Kim DM took Ginger to her room above the gym. Ginger could see the white cat had tried to make the space look pretty with some flowers in a glass and a Japanese screen to hide the litter tray, but it was a still a sad and lonely room above a fight gym. The green neon of the Angry Puma sign flickered through her net curtains.

'You want money, is that it?' Kim DM said as they sat down on opposing ends of an old sofa that smelled of humans.

Ginger took a deep breath. If this didn't work she was going to be in even worse trouble than before.

'Not at all,' she said. 'I just don't want to fight. I spent the first half of my life fighting on the streets. Now it's time to rest. Fighting is so … pointless. You probably think that sounds stupid.'

This last sentence was a teensy-weensy big fat lie. Ginger had read online that Kim DM had said that very same thing on several occasions.

'Go on,' she said now.

There was no telling from Kim DM's hard white face what she was thinking or how she'd react to Ginger's words. Maybe she'd tear Ginger apart there and then and save herself the bother of a big fight in two days' time.

'Well,' miaowed Ginger slowly, 'if I win this fight I'll have to fight another. Then another and another and soon enough I'll have to challenge Sue Narmi for the leadership of the Fur Girls. Or Sue will challenge me. Either way, she'll lose and I'll end up being the chief Fur Girl. That's the last thing I want. I hate the idea of responsibility. Like I said, I want to stay retired. You're young; you're no doubt ambitious; you probably want to lead a gang of alley cats.'

Oops! I just spotted another ginger lie! Because in *Hit Paws*, the catfighting magazine, Kim DM had said she positively *hated* all forms of responsibility and wanted to open a café and call it The Frying Saucer.

'Maybe I do,' said Kim DM, with still no clues in her facial expression. 'So what?'

Ginger swallowed slowly. What if the reporter who'd written the magazine article had been making up Kim DM's words? They do that a lot, you know. Or what if Ginger had misunderstood?

'Oh well,' she thought with a gulp, *'it's all or nothing now.'*

For Ginger was desperate not to have a fight she could only lose. Ivana had been right, there was no way she could beat Kimberly Diamond-Mine. But, at the same time, Ginger didn't want to leave the Fur Girls in the lurch. She had a vision of them starving to death over the winter, unable to enter even the worst hunting grounds. Approaching Kim DM was the only way she could see of getting out of this mess.

'So this is my proposal,' she said. 'We throw the fight. You win. I get to walk away in disgrace and I never have to fight again.'

Kim DM gave Ginger a strange smile. 'I'd win anyway,' she said.

'Eventually you would. But I'd make sure you got a few new scratches you'd never forget. And you can say goodbye to at least one of those beautiful ears.'

Because in *Catmopolitan* magazine, Kim DM had opened up about how lucky she felt to have survived her fighting career with so little injuries. She hoped to do catwalk in later life. She was, after all, a very tall and handsome cat with no fat on her at all. Ginger watched the green neon reflect on Kim DM's muscles and wondered if she'd ever been that toned.

'It's easy,' said Ginger. 'I let you win without injury, you go light on me. Then I walk into the sunset, you carry on fighting for the rest of your life and we're both happy.'

Kim DM looked anything but happy. She stood, jumped down from the sofa and paced around the room, sniffing at the corners and then licking her chest like she'd forgotten Ginger was even there. Ginger waited nervously on the sofa, trying to hide her fear in case Kim DM could smell it. After a few minutes, the white fighter cat joined her back on the sofa.

'I can't believe you're planning to lose,' she said. 'I've always admired you. And now you turn out to be a fraud.'

'Well,' said Ginger, trying not to talk too quickly and thus show her nerves. 'There was one other thing I was thinking. What about if, before the fight, I challenge Sue Narmi for the leadership of the Fur Girls? She'd be crazy not to just pass me her crown, but even if she doesn't, I'll take it from her easily. You do the same with Anna

Fellactic. Then, when we meet on the wasteland, we'll be challenging each other not just for wee-wee rights, but for the leadership of both gangs.'

Kimberley Diamond-Mine sat back with wide eyes. 'Join the Fur Girls and Sourpusses into one gang? But who would they fight then?'

'Exactly!' said Ginger, standing up with excitement. 'There would be no one to fight and peace would rule the streets.'

Kim DM didn't look happy. She sat back in her corner of the sofa and closed her eyes. Ginger watched her nervously, trying to work out how long it was since she'd crossed the wasteland. She was exhausted and keen to get back to the Gertrude Street wharves as soon as she could.

'I have a counter-proposal for you,' said Kim at last, still sitting with her eyes closed. 'My proposal is this. You get out of my apartment and don't ever disgrace either of us again with an offer to throw a fight. You get out of here before I open my eyes, and I will not caterwaul loudly to let the Sourpusses know you're here. I also won't send a message to Sue Narmi to tell her she's got an undercover traitor in her midst. And I won't tear you into pieces until we meet on the wasteland.'

'But …'

'Grab your hat and get out of my flat, you rat!' spat the cat who sat. 'Your chat is tat, like a pat of bat skat. I'll splat you flat on the mat like a gnat, you brat.'

Drat! thought Ginger, but she said nothing. Instead she sprinted across the floor, jumped through the open window and ran down the fire escape which led down to the alleyway. Then, ignoring how hard her heart thumped in her chest, she ran all the way to the wasteland, straight across it and back to the wharves. But no matter how hard she ran, she couldn't escape the truth. Since she had first spotted Kimberley Diamond-Mine training on the wasteland, she had only ever had one plan, and now it had failed.

WHAT A REVELATION!

Now, I'm not actually supposed to tell you about this next little bit because it's Secret Men's Business. And, let's not forget, the whole point about Secret Men's Business is that it's secret. But, in my experience, anything anyone ever calls Secret Men's Business is in reality men behaving like silly little boys and using it as an excuse to get out of the washing-up. Which maybe isn't such a bad idea. You might want to try that next time it's your turn to load the dishwasher? Tell your resident adult you simply can't help, and when they ask why not, look them in the eye and say 'I can't tell you. It's Secret Men's Business'. This works equally well whether you're a boy or a girl, trust me. Put your hands on your hips for added effect, and don't blame me if you get sent to bed with no dinner (although if you're supposed to be loading the dishwasher you've probably already had dinner, so what are you complaining about?).

Hennyway, this next bit is a little secret, but, seeing as it's you, I'll share.

As Tuck stood in the dark, dank and damp depths of the Dell of Hell, he realised he didn't know what to do. He knew what he'd been *told* to do, which was to climb the tree and wait for Bunk to come and find him. But Bunk had told him that before the dogs started barking, and surely he couldn't have known how close they were? Tuck could hear them barking still, and, as he sat at the edge of the dark stream and listened, he heard the barking turn to snarling. Dogs never do that unless they are very close to another animal.

'*Oogy*,' thought Tuck. '*I don't know what to do!*'

But it seemed nobody had told Tuck's legs that, for they were already moving him back towards the spot where he'd last seen Bunk.

'*Oh no,*' he thought, '*I wish I was still a coward when other cats are in danger too, then I'd be safe up that tree near the stream.*'

But even as he thought this, he moved further and further from the stream, and closer and closer to the snarling dogs. Soon he could smell them, smell their wild ways and the drool dropping from their jaws. But the thought of how terrified Bunk must be drew him ever forward. Then, as he climbed slowly over a fallen tree trunk, the dogs suddenly came into view. There were five of them in all: thickset brown-and-black dogs with huge ears and strong jaws. Each of them was baring its teeth, and Tuck could see the drool he'd smelled a second before. None of the wild dogs noticed him for they were all staring at Bunk, who had backed himself against the trunk of a huge fig tree and was staring back at them.

'*Ooh, ooh, ooh,*' thought Tuck. '*I'll have to divert them. If they chase me that will give Bunk time to get away.*'

And he was about to miaow loudly when he suddenly noticed Bunk's eyes. They were red again, but now a far brighter red. A red like the heart of a burning fire. Tuck gasped as one of the wild dogs shot forwards to snap at little Bunk, his teeth reflecting red in the light from Bunk's eyes. But, as he did so, Bunk turned calmly in his direction and the red in his right eye shot out a laser beam.

'HEYOWEEEEEWLLL!'

The dog screamed and fell backwards, its fur singeing and smoking where the laser beam had burned through it. No sooner had he done so than another dog leapt forward to attack Bunk. This time, a laser shot out of Bunk's left eye, and this dog too screamed in agony.

'AWOOO-EEEEE!'

As Tuck watched, two of the other dogs jumped as one, but this time both of Bunk's eyes shot out a beam and caught each dog in mid-air so that they fell, smoking and howling, in front of him. The fifth dog had seen enough and ran barking into the darkness of the trees, its tail between its legs. Slowly, each of the other four dogs picked themselves up from the ground, licked their still smouldering wounds and slunk into the darkness. Before she left, the last of them asked Bunk in a pitiful voice, 'What are you?' But Bunk merely hissed in return and the dog ran away without asking again. Then Bunk turned towards Tuck. Or at least his body did. His face stayed where it was.

'Who's there?' he said.

Then, as Bunk turned further towards Tuck, his face swung in the opposite direction and Tuck saw it was only attached to Bunk's head by a small hinge. Beside the hinge on Bunk's head, where his face should have been, was a series of lights and wires and a circuit board.

'Ooh, my goodness gracious me,' said Tuck. 'Bunk, you're a catbot!'

He jumped down and ran across the snow towards his friend. As he did so, the catbot turned away, sat up on his back legs and used his front paws to snap his face closed again. And just like that he was Bunk again.

'That is classified information,' Bunk said in a rather peevish tone, his underbite more pronounced than ever.

'Oh, thank you very much,' said Tuck. 'But, but, but … you're a catbot!'

Bunk sat down with a miserable look on his face that, even with the rather shocking information now available to us, did look very realistic.

'I'm sure you're very disappointed,' he said.

'Oh no,' said Tuck, who had never been anything with more than two syllables.

'Yes, you are. You thought I was a spy and a secret agent and a real cat. But I'm just a machine. You probably don't want to hang out with me anymore.'

'Of course, I do!'

'Don't pretend. Nobody wants to be friends with a catbot. You know, cat, for a while I was tempted to stay back at the farm, surrounded by cats who didn't know my secret. I can consume food through my mouth and push it through my output cable so, as long as I stick to chocolate, nobody need ever know. Then I thought maybe if I rescued everyone, people would like me as though I was a real cat. But now you know, and you'll probably just want to change my program so I can carry you the rest of the way to safety. Boohoo.'

Bunk said this last word as mechanically as he said everything else, and it took Tuck a while to realise he was crying. Not that there were any tears, sniffs, gulps, sobs or snot. Just those two words and the heartbreaking look on his strange little face.

'Oh, crikey-pants,' said Tuck. 'I won't change your programme at all. Minnie never lets me change the programme at home so I'm quite used to it. And I don't want to be carried; I like running, it's just I need a rest sometimes. And I won't tell anyone about you being a catbot if you don't want me too.'

'Yeah, right.'

'No really,' said Tuck. 'Let me tell you some secrets and then we're quits. Erm ... I'm scared of my own poo and I can't count past ... that one after two, and my second name is Mypantzin.'

'My second name is Tech 2000,' said Bunk sadly.

'Oh well,' said Tuck. 'That doesn't matter. Shall we be Best Friends Forever anyway?'

Bunk looked up, his big round eyes once more yellow, but shiny with what looked like excitement.

'Best friends?' he said. 'I've never had a best friend before.'

'Oh, they're great' said Tuck. 'You get to tell them everything until they tell you to shut up and stop being annoying, and then you have to guess how long it is before you can start talking again, and if you get it right you keep on going until they tell you to shut up again.'

Bunk looked confused. 'But why don't they just listen to everything you have to say as a means of gathering useful data?'

This time it was Tuck's turn to look shiny-eyed with excitement.

'Ooh, ooh, ooh! We're going to be the best Best Friends Forever ever!' he said. 'So, when I was born ...'

And he started telling Bunk his life story, not even hesitating when Bunk told him they needed to continue on through the dell. On and on and on Tuck talked, as he and Bunk walked deeper and deeper into the forest.

WHAT A RORT!*

(*Look it up)

Now that she was a star, Minnie never got out of bed before midday, unless it was to have a quick saucer of milk before going back to bed for some well-deserved rest. But on the day the trouble hit, she was awoken by a strange sound coming from the milk bar beneath her bedroom. It sounded like singing.

'Cor blimey, that's a bit weird, innit?' thought Minnie, ''oo'd want to listen to anyone but me singing a song?'

She turned over in her bed, thinking she'd make a complaint to Lancelot about the conditions she was forced to live in and the selfishness of other people. Naturally, though, she couldn't do this without getting her beauty sleep first, so she shut her eyes tight and tried to think beautiful thoughts.

'Me,' she thought, 'Me, me, me.'

But it was no good. If anything, the sound from downstairs was getting louder.

Now, this may surprise you, but Minnie was not the kind of cat to take interruptions of her beauty sleep lying down. So she stood up. Then she stropped down the stairs and pushed open the door to the bar. She was about to make her feline feelings on noise pollution and poise annihilation known, when she saw what was happening. At first, she couldn't believe her eyes. But then, remembering they'd never lied to her in the past, she was so shocked, so horrified, so outraged, flabbergasted and bowled over that, for once, she stood and said nothing. For there, in the middle of the milk bar, sat Lancelot Soffalot, smiling outrageously at what he was watching on the stage. And there, on the stage, scratching at the scratching post was Minnie's springy-tailed assistant, Dora, dressed in Minnie's best frou-frou, singing her own version of Minnie's best song:

> 'Scritchy, scratchy, scratch,
> Minnie's not a patch
> On me; for against me,
> A fat old cat's no match.

> 'Scratchy, scratchy, scritch
> With me there is no hitch;
> After me you'll be sure
> Minnie was a—'

At this point, Dora noticed who was standing in the door of the bar, glaring at her. She stopped singing and smiled her sweetest wide-eyed smile without any sign of shame or embarrassment.

'Brava!' shouted Mr Ocelot, thinking maybe Dora had forgotten the word 'glitch' and not minding at all. 'Very good, very good.'

Well, mangled moggies, this was too much for Minnie, who at last found her voice.

'What the furball is going on here?!' she screamed,

stomping into the bar and right up to Lancelot Soffalot's face. 'Why is that jumped-up little madam dressed in my ribbons, singing my song and standing on my stage?'

Now, as you can imagine, most cats would be **terrrrrrified** by a furious Minnie scowling and spitting and squealing in their face. But Lancelot Soffalot wasn't any old cat: he was an ocelot, and whilst he'd didn't get cross a lot, when he did, you knew who was boss. A lot.

'It is not your stage,' he said, pulling himself up to his full height and glaring at Minnie with his beautiful big eyes. 'It is mine. And, check your contract, those are not your ribbons. You wore them on my stage, so now they are mine too. And that song is also mine, as per the contract you signed.'

'Rubbish!' said Minnie, who was yet to learn the ins and outs of intellectual property law/ theft.

Mr Ocelot didn't reply at first. He merely produced the contract (which he always kept within convenient reach), and let it unfurl to the floor.

'Read that!' he said, flicking one of his rather frightening claws at the clause which was the cause of his discourse. 'And that. And that. Those songs belong to me now, and I can do what I want with them. You, however, have no rights over them whatsoever. It's all here. And what is also here is that I can terminate this contract with no loss to myself whenever I want. And that, Miss High Maintenance, is now. You are too expensive and too demanding. I have replaced you with a younger, prettier, slimmer and cheaper version of the same act. Which means you, Ms Minnie, are fired!'

WHAT TO DO?

That morning was a hard one for Ginger too. She had pinned all her hopes on Kimberley Diamond-Mine agreeing to her plan, the only ploy she could think of for not abandoning the Fur Girls to a winter of starvation without being torn to pieces herself.

She'd not been lying when she told Kim DM she thought fighting was pointless. She believed it from the bottom of her bellies, even though there were only two of them left. For, underneath it all, Ginger was a peaceful creature—as most martial arts experts are—and whilst she enjoyed fighting as a sport, for anything else she thought it was the most stupid way of sorting out any situation. And I have to agree. A scrap or a slap is generally a trap when a rap or a chat will do.

But what other options did Ginger now have? That morning, as she ran past the wasteland with Killa Heels, she watched the snow on it melting like her hopes.

'You alright, Ginge,' asked Killa. 'You seem distracted. Listen, I shouldn't tell you this, but Sue's asked me to keep an eye on you. Make sure you don't do a runner.'

Ginger picked up the pace so Killa had to struggle to keep up.

'Well, then,' she said over her shoulder. 'Sue doesn't know me very well, does she?'

Killa wasn't the only one who asked Ginger what was wrong that morning. Ivana VeeVee said she looked down in the dumps, and Juliet Balcony asked if she wanted to talk about anything. Even Sue Narmi took her to one side for a pep talk. But all Ginger wanted was to be left alone so she could think things through. Eventually, just before lunchtime, she said she was going for a nap, but instead walked out onto the slushy wasteland.

The thick white blanket that had covered the derelict land for days was melting into ugly brown puddles, and oil barrels and abandoned shopping trolleys were once again showing through. In the distance, Ginger could see the Sourpusses training, the unmistakeable form of Kim DM towering over the other gang members. But they were far enough away for Ginger to believe she was, at last, alone. She tried not to look at the posters which had appeared on warehouse walls and lamp posts overnight. Each of them screamed the same message in garish black-and-ginger letters:

World-famous Ginger Jenkins
returns from retirement
to take on the unbeatable Kim DM!

Ginger sighed and rolled her eyes. She stared at the empty blue sky for a few minutes, then closed her eyes to try and think, or to meditate and see what thoughts came to her, but, no sooner had she done so, than she heard a scratching noise beside her.

'Yer alright there, yer big ginger cat, yer?' said a voice.

Ginger didn't even open her eyes. 'Actually, I just want to be left alone.'

'Aw, come on nigh, did we not say we'd be having a wee chat today?'

Ginger realised she wasn't talking to one of the Fur Girls or, for that matter, any other cat. She opened her eyes and looked around until, in the shadow of an old washing machine lying on its side, she spotted two pairs of shiny eyes.

'This really isn't a good time,' she said. 'Can we reschedule for tomorrow?'

Little brown Bumfluff McGuff stepped into the light.

'Have yer given up hope of getting yer food back, is that it?' he squeaked. 'I wouldn't have had yer down as a quitter. Not after all yer've done.'

'Really,' said Ginger. 'And what exactly have I done?'

'Well, after that big corporal rat there chased us off, we hid in the undergrowth of the forest and watched yer. We saw yer follow them; then we saw yer on that there skateboard and we swam after yer. We've been watching yer for days now, and never was I thinking yer's a quitter.'

'Maybe she's afraid of the Riff Raff rats,' said Fleabomb McGee, poking no more than his fluffy black nose out of the shadows. 'Maybe she realises how evil and bad and big and scary they are. Unlike you, Bumfluff McGuff, with your crazy notions of justice.'

'I do want justice!' Bumfluff snapped at his friend. 'And why shouldn't I? We was supposed to do good honest

195

thieving, and them there Riff Raffs did the dirty on us, so they did. Ten per cent, they told us: ten per cent was for us. We took them to the farm and we showed them the way into the stores and what did we get for it? Nothing, that's what!'

Ginger laughed drily. 'Need I remind you that all that food was ours? You stole from me and my friends, you know.'

Bumfluff scratched behind his ear with his back left leg. 'Ah, yes now, about that. How about we call it quits if I tell yer how to get yer food back? Or rather, how about we stick to the original deal, and yer give us ten per cent, like?'

'You've got a nerve,' said Ginger. 'Look, there's no point in us even talking. I can't get away from here even if I wanted to, the Fur Girls are keeping too close an eye on me. And I don't want to; I have to fight or they'll lose everything. Even if I could get away, I wouldn't be back in time.'

'Tell her!' said Fleabomb, daring to poke his whole furry black head out of the shadows. 'Go on, cousin Bumfluff, tell the big ginger cat she doesn't have to go anywhere.'

'I'm not sure she's interested in knowing,' said Bumfluff, examining his claws nonchalantly. 'I think she's given up, so. Even though her food is right here under her very nose, I don't think she cares about getting it back. Seems to me she cares more about her new friends than her old ones.'

Ginger stared at Bumfluff until, at last, he looked up from his claws.

'Or am I wrong?' he said.

'What are you talking about?' said Ginger. 'What do you mean right under my nose?'

'Right under ye paws!' squeaked Fleabomb.

A shout came across the wasteland and Ginger looked up to see, in the distance, two of the Sourpusses had started scrapping with each other while Kim DM looked impatiently on. When she looked back at the ground beside her again, Bumfluff McGuff and Fleabomb McGee had dis-appeared. Instinctively Ginger jumped into the shadows beneath the washing machine, hoping to catch either of them, but, even once her eyes had adjusted, there was no sign of either rat. She backed out into the daylight again, and ran around to the other side of the washing machine, but there was nothing to see there either. She looked around the nearby wasteland to check where else the two rats might be hiding, but there were only the rusting skeletons of dead bicycles, their wheels sticking out of the melting snow.

'*That's strange,*' thought Ginger. '*They can't have just disappeared.*'

Rolling her eyes, she crawled under the washing machine again—all the way this time—a squeeze she couldn't have managed a few weeks earlier when she still had six bellies. She closed her eyes to let them fully adjust to the dark, but when she opened them again, there was still no sign of either rat. What there was, though, was the entrance to a tunnel.

WHAT A DEN!

Tuck too was in the city that day. But not on its northern edge, where the wide and dirty river skirts the wasteland between the territories of the Gertrude Street Fur Girls and the Citrus Street Sourpusses. Oh massive metropolises, no! Tuck was on the far-eastern outskirts, where the last trees of the Great Dark Forest (or the first, depending on which way you're travelling) give way to a collection of poorly-tended fields, one of which looked like it was full of wrecked and rusting cars. And why did it look like that? Well, durrh, because it was a field full of wrecked and rusting cars—do you think corn or wheat or barley ever looks like that?

Tuck was talking as he and Bunk arrived in the field.

'You see, not all flies taste the same. If you chew on them slowly enough, the blue ones are different from the green ones, especially if they've been sitting on cheese or a sweaty horse's back. I once knew a fly who—'

Bunk held up a paw.

'We will soon arrive at our destination.' It was the first words he'd spoken in hours. 'Let's proceed with caution. Do not try and hide.'

'From what?' said Tuck, who until that moment hadn't considered hiding. 'What is there to hide from? Ooh, Bunk, I'm scared. Let's hide.'

Bunk shot him a stern glance and repeated in his calm

American voice, 'Do not try and hide. They will already be watching us. Just stick close to me.'

Tuck took him at his word, and once again they looked like one black cat with eight legs, two heads and two tails. They were right amongst the rusty old cars now, burnt out wrecks and tyreless, windowless vehicles on all sides. Suddenly, a loud voice boomed out from one of the cars ahead, a burned-out VW diesel.

'You guys lost?' said the voice.

'Agh!' squealed Tuck. 'A talking car! And no verb!'

And he would have run back to the forest if Bunk hadn't held him firm with a not-as-surprisingly-strong-as-it-used-to-be paw on his tail.

'Easy to get lost in such a place,' said Bunk mechanically, struggling to keep Tuck still.

'Looking for a car?' said the voice.

'Thought I might get a bargain,' said Bunk in the same monotone voice. 'Got anything in that category?'

'Password accepted,' said the voice from the car and the lid of the VW's boot popped open. Well, that calmed Tuck down, if only because he was too flabbergasted to do anything but stand and stare. For behind the opened lid was not an empty old car boot at all, but a brightly-lit corridor leading down into the ground.

'Ooh,' he said. 'It's just like *Kitten Impossible*!'

'Stick close,' said Bunk, somewhat unnecessarily. 'And try not to break anything.'

Well, the next half hour passed by in a blur for Tuck. He saw things he'd never seen before and which later he'd struggle to describe. (Lucky for you, I'm an extremely persistent interviewer!) The brightly lit corridor he'd seen from outside led down to a small room where Bunk had to put his face against a hole for a retinal eye scan. That opened a sliding metal door to another brightly-lit corridor, this one running down into the ground more steeply than the first. At the end of that, Bunk had to put his bum against a hole so a machine could sniff it and confirm it was him. That led to another door being opened to—you guessed it—a third brightly-lit corridor, except this one had CAT scans every metre, so that Bunk and Tuck were x-rayed, y-razed and even z-rayed before they got to the other end.

'Oogy,' said Tuck 'Are we nearly there? I'm so excited I need a wee-wee.'

Then, as the end of the corridor came into sight, a panel turned in the wall, so that before Tuck knew it, a very pretty Siamese cat was sitting behind a desk in front of them.

'Visitor?' she said.

'Hiya!' said Tuck.

'Neutered citizen with no political allegiances,' said Bunk.

'We detected remarkably little brain activity in him,' said the Siamese. 'Have you administered a sedative?'

Bunk sighed. 'Why didn't I think of that?'

The Siamese looked down at the papers in front of her.

'And why have you deactivated the hearing in your left ear?'

'Operational necessity,' said Bunk.

'My name's Tuck,' said Tuck. 'We're having a

dangerous adventure in a covered operation. Are you in the FBI too?'

The Siamese cat looked at Tuck, said nothing, then looked back at Bunk who shrugged and gave her an underbitten smile she completely ignored.

'The Board is ready to see you,' she said.

'What?' said Bunk. 'The whole Board?'

As if in reply, another panel in the corridor wall slid open, the space beyond completely dark.

'Can I come?' said Tuck. 'If they're all bored, they'll want lots of visitors.'

Bunk looked at the Siamese and raised his eyebrows, as if asking her permission.

'You better had,' she said. 'I doubt they'd believe you otherwise.'

After the brightness of the corridors, the dark space beyond the sliding panel was a shock. In fact, once the panel had slid closed again behind them, neither Bunk nor Tuck could see a thing.

'There is nothing to fear,' Tuck heard Bunk say in the dark, 'except fear itself.'

'And the dark,' Tuck replied, trying to blink his eyes used to the lack of light. 'And ghosts and other scary things. Oogy, it's so black in here.'

No matter how many times he opened and closed his eyes all he could see was a big white blob.

'It's like someone's shining a light in my eyes,' he said quietly.

'Someone *is* shining a light in your eyes,' said Bunk. And then, in a louder voice he said, 'Agent BunkTech

2000, reporting for debrief on Project Ping the Pongs.'

Tuck heard what sounded like papers shuffling on the other side of the light.

'I can't see you!' he said. 'Could you adjust the light?'

But then he felt Bunk poke him in the ribs and thought maybe he shouldn't talk any more.

'We expected you months ago,' said the voice behind the lamp. 'What happened?'

'I had to, er … work my way deep undercover, sir,' said Bunk. 'It took longer than I expected. However, I have now confirmed the Pongs are experimenting with tasty toxins with which to poison our num-nums. They are now based out of Dingleberry Bottom farm, but I suspect their plan is to kill every cat in the country. I recommend a full and immediate intervention.'

There was more shuffling of papers and Tuck wondered how on earth any cat could read in such darkness. He began feeling his way along the walls. If only he could find a light switch.

'You must return to the farm,' said the voice behind the light. 'There, you must await our instructions. Before you leave, we will give you a new tracking device and a full software upgrade.'

'There is a certain level of danger involved in returning.' Bunk's voice sounded a little nervous to Tuck as he carried on feeling along the walls. 'There appears to also be a plan to create a large black-cat-skin coat. I may need reinforcements.'

'That is not possible in the current economic environment,' said the voice. 'That's why we sent in a catbot. If anything goes wrong, we won't have lost a real live agent, whereas you are expendable. Now what about your visitor? Can he be trusted not to breach confidentiality?'

'Totally,' said Bunk. 'Nobody ever believes anything he says.'

'Gosh,' thought Tuck, *'that's so true!'* As he thought it, he felt his nose press against a protuberance from the wall.

'It's OK, everyone,' he said. 'I think I've found it!'

And then, without waiting for a response, Tuck pressed hard on the big button he'd found.

WHAT A FLIGHT!

Now, where was Minnie last time we left her? Had she got to The Scratching Post yet? Was she still cleaning? Had she started performing? Did she know about Dora and the terrible contract Mr Soffalot had tricked her into? Oh yes! Famished, fatigued, fanfare of fame, flabbergasted, fleeced and fled, all done. Oh, not the 'fled' bit yet? OK, let's do that then:

Faced with the shameless thievery of Lancelot Soffalot, the ocelot, and the equally shameless treachery of her assistant Dora, Minnie fled.

Hooray! There's that that bit done too! There's not really much else to say about it, really. Minnie merely ran to her room to fetch her money (she had, of course, been pilfering from the cash register since the day she'd arrived), gathered together what few possessions she still owned, crammed everything into her teeny-tiny suitcase and flounced out, slamming the door behind her. As she did so, the draft dislodged a calendar which Lancelot Soffalot had hung in the corridor so he could admire its photographs of catresses. Minnie gave it a heavy kick as she passed, but then she noticed the dates it showed.

'My audition!' she cried. 'I can still make my audition! If I can get to the city by this afternoon I'm still in with a chance of the fame and fortune I so deserve.'

This reminded her of the chance which had just been snatched away from her and she felt tears welling up behind her eyes. But would she allow herself to break down in tears about it? Well, yes, actually.

'Oh boohoo,' she whimpered as she ran down the driveway from The Scratching Post. 'Oh, everyone hates me because I'm beautiful! Oh boo-hoody-hoo, boody-hoo, boo-boo.'

Reaching the main road, Minnie realised she had a decision to make. Turn right towards the city and a final shot at fame, or left, back to safety and security of the farm? Stop crying, or carry on crying for a few pages?

'Right,' she miaowed aloud. 'Definitely right!'

The audition was still a few hours away; maybe through some miracle she could still make it. And definitely 'carry on crying', she had plenty more of that left to do. And so it was with tears in her eyes and woeful noises coming out of her mouth that she flounced along the road toward the city.

It was a beautiful winter's day. The sky was blue, there was a breeze in the air and the air was warmer than it had been for weeks. But Minnie's cat senses told her it was going to get colder again, and then much colder than that, before the springtime came.

'At least I've got my beautiful coat,' she said to herself. 'No one can take that away from me.'

And she fluffed it all up and pretended she was a movie star on her way to a rehearsal.

'Oi, Mr Whatsit,' she said, 'I'm ready for my close-up, innit.'

As if in response, she heard the sound of an engine coming along the road behind her.

'*It's a sign!*' she thought, clearly having forgotten what signs really are, and, equally as clearly, not having seen the sign on top of the tall metal pole beside her.

She put down her teeny-tiny suitcase, sat in her daintiest possible manner and let the breeze fluff up her fur. Then, to avoid any potential lack of understanding, she put out a thumb. No doubt it would be Mr Soffalot. He'd probably realised the error of his ways and was motoring after her to beg her to return. Well, she'd make him pay for that!

But the vehicle that came around the corner a minute later was not Mr Soffalot's fancy Purrgeot at all. It was a huge great bus. The driver seemed not to have been expecting a fitter-than-she-used-to-be furry cat sitting at the bus stop and only at the very last minute did he slam on the brakes.

'Hello, puddy-wuddy cat,' he said in that strange way humans have of talking to cats. 'Where you going, puddy-wuddy-dumpkins?'

'Go away, you dreadful man!' said Minnie. 'Do I honestly look like I take public transport?'

The bus driver, who of course only heard 'Miaow, miaow, miaow' shrugged and started up the bus again, leaving Minnie all alone once more on the empty road.

'Oh boohoo, the indignity!' she wept. 'The horrible errors of fate; the wicked way of the world!'

Well, I don't know about you, but I've had it up to here (the rear of my ears) with Minnie's weir of tears, so

I'm going to fast-forward half an hour to when she's finished crying. Here she is, still on the road, walking much more slowly by now, and this time when she hears a bus, she runs full pelt to the next bus stop—sticking out a paw just to be clear of her intentions.

Fortunately for Minnie, the driver of this bus was different from the one she'd met thirty minutes before, or I imagine he may not have stopped. Unfortunately for Minnie, he had the exact same way of speaking to cats.

'Oh, look at the puddy-wuddy-cutey cat!' he said as he pulled up at the stop. 'Where do you want to go, puddykins?'

'Miaow,' said Minnie. 'And step on it.'

And then, without a further word, she walked to the very back seat and lay across it, spreading out as much as she could (which was less than it had once been) to stop anyone sitting beside her. She was in no mood for talking.

WHAT A DRENCHING!

It might have been the warmest day in weeks, but it was still far too cold to be standing around soaked to the skin. But poor Tuck didn't have a choice. Nor, I hasten to add, did the five hundred and fifty-five feline employees of CIA HQ. The VIP's (Very Important Pussies) had been whisked away in a fleet of limousines, but the rest of them were standing woeful and wet in the winter wind, a safe distance away from the disguised entrance to their workplace.

This entrance—which you'll remember was the boot of an old VW—was, nonetheless, a hive of activity. Firecats in shiny helmets rushed in and out, and all sorts of cats in uniforms were miaowing orders at each other and asking to see ID. Not that many of the cats in the field were watching this activity. Oh unimpressed employees, no! They were all glowering at Tuck, or sometimes outright pointing at him, making no disguise of the fact that he was the subject of their hissing and mewling.

'I still don't understand how I made it rain,' said Tuck sadly.

He and Bunk were standing apart from the others in an overgrown corner of the field which ran towards the first (or last depending on your direction of travel) trees of the Great Dark Forest.

'You hit the fire alarm,' Bunk explained for the

fifteenth time. 'That activates the sprinklers and extinguishers. There's so much wiring and weaponry and whizz-bang machinery down there they get very nervous about fires.'

'But I hate the wet,' said Tuck. 'I thought all cats did.'

'Better wet than burned. Uh-oh, here's trouble. Stand to attention.'

The sleek Siamese who had sent them into the dark room was approaching with a fierce look on her face.

'BunkTech 2000!'

'Yes, ma'am.'

Bunk sat up straight with his tail in a perfect line behind him.

'Can you confirm this idiotic individual did not see the faces of any of the Board?'

'He says not, ma'am.'

The Siamese rolled her eyes in a way which reminded Tuck of Ginger, then addressed her next question to him directly.

'Your name is Tuck, I believe?'

'Yes, mammy.'

'Did you see any of the faces of the people in the room with you?'

Tuck looked around him. 'We're not in a room. Are we, mammy?'

'I mean, downstairs,' said the Siamese with a sigh which also reminded Tuck of Ginger, so much so that he suddenly missed her terribly. 'Did you see the faces of the Board?'

'I didn't see anyone who looked bored,' said Tuck. 'I

couldn't see anyone at all. They might have been bored, but it was ever so dark. That's why I was trying to turn the light on. Then suddenly it started raining and everyone was running and now we're outside and it's ever so cold. I've never been an undercover agent before.'

The Siamese gave him an evil stare, then beckoned Bunk away for a few words alone. Tuck could only pick up a few words, or parts of words, but even these he didn't understand: '—iot' and '—upid' and '—nintelligent'. None of it made sense. Finally, the Siamese walked away, no happier than she'd arrived, and Bunk walked slowly back to Tuck.

'You're free to go,' he said. 'I convinced her you hadn't breached security. Other than causing a total evacuation, thereby revealing to the feline fire brigade, the purrlice service and any passing birds the exact location of the headquarters of the most secret organisation in all of cattery.'

'Oh gosh,' said Tuck, smiling for the first time in at least an hour. 'I thought I'd done something wrong. So where are we going then?'

Bunk looked away, the wind pushing his damp whiskers back against his face. '*We* are going nowhere. You can go where you want. I have to go back to the farm.'

'Oh, but you can't go back there! You heard what they said, they said you could die and it wouldn't matter. You're completely expandable.'

Bunk turned back. The wind had made his eyes water.

'This is goodbye,' he said.

'Oh no,' said Tuck. 'I hate goodbyes. Will you write?

Just a paw print on a postcard? Or send me a tweet via the birds? Oh, oh …'

But he could say no more without crying and he knew how Bunk disliked him crying. He closed his eyes tight to keep the tears inside.

'Why are you sad?' he heard Bunk's soft American voice ask.

'Because you're my friend,' said Tuck. 'And I don't want you to get expanded. I want to go on spy adventures with you and talk.'

'So come with me then.'

Well, that made Tuck open his eyes, forget about crying and stop talking, which is a lot of things for an intellectually-disinclined cat to do at the same time.

'What?'

'You heard me, Tuck. Come with me. You're the only friend I've ever had and it would be less lonely if there were two of us.'

'Back to the farm? But what about the Pong man and the Pong woman and the Pong poison plot and all the poor Pong pussies in prison? It's so scary!'

'Your choice,' said Bunk. 'I cannot encourage you to endanger your life. It was nice knowing you. Goodbye.'

And with that he turned and walked away towards the first (or last, depending on which way you're travelling) trees of the Great Dark Forest.

'Oh,' said Tuck, watching him go. 'Goodbye then.'

And not knowing what else to do, he turned and walked in the opposite direction. Then he walked to the left a bit so he didn't have to get too close to the glowering glares and still stormy stares of undercover cats caught unawares. Then he walked to the left a bit more to avoid a group of muscular white toms dragging a rather long hose pipe. And then he walked to the left even more to avoid a group of tabbies comforting a young ginger who'd nearly been trampled in the evacuation. And then even more to the left … just … because … until soon he found himself facing in his original direction. He could see Bunk making his way through the rough grass at the edge of the car yard, back toward the forest. Even now, in the middle of the day, the shadows between the trees looked ominously dark, and Tuck knew he would lose sight of Bunk as soon as he got close to them. He stood there, watching, hoping Bunk would maybe turn around so he could give him a little wave. Then he stood there a little longer, wondering where he was supposed to go. He knew it wasn't very far to the city centre, he could probably get there in a night's travel. He'd certainly be able to find something to eat, and maybe he'd even find somewhere warm and snuggly and safe to sleep. But what was he supposed to do then? He had no idea where Minnie's audition was, or when, and he'd given up hope of ever seeing Ginger again. He suddenly realised he'd never felt so lonely and unloved in his whole life. He tried to imagine what Ginger would say to him now if she was by his side, but instead he found himself thinking what Bunk would say.

'There is nothing to fear,' he whispered. 'Except fear itself.'

Then, 'Hang on,' he said, as if he'd just had an idea.

And then 'Hang on!' he shouted, so that those cats

who'd forgotten he was still there turned and scowled at him again.

'Hang on, Bunk, hang on!' yelled Tuck, and before he knew it he was running as fast as he could across the overgrown field of burnt-out cars, chasing after Bunk, desperate to catch him before he disappeared into the dark shadows of the trees.

WHAT A HOLE!

Ginger too was about to enter the darkness. She was sure that Bumfluff and Fleabomb had disappeared down the tunnel she'd found, but who knew what else was down there? OK, that's an easy one. Bumfluff and Fleabomb knew, but you get the point.

'*Oh well,*' she thought. '*Here goes.*'

And with that, she put first her head, then her front legs, then her tight and toned torso, and then her back legs and, last of all, her tail, into the black mouth of the tunnel. It took a second or two for her eyes to adjust to the new level of darkness she found there, but (unlike Tuck's eyes with a light shone at them) soon enough they did. Not that there was much to see, just a long dark hole boring down through the ground. But **pooeeey!!!** What a smell! It smelled like rats and wee and worms and bin juice, but mostly rats. The tunnel ran steeply downhill, and, as Ginger crept slowly along, it became wider. Soon she heard the sound of trickling water and could make out, a long way ahead, a faint glow of light.

'Be brave,' she said to herself. 'Feel the fear and do it anyway.'

On and on she crept in the darkness, knowing neither what she was treading on, nor where she was going. All she knew was that the noise of running water was growing louder and louder; and there were other noises too: scuffles and scruffles and scraps and scrapes and squeaks and scratches and drips. But above all of those were the smells. Not only the pongy smells like before, but scrummy, scrumptious, delicious smells. Maybe it was that which encouraged her forwards. Certainly, it made her belly ache.

Soon enough—well, soon enough for you and me, but for Ginger it felt like ages—the tunnel ahead of her began to curve and the glow of light grew stronger. Ginger flinched as she suddenly saw the source of the light: a huge chamber with a ventilation shaft dug out of the ceiling, that obviously ran all the way to ground level. Now Ginger was really nervous. What kind of animal could dig tunnels and was also smart enough to think of ventilation shafts? Well, there was only one way to find out, so Ginger continued to crawl slowly forward.

As she did so, she discovered the space ahead of her wasn't a chamber after all. It was simply another tunnel, but this one was much, much, larger than the one she was in. It had curved concrete walls and was so big a fully-grown human could stand in it. Her small tunnel ran into its side.

'*Oh!*' thought Ginger. '*It's a sewer!*'

She realised she was approaching one of those huge tunnels which run under all cities to take away all the water humans waste and all of the waste that comes out of humans. The tunnel Ginger had crept down ended as a small hole in the sewer wall and, as she leant in and looked along it, she saw there were other small tunnels opening into it too. But this was nothing compared with what she saw on the sewer floor. It was like looking down from a second-storey window onto a busy street. But, whereas if you or I did that, we would see humans and cars, what Ginger saw was rats. Hundreds and hundreds of rats. And all of them were busy. Some were pushing little trolleys with boxes on them; some of them were pulling little trays with boxes on them; some of them were floating boxes in the deeper water in the middle of the sewer floor. And every single one of the boxes smelled delicious, so delicious they even cancelled out the pooey smell of the sewer. Then Ginger noticed what was written on every single box: *Destination: Dingleberry Bottom.*

Ginger gasped. What could it all mean? If the Riff Raff rats, with Fleabomb and Bumfluff's help, had stolen their stores *from* the farm, why on earth would they be sending them back there?

'Maybe yer still interested, so?' said a voice right behind her.

Ginger gave such a jump that she nearly lost her footing and fell into the sewer full of rats below her. She crawled backwards into the dark, then pressed herself against the smaller tunnel wall to let her eyes adjust again.

'Watch out,' she said to Bumfluff McGuff once she could make him out. 'I might eat you.'

'Yer watch out,' said Bumfluff. 'I might squeal and yer'll have ten thousand rats on yer tail.'

Ginger thought about it. She couldn't remember how far it was back up the tunnel to the wasteland, but she wasn't convinced she could outrun rats in such a confined space. And there was no cat in the world who could defend herself against so many of them.

'What's happening down there?' she asked, nodding toward the sewer.

'See,' said Bumfluff looking behind him. 'Didn't I tell yer she'd be interested?'

'Ay!' Fleabomb's voice came out of the darkness and soon his shiny little eyes appeared, his furry black body still invisible in the darkness. 'And didn't I tell ye she might eat ye, like?'

Bumfluff gave a ratty little smile and turned back to Ginger.

'What yer see down there, big ginger cat, is a major trade agreement. It seems Mr so-called King Rat has done himself a big fat deal. Turns out, some major cat food producer wants all the food what cats find delicious from the entire region. "Get it by hook or crook", that's the motto, apparently. Well, King Rat's a crook all right. Word on the street is there isn't a food store in the city that hasn't been pilfered. And, as we both know, he's also branching out into the countryside.'

'With your help,' said Ginger with a frown.

'Oh, yer can't blame us,' said Fleabomb. 'They made us a lovely offer so they did, and it wasn't like we had to—'

Ginger heard Fleabomb suddenly scuffle, and then watched as Bumfluff scuffled too, sitting up on his back legs, his nose twitching the air, his shiny little eyes wide and his tiny brown ears alert.

'Someone's coming,' squeaked Fleabomb.

'What?' said Ginger. 'From where?'

But when she cocked an ear she could hear it too. The

unmistakeable noise of two or three rats, scampering down the dark tunnel towards them.

'Negotiate,' said Fleabomb quickly. 'King Rat loves to negotiate.'

And with that, he ran past Ginger, Fleabomb close on his heels, towards the lower end of the tunnel. Then, before she could say another word, the two country rats disappeared over the edge and down into the sewer.

WHAT A DIFFERENCE!

'We are to let ourselves be recaptured,' Bunk explained to Tuck as they walked back through the Great Dark Forest. 'I have had a system upgrade with a new tracking device, a new navigation device, and a new communications device. Once we have identified what the Pongs are doing, we will send a message back to CIA HQ for them to determine an appropriate course of action.'

'Ooh, goody, goody, gumdrops,' said Tuck, who had no idea what Bunk was talking about. He was so happy to be having an adventure with his friend again that he couldn't listen properly over all the happy noises in his head. 'And then will we live happily ever after?'

'There is a 3.72% chance of that outcome,' said Bunk.

'Awesome,' said Tuck. 'Shall we sing a song?'

The Great Dark Forest didn't look at all scary to Tuck today. He was with his best friend in the whole world on a second secret mission, and they were, like, total undercover cats. He was so happy he started to sing:

'I'm a spy, I'm a spy
No one can deny,
So, don't you try
Or even ask me why

'I'm undercover
With my brand new brother
You can't tell us from each other
As if we had the same mother.'

And Bunk seemed happy too, because he started to harmonise as if Tuck was singing in tune and anything rhymed. Bunk sang:

'I have no strings to strum,
So I will simply hum
With my friend who isn't dumb,
Although he can't do a sum.

'I shouldn't be dishing,
But we're on a mission.
It isn't nuclear fission
But Pongs under suspicion!

'I used to be glum,
But now life's so plum.
Tuck's more than a chum,
He's my bro' from another mum.

'Look how the trees glisten,
Like a painting by Titian.*
I'm clearly not wishing
To be away from this mission.'

(*Look it up)

As Tuck and Bunk crossed the forest, on and on through the afternoon, the air around them grew steadily colder. The snow, which over the previous days had softened, began to freeze again into strange jagged shapes, and the puddles of slush beside the path grew crackly and stiff. Tonight, it was clear, more snow would fall. Fortunately, Bunk's system upgrades meant he could direct them back to Dingleberry Bottom farm in significantly less time than they had needed to travel from the farm to the CIA HQ. In fact, it was no more than a couple of hours walk across a narrow stretch of the Great Dark Forest before Tuck said, 'Gosh, this looks like the road near our old farm.' A little while later, he said, 'Gosh, this looks like the driveway which runs off the road down to our old farm.' And a little while after that he said, 'Oh, look at those roofs! They look just like roofs at Dingleberry Bottom.' Then he and Bunk reached the point of the driveway where it dipped suddenly down to the farm buildings, and Tuck said, 'It *is* Dingleberry Bottom, what a coincidence! But, oh! What have they done? It looks so different!'

This was an understatement. In the short time Tuck had been away, the farm had had a complete makeover. The old barn, which used to lean at a forty-five-degree angle towards the ground, had been pushed straight again, held upright by six long beams of wood. The smokehouse had been painted in yellow and black diagonal stripes and now had a sliding window which faced down the driveway. Outside the window was a yellow metal bollard and attached to the bollard was one end of long wooden barrier which stretched across the driveway in a most foreboding way. As for the open-fronted farmhouse, it was barely open-fronted at all. Two humans in yellow helmets were standing on scaffolding building a thick new wall along its front, and were already halfway up the second level.

But the biggest change of all was to the stables. The once ramshackle building looked shiny and new. The hole in its side had been repaired with clean new bricks, and the wall which faced the farmyard was now made of metal-framed glass. Behind the glass was a huge, shiny, silver machine. Bunk's bionic eyes could see the machine had *Animal Skinning Device* written on it, although, of course, Tuck couldn't see that far, and even if he could have, he wouldn't have been able to read it.

'What have they done to the farm?' Tuck cried. 'It looks so horrible!'

No sooner had he spoken, than he and Bunk heard a loud whistle. Immediately the two humans building the wall on the farmhouse stopped and began to climb down to the farmyard. Other humans, all of them in hard hats and most of them with big bellies, appeared. They came down from the roof of the stables, out of the upright barn and through the doorway in the half-built farmhouse wall. One of them was Mr Pong, his tall and gangly frame recognisable from any distance, and, as Tuck watched with eyes so wide they hurt, Pong entered the smokehouse. The other men climbed into a truck and a car and, once Pong had raised the barrier which stretched across the driveway, they drove out, the engines of their vehicles growing louder as they approached Bunk and Tuck.

'Hide!' said Bunk, throwing himself under the nearest bush.

Tuck followed him sadly.

'They've ruined my home,' he said, not even flinching as the car and the truck rolled noisily past them along the driveway.

'I caught a panorama image of the whole thing,' said Bunk. 'I've relayed it to HQ for processing. Did you notice the lorry we were locked in has gone? I wonder what has happened to the other cats?'

Tuck said nothing. He stared sadly at the ground in front of him. He didn't think he could be any more upset, but as he and Bunk continued down the driveway towards the farm, he found he was wrong. Bunk was using long words like 'recapture' and 'compliance' and 'submission', but Tuck didn't have the energy to ask what they meant. He trudged along beside his catbot friend, thinking how now it was less likely than ever that Ginger or Minnie would want to come home and stay. Things were never going to be the way they had been before. Then, as they approached the farmyard, he looked up and gasped. Where their lorry had once sat, was a large pile of rubbish. At the bottom it was mostly building materials and dusty rubble, but at the top were all the things the humans had carried out of the farmhouse. Second from top was Tuck and Minnie's old chest of drawers from the attic.

'Our bedroom!' squealed Tuck, desperately trying not to cry. 'And … but … oh!'

He was lost for words. For there, on top of the chest of drawers, at the very top of the pile, the humans had thrown

Minnie's television: its screen smashed and its wonky aerial snapped in half. The sight of it felt like a stab in Tuck's heart. He'd been so busy having adventures he hadn't really had time to miss his prissy miss who he liked to kiss, but now—at the sight of her beloved television—he broke down in tears.

'Oh, Minnie,' he cried. 'Where are you? What has happened to you and Ginger and our lovely home?'

WHAT AN ARRIVAL!

Well, dozing dust-rags, it's a good job Minnie couldn't hear Tuck crying her name and asking where she was just then, or else she'd have had to lie. For Minnie was far too much of a glamour puss to shout out, 'I'm on a bus.' But on a bus she was, snoring gently. Maybe it was the stress of discovering her betrayal; maybe it was exhaustion from crying; maybe it was the gentle lull of the back seat above the throbbing engine. Whatever it was, no sooner had she lain down than she'd fallen into a deep and dream-filled sleep. But, did she dream of fame and stardom? For once, she did not. She dreamt she was back at the farm, watching television with Tuck and Ginger. They were watching Dora and Lancelot Soffalot in a Christmas Special, singing Minnie's songs and bowing to the applause of thousands of their adoring fans.

'No!!!'

Minnie woke up screaming.

'You all right, puddy-wuddy cat?' the driver shouted back from his seat. 'You want the next stop?'

Minnie looked out of the window and was amazed to find herself right in the middle of the city.

'I made it!' she yelled. 'Oh, to be back in town, how glamorous, how glorious, how gluttonous. But, oh my goodness, what time is it?' She stared out of the window

225

until she made out a clock on the tower of an old stone church.

'Oh, crispy cod flakes!' she squealed. 'I've got to be there in less than an hour! Stop! Let me off this blooming jalopy.'

And she grabbed her teeny-tiny suitcase and ran to the front of the bus, holding onto the huge vibrating gear stick as she tried to get the driver's attention. But the gear stick was bigger and stronger than Minnie, and it wobbled her and wibbled her and wabbled her and wubbled her as she spoke.

'Ta-a-a-a-a-a-ke me-e-e-e-e-e   to-o-o-o-o-o-o the-e-e-e-e stu-u-u-u-u-udioo-o-o-o-s of the Fe-e-e-e-e-e-line Broadca-a-a-a-a-a-a-tting Company-y-y-y-y-y,' she said.

But, of course, all the bus driver heard was 'Mi-i-i-i-a-a-a-o-o-o-w.'

'Puddy-wuddy cat want to get off?' he said, slowing gently before opening the doors. 'You're not the first cat to want this stop this week and you won't be the last.'

Unfortunately, the driver's foot then slipped off the brake so that the bus jerked hard forwards.

'Oopsadaisy!' he said, bringing the bus once more to a very sudden standstill by jamming his foot on the brake. Unfortunately, the result of this was that Minnie fell backwards down the bus steps—**plunk, plunk, plank, splonk**—before landing in a dirty puddle—**SPLASH**! And as if that wasn't humiliating enough, her teeny-tiny suitcase followed her out and landed on her head. **Bonk!**

'Ow!!! 'ow blooming well dare you!' she screamed at the bus driver, 'Do you know 'oo I am?'

'Miaow, to you too,' said the driver, 'See ya, puddy-wuddy cutey-pie.'

And with that he closed the bus doors and drove off, splashing through another puddle which completely soaked the bits of Minnie which hadn't been soaked by the puddle she'd landed in before. And as if *that* wasn't bad enough, Minnie soon discovered the puddle wasn't rain water. It wasn't water at all! It had been made by a travelling salesman's poodle earlier that morning. Well, pongy pools! I don't know if you've ever paddled through a puddle of peddler's poodle piddle, but it's not very nice.

'Look at me!' screamed Minnie. 'Look at my beautiful fur! I can't go to an audition like this. I stink! Oh boo-hoochie, karoochy-boo.'

Then she heard a giggle behind her. Then another giggle, then another, and soon a whole host of giggles. Minnie swung around, willing to fight whoever made light of the sight of her plight, but the surprise which met her eyes made her stop and stare. For there, not twenty metres away, was a queue of the most glamorous pussies she'd ever seen. There were beautiful Burmese, perfect Persians, slinky Siamese, tantalisingly-taut tabbies, jaw-dropping gingers and magnificent moggy mixes all standing in a line. Every single one of them was primped and preened and beribboned and backcombed to within an inch of their lives and all of them—at least all of those who had seen Minnie's less-than-graceful descent from the bus—were laughing at her. With horror, Minnie read the sign which stood at a street corner where the line ran out of view:

Kitten's Got Talent.
Auditions
Estimated queue time from this point:
four days.

Minnie gasped, ignoring the puddle pong which immediately entered her nostrils, and ran to the corner. The line of beautiful cats ran on and on down a very, very, very, very, very long street until it reached a huge FBC Studios sign, tiny in the distance.

Now, as you may or may not have noticed, Minnie may have many minor mundane flaws, but a lack of quick-thinking and ruthless ambition are not amongst them.

'Agh,' she screamed. 'Agh, help! My suitcase landed on my head and I think I'm about to explode sticky cat guts over everybody in sight!'

Well, primping preeners, can you imagine the effect this had on the carefully caticured crowd? Every one of them stopped giggling and started screaming, careful to maintain their place in the queue.

'Get her out of here!' bellowed a Burmese.

'Call the police!' miaowed a moggy mix.

'Call security!' growled a grey-stripe.

And they kept on screaming until a group of two tortoiseshell security cats did indeed come running down from the front of the queue.

'Help me, help me, I need water, I need rest, I need to get into that studio,' cried Minnie.

Well, what with the screaming crowd and the manipulating Minnie, the security guards thought they better do what they were told. They put her on a stretcher and carried her at a trot up to the corner and down the very, very, very, very, very long street (Minnie winking at the queue as she passed), right into the foyer of the Feline Broadcatting Company.

'Don't worry, miss,' one of them said to Minnie, holding his nose against the wild whiffs of wet wee-wee coming from her fur. 'We'll get you to a doctor.'

'I *am* a doctor,' said Minnie, for whom the truth had scant value at the best of times, let alone at the worst of them. 'You've no time to waste, save me if you can! I need a nice warm bath, some flea-dirt remover, a can of hairspray and a squirt of Chanel No 5, stat.'

'Er …' said the larger of the two tortoiseshells. 'Are you sure you're a doctor?'

'Do you want a death on your hands?' Minnie screamed and with that she fell off the stretcher in a rather dramatic backward faint with a double salto.

Well, miraculous makeovers, to cut a long story into a not-quite-as-long story, Minnie ended up arriving at the front of the queue half an hour earlier than her allotted registration time and looking not far off her very best. She had, after all, done so much exercise in the previous days, that she was close to her ideal weight. But, aside from that, in the time between shooing the security men out of her sickbay and leaving the room herself, she had achieved such a magnificent metamorphosis that even the two tortoiseshells—who by that time had worked out her ruse and were on their way to eject her from the building for queue-jumping—didn't recognise her as she flounced past in her fluffy and fully-furred finery.

'Ripperton-Fandango!' she said to the rather handsome tom, barely more than a kitten, who was holding a clipboard at the front of the queue. 'Minnie T. Ready for my close-up!'

'Mm,' the young tom consulted his clipboard. 'Yeah, you've been bumped. Your audition's been moved to tomorrow. But you may as well get in the queue now. It takes twenty-four hours to get to the stage.'

And with that he beckoned to a whole new queue of cats which stretched down the corridor behind him. For a second, Minnie was downhearted. Did anyone understand how much effort it took to look this fabulous? Could see keep it up for another twenty-four hours?

'Yes, I can!' she said out loud, much to the surprise of the tom who hadn't, as far as he could remember, asked her a question. 'In fact, I can be fabulous for however long it takes.'

And with that, she pushed past the handsome young tom and, for once in her life, joined the queue.

WHAT A SITUATION!

Ginger, at that precise moment, was not feeling quite so fabulous. In fact, she was downcast, downhearted, downtrodden, down underground and generally just down. She was sitting at one end of a collapsed overflow pipe which had once run into the huge sewer she'd looked into that morning. And, as if that wasn't depressing enough, she was being guarded by a particularly nasty rat who went by the name of Binjuice Jones. He was grey with black streaks and had two huge front teeth sharpened into vicious-looking points. His eyes were hidden under the visor of his flat black leather cap, and every so often he'd reach under his cap, pull out a hip flask and sip on what to Ginger smelled like turpentine. Each time he did this he'd burp happily in a very sloppy and grotesque manner and say 'Scuse me', as if Ginger was in any position to excuse the perp's chirpy slurpy turps burps.

No doubt you're wondering how Ginger got into such a position? You're not? Oh well, let's talk about dice instead. Oh, you were joking? Well, I wasn't. Did you know the opposite sides of any die (which is the singular of dice) add up to seven? And did you know that if you're throwing two dice, seven is always the most likely total score. Fascinating, mm?

OK, back to Ginger.

After Bumfluff McGuff and Fleabomb McGee had

scrambled away and merged in with the traffic of rats in the sewer, Ginger had waited anxiously to see who was coming down the tunnel. She sat there, summoning up her courage and practising what she was going to say. But all she could think of was what BumMcG and FleaMcG had suggested. Negotiate. Well, it wasn't long before she had to.

As the scuttling, scuffling paws got closer and closer to her in the dark, Ginger realised the rat who was approaching was of an almighty great size. And of a familiar scent. Ginger could even smell her breath by the time the rat squeaked 'Paws up!' in a raspy voice. Ginger didn't turn around.

'You must be Corporal Punishment,' she said doing her best to sound bored, and not putting her paws up at all. 'I've been waiting for you for ages. Does the King like to be kept waiting?'

There was a hesitation behind her, then the raspy voice spoke again.

'I said put your paws in the air. Where I can see them.'

Ginger had to hide her sigh of relief. Now she was sure it was the huge rat she'd spied in the forest. She turned and looked at the Corporal. Up close, she was even scarier than Ginger remembered. She had thick scars across her face, and her teeth looked very menacing. She wasn't much smaller than Ginger herself, but she looked a lot musclier, meatier and meaner. If anything, she reminded Ginger of Kimberly Diamond-Mine. Ginger leaned against the wall of the tunnel and lifted a front paw, but only so that she could give one of her best claws a cool and calm inspection.

'Do be a love, Corpie, and let the King know I'm here. We have a deal which needs tying up. Don't worry, I don't bite.'

And with that she gave a huge yawn which also happened to show off all of her teeth. When Corporal Punishment spoke again, she didn't sound quite so confident.

'What's your name?'

'Ginger.'

'And the King is expecting you?'

'He's expecting someone. He didn't know it was going to be me. Maybe you should take him a message and tell him I'm here?'

Well, the Corporal did just that, but only after she'd called Binjuice Jones down the corridor and ordered him to take Ginger to 'the holding room'. To do this, Binjuice had marched Ginger halfway back up the tunnel she'd crawled along, and down an off-shoot she'd not even noticed on the way down. It was at the bottom of this smaller tunnel—even darker and danker and durkier than the first—that they found the dead end in which Ginger now sat. Corporal Punishment, she hoped, had gone to find the King.

And what was Ginger supposed to do when he arrived? Say she'd made a mistake and was actually looking for the loo? Attack him and let herself be mauled by his guards? Pretend she was a strange species of big fluffy ginger rat? **Cripes!** What an uncomfortably confusing and consistently confounding conundrum.

Ginger sniffed around the back of the collapsed overflow pipe, but there was definitely no escape there. And even if there had been, it would only have been an escape into the main sewer.

'Stop panicking,' Ginger told herself. 'Sit and think quietly.'

This, I have to point out, is always extremely good advice. No matter the situation, you'll probably find a solution more quickly by sitting and thinking than by running around and screaming. Unless, of course, you're being pickpocketed in a crowded train, which, I need not point out (but, ooh, I just can't help myself), Ginger was not.

It was over an hour before Ginger heard anything, and when she did it was, at first, no more than the unmistakeable sound of rat claws on the tunnel floor. She listened carefully and worked out there were two rats approaching her cell. She swallowed hard and sang under her breath the song she always sang when she needed to feel brave:

'I'm a survivor,
Like Lady Godiva.*
Bet you a fiver,
I'm better than MacGyver.*
I won't take a dive or
Slip on my saliva,
Like a bee in a hive-ah;
I'm a survivor.'

(*Look it up!)

Ginger had barely finished the second verse when she heard Binjuice Jones grunt out an exclamation.

'Who goes there?'

'Food for the prisoner, special orders, so,' said another rat who Ginger couldn't see.

'Food for the prisoner? What about food for the guard, I'd like to know. And what's that?'

'Water for the prisoner, like,' said a third voice.

Ginger crept forwards to try and see past the guard, but he saw her and snapped at her with his sharpened teeth.

'Get back there!' he squeaked, staring at her with his pink eyes. Ginger considered biting his head off, but she knew she'd soon have a hundred more rats on her if she did. She retreated to where the roof of the overflow pipe had caved in. Once more, she heard Binjuice Jones talking to the two rats she couldn't see.

'You got passes?'

'Glasses?' said one of them. 'What would I be wanting with glasses? Down here, where it's so dark I can hardly see at the best of times, and even if I did have a pair, someone would be after stealing them?'

'I said passes!' said the guard.

'Classes? said the other out-of-sight rat. 'Nigh, ye don't have to be going to classes, like, to deliver food to a prisoner. It's a non-skilled occupation.'

Clearly, Binjuice Jones couldn't be bothered with this pass-class-glass-larceny farce.

'Oh, don't bother,' he said. 'You want to see the

prisoner, be my guest. Let's see how you react then.'

Ginger, who had by now recognised the voices, not to mention the idiotic banter, of the two delivery rats, stayed at the very back of her cell as—you guessed it—little brown Bumfluff McGuff, with a plastic bag of water, and fluffy black Fleabomb McGee, with a small cloth sack of num-nums, crept in.

'Cheeses, it's dark in here,' said Bumfluff. 'Yer could poke me in the eyes with a sharp stick blinding me entirely, and I wouldn't know nothing about it until I got back outside. How are yer, yer big ginger cat, yer?'

'What are you two doing here?' Ginger hissed at them. 'You'll ruin everything.'

'Nigh, hi'd you like that?' said Fleabomb. 'I told ye she wouldn't be happy. Let's go, it's too dangerous here.'

'Settle, petal,' said Bumfluff. Then to Ginger he winked and said, 'Will yer not calm down? Here we come to tell yer that all is fine, and we're hatching plans, and we've not forgotten yer, so, and all yer can do is ask what we're doing here. We're communicating with yer, that's what.'

'OK,' whispered Ginger. 'So what's the plan? How are you going to get me out of here?'

'Patience, patience,' said Bumfluff. 'Yer've only been in here a few hours, ginger cat. Dem plans I mentioned, dem's being hatched. They're not quite hatched as yet. We—'

But before he could say another word the guard yelled in to them.

'What are you doing in there? Prisoner, show yourself.

If you've eaten those two you're in big trouble.'

'Yikes!' squeaked Fleabomb. 'Let's go!'

'We'll be back,' said Bumfluff.

And, leaving the food and water with Ginger, the two rats disappeared out into the tunnel.

'We was just looking at the tiger, so,' Ginger heard Bumfluff saying to the guard. 'Seeing as we've not got one in the zoo back home.'

'Nor in the local park, like,' said Fleabomb. 'Nor even in the local pet shop as far as me memory serves me. Isn't it funny how everything is always so disappointing in the flesh? I was expecting something grander.'

'Get lost,' said the guard.

Well, scuttling scaredy-rats, he didn't have to ask twice. Not that the first way he said it was much of a question, really, was it? (That, I hasten to add, *was* a question.)

SCARYWAY, the two rats scampered off to finish hatching their plans, or at least Ginger hoped that's what they were doing. For the next thing she heard was a distant shout of 'Make way for the King!'

WHAT A FADE OUT!

Tuck too was in a dark prison. Not *Tuck 2: The Sequel*. For *Tuck 2: The Sequel* to be in a dark prison, we'd need *Tuck 1: The Movie* to be conceived/ written/ produced/ released to huge critical and commercial success (one can only hope). And, not only that, we'd need to end up with Tuck, in *Tuck 1: The Movie*, being caught and thrown in a dark prison. Which, coincidentally, is exactly what *has* happened to poor Tuck since we saw him last. Or, not that coincidentally really, seeing as that was the plan, even if Tuck hadn't listened to it. Of course, if Tuck had listened to the plan, I suspect he might have screamed a little less loudly when Mr Pong, spotting him staring at the rubbish heap, suddenly emerged from what had once been the smokehouse with a large black-cat-catching net in his hands.

'Aggggh,' Tuck yelled with the most miaow-power he could muster at that hour. 'Bunk, it's the Pong man. Run!'

And, perhaps if Tuck had been listening to the plan, he wouldn't have panicked quite as much as he did, and run completely the wrong way right into the cat-catching net. Or maybe he would, if you think about it (do try.) As for Bunk, of course he didn't run at all. He simply succumbed with full compliance, as agreed beforehand, and allowed himself to be recaptured.

'You're acting is superb,' he whispered to Tuck as Mr Pong carried them both in the net towards the barn and, there, in the dark shadows at its far end, threw them into a cage. 'He'll never believe we actually *meant* to be recaptured. Oh look, this is where all the other cats are.'

Sennyhoo, as I was saying, Tuck too sat rotting in prison. That's a funny expression isn't it, 'rotting in prison'? I mean, just because you're in prison, there's no excuse for rotting. You're not a tomato which has been left at the back of the fridge for too long. You might want to remember that next time you're in prison: 'I am not a tomato.' Actually, you might want to remember that the whole time. Maybe go out and get a T-shirt with 'I am not a tomato' printed on it. Or stick a Post-it note on your bathroom mirror or your phone. You are, after all, not a tomato. (Apologies to any tomatoes who may be reading this book).

Where were we? Oh yes, Tuck was sitting in his cage, not rotting, but definitely snotting.

'Ooh, noo,' he sniffed. 'We got caught!'

The cages at the dark and shadowy end of the newly upright barn were arranged in much the same fashion as they had been in the lorry. Bunk and Tuck were in adjoining cages. Opposite them were the Principessa Passagiata Pawprints from the posh part of Palermo, Matt, the fat cat, and Butch. And, just as they had been in the lorry, all the other black cats, who were far too many to name with any attempt at character development, were housed further down the rows of cages.

'Where have you been?' asked Butch when he saw first Tuck and then Bunk locked up in their cages. 'Darling, please don't tell me you fell for all his nonsense about being a secret agent? Let me guess, he tried all his "I'll get you out of here" rubbish on you and you fell for it. Oh dear!'

'Bunk is a secret agent!' said Tuck. 'Leave me alone. Boohoohoo.'

Principessa Pawprints smirked and then set about cleaning her ears in a most condescending manner.

'Pah!' she said between licks. 'Secret agent indeed-a!'

'He *is*,' said Tuck. 'It's confidential. He's in the CAI, which is more important than the FIB, and we had adventures and we went to the super-secret HQ in a location which must never be revealed in Bodgkin's Car Yard next to the Great Dark Forest, and we've come back to take photos and rescue you all. Tell them, Bunk!'

But Bunk said nothing. He was sitting very quietly in a corner of his cage, struggling to keep his eyes open.

'You've both made ever such a fool of yourselves,' said Butch in his light and lilting voice, as he played with his gold medallion. 'Plus, you've missed out on some lovely num-nums.'

'Yeah,' said Matt, the fat cat. 'And it seems even your friend isn't looking so clever now. He looks like someone who's a bit embarrassed to be discovered as a fraud.'

'He is not a fraud!' Tuck spat at fat cat Matt. Not that the latter gave a rat's gnat for his chat.

'Really?' he said. 'So why is he looking so sheepish then?'

Tuck turned and looked at Bunk.

'Tell them,' he said, but still Bunk said nothing. His eyes were almost fully closed and he seemed barely able to move. 'Bunk, what is it? Bunk, are you feeling OK?'

Tuck pushed his nose up against the wire between their cages.

'Sunlight,' whispered Bunk. 'Need sunlight. New software very draining on batteries. Need a solar recharge. Need sunlight.'

'What?' said Tuck. 'Bunk, are you OK?'

'Turning off now to conserve power. Speak tomorrow. Click, zzzz.'

And with that, Bunk closed his eyes and lay as still as a corpse.

WHAT A CHEEK!

Miaownwhile, way back in the centre of the city, Minnie was preparing herself for her own big moment. She had been in the queue for hours now and the effort of maintaining her fabulosity was beginning to make her tired. Behind her, a fluffy little Persian Blue was practising his scales. '*Miaow, miaow, miaow, miaow, miaow, miaow, miaow*,' he sang in such a perfect run-through of the scale of A minor that Minnie began to feel a little nervous. For the very first time, it occurred to her that global stardom might be more than one audition away. She tried practising her own routine: a rather saucy version of 'Scritchy Scritchy Scratchy' with a few tremolos thrown in. Defying Mr Soffalot's legal hold over the song made her feel better immediately and she practised some of the trickier lines a little louder.

'What key is *that*?' said the Persian Blue with a smirk. 'B-careful?'

'D-saster, more like' said the cat in the queue behind him, a long-legged ginger wearing a tiara.

'Lick my tail!' said Minnie, before giving them each a withering glare and turning her back on them. Now she was more nervous than ever.

The queue of cats ran along three long corridors of the FBC studios before reaching the room where the auditions themselves took place. This was a humungous great sound studio with a stage at one end. Here, the queue snaked back and forth, so that whoever was on stage could be seen not only by the judges, but also by the first hundred or so cats in the queue. Well, if Minnie had thought she was nervous before, she was doubly so when she reached this room. As she entered, the cat on stage—a strongly built tom who reminded her of Tuck—burst into tears, before running from the stage. The cat ahead of Minnie, a small white cat with an obvious eating disorder, told her the tom's version of 'Just Kitten Around' had drawn such scorn from two of the judges that they'd started spitting at him.

'Lorky lummocks, that's bit much, innit!' said Minnie, who never in her life before had ever thought anything was a bit much.

'That's nothing,' said the white cat. 'The tabby who was on before him got booed off by the cats in the queue.'

Minnie felt her stomach contract. Looking back, she saw the Persian and the ginger in the queue behind her had also grown quiet at this news.

'Well, that's just disgraceful' she said. 'We should all stick together—'

But no one knows how cunning and manipulative she was going to be next because the white cat interrupted her.

'Oh, this is number three thousand and forty-two coming up now. She's one of the favourites to get through.'

And, as one, they all turned and waited for the next cat to walk onto the stage. There was a murmur of anticipation amongst the queue, and then Minnie thought she was going to be sick as no one other than Dora walked out from the wings.

'How did that—'

But again, she was interrupted, and we will have to guess what very rude word she was going to use, because the entire queue made a collective 'Aw!' noise. The words 'cute' and 'adorable' and 'lovely' were heard amongst the general kerfuffle. Then all the cats in the queue grew quiet again. Even Minnie, who was—for the second time in her life—utterly lost for words.

'What's your name, sweetheart?' said the lead judge in a thick Manx accent. As he leant forward into the light of the lamp on his desk, Minnie saw it was none other than Mickey Manx.

'D … D … Dora,' said Dora.

'And what are you going to sing?' said Mickey Manx. 'Come on now, don't be shy. Have you got a song?'

Dora nodded silently, clearly shocked by the sight of a hundred cats staring at her. Then she remembered the judge had asked her a question.

'It's … it's … my song, it's … called 'Scritchy, Scritchy, Scratchy'.'

Minnie emitted a tiny scream. 'That little … That conniving …. That thieving …' she said, struggling to finish her sentences because she was so **FUUUUUUUURIOUS**. The cats ahead of her hissed at her to be silent, but this made her all the more angry and she started pushing past them, determined to get to the stage. Before she'd progressed more than a metre, cats screeching and spitting as she pushed past, the music to 'Scritchy Scritchy Scratchy' came over the loudspeakers. Everyone watched in anticipation as Dora stood there, opened her mouth and stayed silent.

'Can't hear you!' shouted a tall brown cat in hoop earrings, before screaming as Minnie shoved her out of the way.

'Scritchy?' Dora sang in a very weak voice, before falling silent again. 'Scratch?'

It was another minute before someone in the crowd booed. But as soon as they had done, it started a chorus of caterwauling.

'Get her off!' shouted a mean-looking grey-stripe cat before saying 'Oof!' as Minnie trampled him out of the way.

Next, the music fell silent again and Mickey Manx stood up and turned to the queue.

'Seeing as she's so cute, we'll give her one more chance,' he shouted to the cats waiting to perform themselves. 'What do you reckon, folks?'

But before any of them could answer, there was an altercation at the steps which led up to the stage. Two of the tortoiseshell security cats had been pushed out of the way by a rather large and extremely angry cat of many colours who now appeared on the stage beside Dora. The entire crowd gasped to see two cats of such very different sizes looking so alike. Wondering what all the fuss was about, and why, for once, he wasn't the centre of attention, Mickey Manx turned back to the stage.

'Wow!' he said, his beady little eyes already alight

with commercial possibilities. 'I'm so sorry, Mrs Dora's Mother, we didn't realise it was a double act. We should never have started without you. Let's take it again from the top.'

'Mrs Dora's ... how dare you!' said Minnie. 'A double act!? A double act!!! Oh ... a double act, that could work.'

And then, as if there had never been any bad blood between them, Dora pushed her nose up against Minnie's chest and said loudly, 'Oh, Mummy, I thought you'd left me all alone.'

Well, just then Minnie would have happily bitten off Dora's pretty little head, if it weren't for the fact that every cat in the room said '**AWWWwwww. So cuuuuuute.** Aren't they adorable!'

Well, misplaced maternal mutterings, Minnie had been called many things in her life by other cats, but 'adorable' was not one of them. She put on her best smile and wrapped her tail around Dora's little body.

'I'm going to kill you if this doesn't work out,' she said through gritted teeth, so quietly that only Dora could hear it.

'Ah si,' Dora whispered back. 'But we go fifty-fifty on sales and global merchandise if it does?'

Then, before Minnie could negotiate a better rate, the music for 'Scritchy Scritchy Scratchy' started up again.

WHAT A NEGOTIATION!

'Make way for the King!' came the cry, at first from far away, then closer and closer, until Ginger could recognise it was Corporal Punishment's voice shouting.

'Make way for the King!'

Even deep in the dark, dirty and dank tunnels of the rat kingdom, not to mention deep in doo-doo, Ginger was still cynical enough a cat to roll her eyes. Make way for the king, what rubbish! There wasn't anyone in the way, just a long and empty tunnel and the vicious rat guarding her cell.

'Make way for the King!' came the cry even more loudly now, accompanied by the scratchy tread of several heavy rats. That made Ginger stop rolling her eyes and start gulping. This was her big moment and, whereas Minnie would be disappointed if her big moment didn't work out well, Ginger would be dead if hers didn't.

'Make way for the King!'

This time Corporal Rat's husky voice boomed right outside Ginger's cell.

'You only have to say excuse me, Corporal P,' Ginger heard Binjuice Jones say. 'I'm happy enough to move … ow!'

Well, painful punches, we will never know what made him say 'Ow!' because Ginger couldn't see, but suffice to say he went scampering out of the way. Ginger took a breath and waited. And waited. And waited a bit more.

'Someone still in the way of the King?' she called out in the end.

Corporal Punishment's head appeared around the corner. 'He's just coming,' she said, clearly a little embarrassed. 'You must excuse him, he does get very busy … Oh, here he comes now. Make way for the King!'

Ginger heard the noise of the heavy rats who had accompanied the Corporal down the tunnel shuffling quickly to one side (like, they hadn't heard their boss telling everyone to make way since the beginning of the blooming chapter!), took another deep breath and prepared herself for coming face-to-face with the famous King Rat.

'Oh hello,' said the very small and friendly-faced white rat who entered her cell.

'Morning,' said Ginger. 'King on the way is he?'

The white rat laughed a rather soft and gentle little white laugh. 'Oh, I am the King. So sorry to disappoint you. But, you know, good things do come in small packages, ha, ha, ha. Now, you wanted to see me?'

'You're the King?'

'Ha, ha. Yes, indeed. Now how can I help you?'

Ginger couldn't help but feel relieved. She had expected to come face to face with the biggest, meanest, most terrifying rat in the history of the universe. This little fellow seemed quite charming.

'Well, I don't mean to be rude,' she said, truthfully for once, 'but it seems you've been taking from us when you're supposed to be sending to us.'

King Rat looked at her and said nothing. This, you should note, is one of the key tricks of good negotiation.

Just because the other person stops talking doesn't mean you have to start. It works particularly well on the phone. If you want to shake someone off their balance, stay silent and see what happens. Unless, of course, you're talking to Tuck. Fortunately for Ginger, she was well aware of the trick, being an arch-negotiator herself. She had once negotiated for a hated waiter whom a feted curator had slated and berated for plating his skate too late. She might be deflated and incarcerated, but now she waited and said nothing.

'Go on,' said King Rat at last.

Ha! There he had her.

'I represent Dingleberry Bottom Inc.,' she said. 'Your client.'

'Whose name is …?'

Ginger let her face look calm and calculating. In fact, she was wracking her brains to remember what had been written on the 'For Sale' signs. Ping? Pang? Pung?

'Don't fool around with me, King Rat. You know who I mean. Mr Pung wants to know why you are stealing from his smokehouse. He's sent me here to negotiate.'

The little white rat laughed his soft and gentle little white laugh again.

'Well, they say a cat may look at a king. We weren't aware we had stolen from you. As you know, we run a big operation here, there are bound to be mix-ups. We apologise. What kind of negotiation were you thinking of?'

'A return of the goods, cost free,' said Ginger. 'Mr Peng wants me to accompany them until arrival.'

King Rat's little white nose twitched as he seemed to think about it.

'Tell me, how did you find out about this … let's say, this *error* in our logistics chain?'

'I discovered it myself,' said Ginger proudly. 'I caught your foot soldiers red-handed and followed them to the city.'

The white rat laughed again. 'Oh, what a very resourceful cat you are. And what a brave cat too. So you saw them taking from your farm and without a second thought followed them all the way here?'

'Yes,' said Ginger.

'So when exactly was it that your employer asked you to come and negotiate with me?'

'Er …'

'And how is it possible you don't know his name is actually Pong?'

'Er …'

'And how is it you were found in a small access tunnel, not the main sewer tunnel through which all goods are delivered?'

'Well …'

'Enough!' said the friendly-looking little rat. 'You bore me. You are obviously an opportunist looking to profit from my organisation's labour. You will be executed in the morning. Corporal Punishment, relieve the guard who was on duty and send two new rats in his place. Position two more rats every few metres up the tunnel from here. See that this cat has no chance of escape. I will retire to my nest to think of a suitably vile way of killing her.'

And with that he disappeared out of the cell, leaving Ginger alone in the dark.

WHAT A LET DOWN!

Bunk stayed switched off all afternoon. He lay so still and silent that even Tuck didn't bother miaowing at him.

'What's with your friend?' said the fat cat, Matt, as he washed his tail. 'Tired of lying?'

'Leave him alone,' said Tuck. 'He's travelled a long way to make sure you all escape. He needs to rest.'

Well, that set all the other cats off laughing, even those further down the row who Tuck couldn't see.

'Help us escape?' laughed Principessa Passagiata Pawprints. 'Look at him-a. He can't even-a move-a, he's-a catatonic with shame!'

'Help us escape?' laughed fat-cat Matt. 'He can't even stand up. Hey, secret agent, secrete this!'

And with that he threw a big clump of litter across the aisle. It sailed through the air, through Bunk's cage, and landed hard on his head. When Bunk didn't even react to that, the laughter in the cages around Tuck fell silent.

'Is he all right?' someone asked.

But Tuck just glared at the other cats. Let them think what they wanted. Let them think they'd killed Bunk with their nasty jokes and not believing him. What did it matter? They were all doomed anyway.

The rest of that afternoon passed more slowly than any

hours had ever passed for Tuck. Even more slowly than the previous winter when he and his friends had nearly starved to death on the farm. Because at least then he had friends. Now he was just surrounded by cats who laughed at him, and by Bunk, who was at best unconscious, if not dead. For hours on end, Tuck sat silently. He watched the shadowy back of the barn growing shadowier still, as the scant daylight from the huge barn door drew further and further away. It was properly dark by the time Tuck heard a beep beside him, and then another beep and a whirr. He stood and cautiously approached the mesh between his and Bunk's cage. Then he watched with amazement as Bunk opened his big round yellow eyes.

'You're alive!' said Tuck. 'Oh, my goodness, I thought you were dead and I wouldn't know what to wear to your funeral because I always wear black and I wanted something special to show how sad I am. I was thinking pink wasn't appropriate and maybe cornflower blue would be too difficult to come by.'

'Sunlight,' said Bunk slowly. 'Need to recharge.'

'Don't speak,' said Tuck. 'I'll …'

Before he could say anything else, there was a very human noise from the other end of the barn. Tuck pricked up his ears and tried to resist moving to the back of his cage. Suddenly Mr Pong's long, thin face (above his longer, thinner body) appeared between the two rows of cages. He was carrying a tray full of din-dins.

'Miaow, miaow, miaow!' All the other cats started up mewling, as if they'd never learned not to eat anything Mr

Pong put in front of them. 'Yum, yum, yum. Miaow, miaow, miaow!'

Bunk said something else, but Tuck couldn't hear it.

'Wait for later, Bunk,' he said. 'Save your energy. Don't speak.'

Tuck watched Bunk barely lift his head as Mr Pong put his hand through the flap in his cage and leave a bowl of food inside. But then Tuck's nose realised something unusual was happening. His stomach was rumbling, his nose was twitching, he was salivating.

'Ooh, ooh,' he said. 'I think this food is OK to eat. It smells really good.'

Tuck looked around and saw the other cats were thinking the same thing. Those who had already been given bowls were sniffing it closely and purring.

'No,' Tuck heard Bunk say quietly. 'My detectors are still detecting poison. It's just he's lreant to hdie the sleml of it.'

'Oh no!' said Tuck. 'Bunk, your spelling's gone like mine. Stop talking, save your energy.'

'Don't let tehm ate eeeeeeet ...' said Bunk, as a big puddle of drool came out the side of his mouth.

'Oh no!' said Tuck. 'Don't power down again, Bunk. I need you to be clever. I need you to save us. I can't stop them eating it by myself.'

'You are clveer,' said Bunk in a strange slow-motion voice, the saliva dripping from his mouth. 'You are as clveer as you thnik you arrrrrrrrrr.'

'No, no, I need you!' cried Tuck. 'I need you to be in charge and tell me what to do!'

As if in response, Bunk suddenly sprang up on all fours and his head span all the way around while his yellow eyes rotated in opposite directions. When he spoke it was in a high-pitched voice, the words pouring out so fast Tuck could barely understand.

'Be cool, you fool, I don't want a duel. Rule the school to stop them eating gruel while I unspool in a pool of drool.'

And with that Bunk fell down again, his legs and tail at strange angles, his eyes wide open, his whole body flat and silent and still.

WHAT A TURN UP FOR THE BOOKS!

At purrcisely the same time, back in the city, Dora was also lying flat and silent. But not because she was a black bot bitterly battered by flatter batteries; not a bit. Dora was lying flat and silent under the weight of Minnie's front paws. The two cats had left the stage to thunderous applause, which is a strange expression, if you think about it. I mean, what are people clapping with to make a sound like thunder: canons?

Hennyhoo, no sooner were they off the stage and in the wings than Minnie dragged Dora behind a curtain and pinned her to the ground.

'You thieving little minx!' she spat. 'It's not enough that you steal my songs and steal my job, now you want to steal my chance of fame too! Well, I've got news for you, kitten. No one gets between Minnie and what Minnie wants. You understand?'

Dora said nothing. She just looked up at Minnie, her pretty little eyes wide open, her ears slightly squashed against the floorboards.

'Do you understand?' Minnie said again.

Still Dora said nothing, until Minnie said a very, very, very rude word, hissed in Dora's face, and removed her not-as-substantial-as-it-used-to-be weight from Dora's little body. Immediately, Dora sprang to her feet and took a step or two backwards, towards the curtain hiding them from everyone else in the wings.

'Sorry,' said Dora. 'But I am like you, I want get ahead. Problem is for me, I have no talent, so I think to take yours. You have enough to spare, I think.'

'Nice try,' said Minnie, struggling to resist the compliment. 'But take someone else's. How did you even get down here before me?'

'I take first bus who come,' said Dora. 'They say I am so cute I can ride for free. I see him stop for you and I hide, but you no get on bus.'

'But why didn't you stay up at The Scratching Post? You had my job after all.'

'Oh no. That Mr Soffalot, the ocelot who scoffs a lot, he want me to sign crazy contract only an idiot cat would sign.'

Dora smiled sweetly in a way which made Minnie want to pin her to the ground again, this time pummelling her ears until she screamed.

'I don't ever want to see you again in my life,' Minnie said. 'Got it?'

Dora's eyes opened even wider. 'But where will I go? What will I do?'

'Oh,' said Minnie, with a soft voice. 'Don't you worry, sweetheart. The answer to both of those questions is really easy. It's "I don't care." Now get out of my sight and don't ever cross my path again. Not if you like the idea of keeping your looks. Go on, get lost!'

And with that Minnie made a swipe at Dora which made her jump backwards in fright. But before Dora could turn and flee, the curtain behind her was swept to one side and Mickey Manx appeared behind her.

'There you both are!' he said, his overly-whitened teeth a glimmer of gleaming glamour in the glum and gloomy space. 'What are you two up to?'

'Oh, Mr Manx!' said Minnie. 'Oh, what an honour. Oh my, I was just telling Dora not to get lost.'

'What a caring mother,' said Mickey Manx, patting Dora patronisingly. 'What a wonderful role model. Such looks, such talent, and a soft motherly heart to boot. How moving, how meaningful, how massively marketable.'

'One does one's best,' said Minnie. 'And can I just say I have always been your greatest fan. I've so often dreamed of meeting you. You're even more handsome in the flesh, if you don't mind me saying so.'

'One does one's best,' said the Manx, looking rather uncomfortable.

'Back home in Andorra,' said Dora, 'we have a Juan. He always does Juan's best too!'

Mickey Manx's teeth flashed as he laughed, lighting the space around him.

'Oh, but she's adorable. You must be so proud.'

'I am!' said Minnie, flicking her tail in a way which she knew was fetching. 'But my dear darling Dora is doing direly. She's drooping and dreary, aren't you, dearie? She was just off for some rest, weren't you, sweetie? Yes, you were. So run along and leave Mr Manx and me to talk.'

'I …' said Dora.

'Run along' said Minnie.

'But …'

'Off you go …'

'It's just …'

'Bye then.'

'Can't I …'

'Bedtime!'

'If …'

'Toodle-pip!'

'Not a bit of it' said Mickey Manx, laying a paw on Dora's back. 'Dora should be here to hear this too. I have an offer of fame and fortune for you. There's no need to wait for all the other stages of this silly competition. I'm willing to offer you a contract right here and now so we can get on with lighting up the lives of all those poor pussies out in the real world!'

'What?' said Minnie. 'A contract! For me?'

'What?' said Dora. 'A contract! For me?'

Dora and Minnie looked at each other, then they both looked at Mickey Manx.

'A contract for who?' said Minnie.

'A contract for whom?' said Dora, who, having learned her yammer from a crammer, had better grammar than her mamma. Mickey Manx's teeth shone again and his whiskers wobbled and his stripes shook. Being a Manx cat, he had a very short tail, but even this twirled slightly as he laughed.

'For both of you!' he said. 'You'll be my first double act and I have high hopes for you. There's no time to waste. We'll launch you this weekend on *What's New,*

Pussycat? Then it'll be work, work, work. Endless hours of rehearsals and tours and appearances and recordings. But never fear, you'll both be together the entire time. You'll never be out of each other's sight!'

'Er …' said Minnie. 'That's …'

'That's fabulosa!' said Dora.

'That's …'

'We see a contract, yes?'

'That's …'

'Because we want fully copyright, trailing commissions on recordings, guaranteed payola, separate trailers and an annual non-performance-related fee, por favor!'

'That's … my girl,' said Minnie.

And, for the first time in a very, very, very long time / **ever**, Minnie considered the pussibility she might not be the smartest cat in the room.

WHAT A PLIGHT!

Ginger didn't sleep that day. She had always imagined her last hours would be spent lying in the sun, and maybe eating her favourite food—not imprisoned by rats deep underground. She tried to keep her spirits up, but all she could think was how she'd let everyone down. Tuck and Minnie, back on the farm, would probably starve to death over the winter. As for the Fur Girls, Ginger had lost track of time, but she knew the fight would be starting soon. When she failed to show up, the gang—or her friends, as she now thought of them—would forever think her a coward. Nobody would even know she was dead. Ginger tried not to think of what form her execution would take, for what was the point in worrying about that? It was better to try and meditate and enjoy what little time she had left. But even in the quiet dark of her cell she couldn't concentrate. There was a dripping noise somewhere, the unchanging faint light from the end of the tunnel, and every few hours the changing of the guards.

'The prisoner is yours,' she heard one of them say as he went off-duty. 'She's quiet in there, but watch out. She's got the look of a mouser about her.'

'That's right,' said the other. 'She's an absolute monster.'

Ginger rolled her eyes. The guards who were going off-duty hadn't even seen her: they were just trying to frighten whoever was taking over. From the sound of the new guards' voices, it hadn't worked.

'Ah, sure, we're very careful of cats where we come from, so,' one of them said. 'I once had an aunt who asked a cat for advice on punctuation. The cat told her she couldn't give a rat's asterisk and ate my aunt then and there. Which was very rude, now, if yer ask me.'

'My own father lost his tail to a cat, like,' said the other. 'I asked him what happened and he said there was a tale to it, but as he no longer had his own, he didn't feel he could share.'

The reaction of the departing guards to this nonsense was so rude it simply cannot be typed, at least not by my delicate fingers. And even if it could be typed, it would be too rude to be printed, and even if it could be printed, it would be too rude to be published, and even if it could be published, it would be too rude to be sold, and even if it could be sold it would be too rude to be read by someone of your young and impressionable age. Which is a lot of 'evens' and an equal amount of 'ifs', so just face it, you'll never know. Suffice to say, it was rude. Ginger didn't care. She knew to which two rats those two voices belonged, and, if you don't know too, then all I can say is maybe I should have typed the rude thing after all because you probably wouldn't have got it anyway.

'Bumfluff!' she hissed happily as soon as the other guards had scampered away. 'Fleabomb, is that you?'

'I should hope it is us,' said Bumfluff McGuff, the faint light catching his shiny little eyes as he appeared in the cell. 'Or, sure, yer'd have blown our cover to anyone who wasn't us.'

'I thought cats were supposed to be discreet,' said Fleabomb, appearing beside him. 'Just because ye're about to suffer a gruesome, lingering and horrible death, doesn't mean we have to too, you know.'

'Thanks for reminding me,' said Ginger.

'Oh, sure, it was nothing.'

'You know,' said Bumfluff, looking at his cousin, 'yer too modest, FB.'

'I was being sarcastic,' said Ginger.

'Well, there's no need for that, now, is there?' said Bumfluff. 'I once had an aunt …'

'The plan!' hissed Ginger. 'How are you going to get me out of here?'

The two rats looked at each other.

'Is she joking?' said Fleabomb.

'Is that the sarcasm again?' said Bumfluff.

Then to Ginger he said: 'Come here till I tell yer, this *is* the plan. We're here, are we not? We're yer guards. So go on, be our guest now, escape. We're not going to stop yer. Off yer go.'

'But what about the other guards further up the tunnel?'

'What about them?' said Fleabomb. 'Surely ye can't mean us to replace them too?'

'Well, I thought you might at least consider getting rid of them. Otherwise I won't get very far, will I?'

Ginger watched Fleabomb and Bumfluff thinking about this.

'Could ye not be killing them at all?' squeaked Fleabomb after a while. 'I think that's what most cats generally do.'

'I could kill one or two,' said Ginger. 'Maybe even get past three or four. But with all the noise they'd make, by the time I got up to ground level I'd … Oh, hang on! Mm. And then they'd …   And then I'd … Mm, that could work!'

'Is she after having a catniption?' said Fleabomb staring at her with his head on one side. 'Has she succumbed to the strain of staring death in the face?'

'She's certainly succumbed to something,' said Bumfluff. 'I think she's having a wee whitey.'

'Got it!' said Ginger so suddenly both rats remembered she was a carnivore after all. They looked at each other nervously and took several steps backwards.

'And what would *it* be, now?' squeaked Fleabomb, with a little tremor in his voice. 'Would *it* be a good thing, like cheese, or a bad thing, like, a disease that makes you hungry all of a sudden?'

'I mean, I've worked out how I'm going to get out of here,' said Ginger. 'Are you ready to hear all about it?'

'No,' said Bumfluff. 'I've got to go and do my hair.'

'And I think I may have left something under the grill, like,' said Fleabomb.

Ginger stared at them until she remembered she wasn't the only animal in the world who could be sarcastic. After all, if sarcasm is the lowest form of wit, there's bound to be more of it underground.

'OK,' she said. 'Now listen carefully. You need to do exactly as I say. First of all, I'll need a pair of sunglasses and a bus timetable.'

WHAT A SONG
AND A DANCE!

Tuck gasped and didn't know what to do. Bunk, who he'd been banking on, had gone from bonkers to blank in the blink of an eye.

'Oh, Bunkette,' he yowled. 'Talk to me. Say something. Do something!'

But Bunk lay where he had fallen, nothing more than a thick fur coat around some rather clever wiring. Then Tuck yowled again, realising he was about to watch all the other cats around him meet their ends too. None of them had noticed what had happened to Bunk. They were all too busy concentrating on the yummy food Mr Pong had put in their cages. As Tuck watched in horror, Principessa Passagiata Pawprints started to lick at the meat.

'No!' shouted Tuck. 'Don't! It's poison!'

'Please don't-a take that-a tone with me,' said the Principessa sniffily. 'It doesn't *smell-a* like poison.'

Fat-cat Matt was sniffing his food too.

'I know the man's always given us bad food in the past,' he said. 'But maybe they've switched it around? Maybe it's the woman's turn to give us the bad food now. Which means if we don't eat this, then we'll go hungry tonight.'

'Oh, I do so hate to be-a hungry,' said the Principessa in a very princessy way.

'And since when were you such an expert on poison anyway, Tuck?' said Butch, picking up a piece of the meat on his paw. 'Why should we listen to you?'

'Bunk told me!' said Tuck, and for the first time the attention of all the other cats turned to Bunk.

'Ooh, lore!' said Butch. 'What's happened to her then?'

'He looks-a strange,' said the Principessa, squinting across the space between the cages. 'Is he sleeping with his eyes-a open?'

'Oh my Cod!' shouted fat-cat Matt. 'He's dead.'

'She's corked it!' said Butch.

'He's expired!' said the Principessa.

And all the other cats down the row of cages said other variations on the same theme, which wasn't surprising really, given it was a slow news day.

'What happened?' they all asked each other.

And then they asked Tuck.

'What happened?'

But Tuck was too sad to tell them. All he could think of was that his new friend Bunk, the only cat in the world who'd ever thought he was clever, was no more. 'You're as clever as you think you are,' Bunk had said. But Tuck didn't think he was clever at all, which meant he wasn't.

'Did he eat the food?' said Matt, the fat cat. 'Is that what happened?'

'Oh!' said Tuck quietly, under his breath. 'Oh, er … Yes! Yes, he ate the food.' Then he said it louder. 'He ate the food!' And then he shouted it. 'He ate the food! He ate the food! He said it smelled good, but as soon as he'd eaten it he realised the truth, and then he died.'

Well, that set a cat amongst the pigeons. Oh no, that doesn't work. It set a pigeon amongst the cats? Well, you get the picture. It set them all talking at once and had them backing away from their food quicker than you can say 'ghastly agonising death if you eat it'. Butch started wiping the meat off his paw onto the floor of his cage and Principessa Passagiata held her nose even higher than normal, as if she could suddenly smell the poison after all. Tuck even saw fat-cat Matt putting his paw down his throat to sick-up a bit of food he'd obviously eaten.

'But why do they want to poison us-a?' cried out the Principessa. 'What have-a we ever done-a to them-a? And how will we ever getta out of here-a?'

'We'll get out tonight,' said Tuck. 'I know how; Bunk showed me. I just need the pin from his collar. Until then we have to be calm.'

'Calm, darling?' said Butch, looking at all the panicked cats around him. 'Are you nuts? What are we supposed to do, play dead?'

'Play dead?' said Tuck. 'Oh, er … Yes! Yes, play dead. Hide your food and play dead! Then maybe they'll leave us alone.'

Well, the cats took some convincing of this. But Tuck didn't have to convince them all by himself. Butch thought it was a fabulous idea, probably because it had been his idea in the first place, and Matt, the fat cat, and a few of the others agreed too.

'But I always wanted a state-a funeral,' whimpered the Principessa. 'With a horse-drawn-a carriage and-a white-a lilies.'

Butch pointed out that lilies are also poisonous to cats, which so weakened the Principessa's argument that it even shut her up for a bit. Still, the debate amongst the other cats went on and on, until suddenly they heard footsteps outside and the familiar voice of Mrs Pong approaching.

'Dong-ding, ding-dong, the dinner gong sounds so wrong!'

'Quick' said Tuck. 'Play dead now!'

And with that he fell in a heap, closing one eye, but keeping the other one open so he could check all the others had lain down too. And they had! Even Principessa Passagiata Pawprints dropped gently to the ground in a graceful swoon. Tuck closed his other eye and heard Mrs Pong's footsteps approaching his cage. Then he heard her shrill voice.

'**Willeeeeeeeeeeeee!!!!** Willy-woo my darling, you've done it! Come here now, come and see! Oh, at long, long last you've done it, you clever, clever man!'

Tuck lay still, not knowing what to do. He still didn't feel very clever and he was worried that maybe he and the other cats would be thrown into the rubbish or—horrors!— onto a bonfire or buried or something. But before he could think of anything else awful which might happen, he heard footsteps rushing towards the barn and then the nasty nasal voice of Mr Pong.

'I don't believe it! I don't believe it! Success at last!

Oh, oh, success at last! You know what this means, don't you, Frances? We can mix it into all our cat food and then start distributing it. We'll give it away for free!! I'm going to be known forever as the man who rid the world of cats. Oh joy, oh wonder!'

Tuck felt a horrible prod as Mr Pong poked one of his long thin fingers through his cage.

'Still warm,' he heard Mr Pong say. 'Oh, Frances, my dearest, do you not mind too much that you can't fatten them up any more to get the maximum amount of fur?'

'Oh, not at all Willy-woo,' Mrs Pong replied. 'They're plenty fat enough. And with winter being so cold already, it's the perfect time to skin them for my beautiful fur coat. Oh, it's a momentous occasion, my darling; you must be so proud.'

Then Tuck felt the ground under the cages vibrating and heard the sound of heavy footsteps. He opened one eye the tiniest amount possible and saw the Pongs dancing in the aisle between the cages, Mrs Pong's red hair flying out behind her as her tall and skinny husband spun her round and round.

'A world free of cats!' laughed Mrs Pong, revealing every one of her yellow teeth. 'My darling Willy, I'm so happy for you.'

'And a beautiful coat of fresh cat fur,' said Mr Pong. 'My beautiful wife deserves no less.'

And with that, the two Pongs waltzed down the corridor to the darkest end of the barn, and then back up again, continuing all the way out of the doorway and into the freezing night.

WHAT A LAUNCH!

The next morning the city woke to find itself, once again, covered in snow. Down on the streets, this was crushed in a rush to mushy slush by human feet and cars, but higher up it remained as pristine and pure as … well, as the driven snow, I suppose. Mickey Manx lived on the top floor of a very swanky building even closer to the city centre than the studios of the Feline Broadcatting Company. In fact, he lived on the roof, and that morning he invited Dora and Minnie up there to look at the view and talk business.

'Oh-ee,' said Dora when she arrived. 'The city, it so beeg.'

'Big!' hissed Minnie in her ear. 'Not "beeg". If you're going to pretend to be my daughter, you're gonna 'ave to learn to talk proper, innit?'

'Gonna after learn ta talk proper, eeneet,' said Dora, trying to get her little mouth around the sounds. 'Gonna after …'

'Now, ladies,' said Mickey Manx, smiling his brilliant smile. 'Let's get down to business. Manx Records has agreed with Manx Television Productions that, rather than go on *What's New, Pussycat?*, you can appear on *Mickey Manx's Back To Your Roots* to launch your careers. The only trouble is, there are no slots available for the next two months.'

'Two months?!' said Minnie. 'I want to be famous now!'

'Two month?' said Dora. 'I will not be so cute in two month. I need exposure now!'

Mickey Manx licked a paw and wiped it over his ears distractedly as he looked out over the city. He was obviously deep in thought.

'Well,' he said, 'one of the new faces from tomorrow's episode has come down with cat flu. But I'm not sure you're ready. We need to …'

'We're ready!' said Minnie and Dora at the same time.

'Well said,' said Dora, determined to get the last word in.

'I know,' said Minnie, achieving the same.

Mickey Manx wasn't convinced.

'I don't know. I mean, we'd have to find a location.'

'But you always go back to where cats come from,' said Dora. 'Is easy, we go to Andorra. I'm from a leetle town in the mountains, very beautiful, lots of skiing.'

'Andorra!' said Mickey Manx. 'Even if we could get there in time, it would blow the budget. What about you Minnie, where are you from?'

Well! Minnie, as we all know, was born under a house in a very unpleasant part of a rather horrible town. Visiting Andorra might blow the budget on plane tickets, but visiting her birthplace would blow the budget on replacing everything that got stolen during the shoot. Mickey Manx might not have much of a tail, but that wouldn't stop someone in Minnie's home town from stealing it.

'Well,' she said …

'Please tell me it's somewhere picturesque?' said the Manx in a frustrated tone. 'Somewhere with trees and fields. Everybody wants a bit of escapism, and as the majority of cats live in cities, somewhere in the countryside would be perfect. Somewhere rural and—'

'The farm!' squealed Minnie.

Mickey Manx looked at her. He didn't like being interrupted.

'I come from a farm, Mr Manx,' she said with the closest thing she could achieve to humility, which wasn't really close at all. 'It's very beautiful. It's called Dingleberry Bottom, and there are no humans on it, just my family. I'm a simple girl: I just like to make up songs when I'm in the fields picking flowers.'

Dora put her head on one side. 'You said ...'

Minnie put a paw over Dora's mouth. 'Oh, it's the birdsong I miss the most. When I'm not eating birds, I do love to listen to them sing. I love to walk through the fields with the grass tickling my belly. Or through virgin snow on a day like this. I like to sit high in a tree. I'm thinking a panning angle from a helicopter with a soaring orchestra in the background. Yes?'

Mickey Manx's eyes were wide open and, if you'd been there, you'd have seen little dollar signs in them. 'And?'

'Oh, and maybe some rabbits in the field talking about how well we all get on. And maybe Dora and I are walking across the farmyard/ dance floor—'

'Yes, yes, yes!' cried Mickey Manx. 'Like mother, like daughter, you are both such geniuses! Tiddles! Tiddles, are you here? Get me a camera crew and a helicopter. We're going to …?'

'Dingleberry Bottom,' said Minnie.

'Tiddles!' Mickey Manx shouted again. 'Where is that tom?' And he disappeared down the stairway to his office.

Minnie walked to the edge of the roof, looked over the city, and shook her hair in the cold breeze. She couldn't *wait* to see the look on Ginger's face.

WHAT AN EXIT!

If Minnie had bionic eyes, or binoculars, or maybe even a particularly good pair of bifocals, she would have seen an interesting pattern of movement far below her on the snowy city streets. All the people were rushing around in their normal way, carrying bags and looking important. All the cars and lorries and buses were moving in all directions too, honking and beeping and braking and belching out gas. The pigeons were flying in random directions, and most of the dogs were lifting their legs on corners or being dragged along behind their owners. So far, so normal. But what, I hear you ask (yes, I do), about the cats? Were all the cats in the city idling around or strolling in different directions? They were not. For almost all the cats in that huge city—at least those allowed out of the house—were travelling in more or less the same direction. And that direction was north: towards the wasteland beside the river.

Ginger's disappearance had been big news on the Catnet. For the first time in the history of the Fur Girl/ Sourpuss stand-off, it seemed possible that a contender might not turn up. At first, the Gertrude Street Fur Girls denied Ginger had disappeared at all and blamed the Citrus Street Sourpusses for making the whole thing up. But when the Fur Girls were unable to present Ginger for the pre-fight press conference, and the media storm grew stronger, at last they had to admit the truth. Not only had Ginger disappeared, she had disappeared *into thin air* which, as we all know, is significantly more difficult than disappearing into air of a standard thickness.

Of course, there were claims of conspiracy on both sides of the wasteland, but the truth of the matter was clear for all to see. Nobody knew what had happened. And so, as is the way of the modern world, when there is no clear answer to a news story, that story grows and grows. Or, as it was in this case: growls and growls.

It seemed there wasn't a cat commentator in the world who hadn't a strong opinion of what had happened. Ginger, or rather the lack of her, made the front cover of *The Times*, *The New York Times*, *Time Magazine* and even *Thyme Weekly*, the herbalist magazine. And then, just as the story was ready to be replaced by a celebrity baby or a political scandal, things took a new twist.

It was heard first amongst the city birds, all tweeting gossip of the fight being on after all. Ginger, it was rumoured, had reappeared and was planning to represent the Fur Girls, but no further details were known. Next, an official communication came from Gertrude Street. The Fur Girls had heard from an unusual but verifiable source that 'the big ginger cat there would be wanting to do the scrap on Tuesday night, so.' Soon after that, posters started appearing all over town. Written in a strange ratty scrawl, they invited everyone to the wasteland to watch the fight of the century:

Witness the return of Ginger Jenkins at twelve minutes to num-nums

*on Tuesday night and find out where she has been these
last few days!
A once in a lifetime opportunity, like!*

Well, malicious marketing manoeuvres, you can suspect the cynicism with which this news was met. It varied from comments that Ginger's whole disappearance had been a publicity stunt in the first place, to suggestions that the Fur Girls had deliberately delayed the fight so Ginger could gain some extra weight:

Fur Girls Cringe!
Win In Dingy Fringes
Hinges On Ginger Ninja's Binge.

Some even suggested that it was Ginger's reappearance that was the hoax. But the latter couldn't be true because, next, the Sourpusses issued a statement. The Fur Girls had confirmed the bout was on and that Ginger would be there. Until then, no prowling rights would be relinquished.

Can you conceive of the amount of fuss this caused on the Catnet; how many Licks it got on Furbook? Online felines blogged about nothing else and, soon enough, all the cats in the city were off to the wasteland to see what there was to see. Even the super-cool cats, who pretended not to like anything popular and preferred to talk about things no one else had seen and places no one else had been, even they could be spotted slinking along the side of buildings in a northerly direction.

Minnie and Dora and Mickey Manx, on the other paw, high on the rooftop making plans for stardom and fortune, were perhaps the only felines in the metro area not to have heard the news. Mickey Manx's secretary, Tiddles, was to blame. One of his chief responsibilities was to keep his boss current with all trending news, but Tiddles had been in such a rush to make his own plans to see the fight himself, he'd forgotten to tell Mr Manx anything about it. Which just goes to show how you should never rely on your staff.

Thirty feet below the wasteland, Ginger lay in the dark breathing deeply. She had not heard from King Rat, but Corporal Punishment had been strict in ensuring she was closely guarded at all times. The rats who guarded her now were the Corporal's most trusted henchmen, the rats Ginger had first seen in the forest: Private Dubious Staines and Sergeant Vicious Lee Scard. She could hear their wheezy breathing. Other than that, she could only hear her own heartbeat.

It was very difficult for Ginger to tell the time in the unchanging light underground, but she knew in her gut it would soon be time for her to escape. Which also meant, if her plan did not come off, it would soon be time for her to die. She sat up as well as she could in the dead-end pipe and closed her eyes tightly. She thought of her beloved Major waiting for her in Purrvana. She thought of Tuck and how sorry she was she would never see him again. She thought of Minnie and the Fur Girls, but these thoughts were interrupted by the voice of Private Staines squeaking outside her cell.

278

'Here you blooming well are!' he was saying to a rat coming down the tunnel. 'What time do you call this?!'

'Now, we call it ten past seven, so,' said a familiar voice. 'What do you call it?'

'Or are you not familiar with the names of the times, like?' said another familiar voice.

'You was supposed to take over from us at seven,' said Sergeant Scard. 'You're late. Here, don't I know you?'

'I doubt it,' said the first familiar voice. 'But you might recognise me from the telly, so. I do a lot of adverts.'

'Humph,' squeaked the Sergeant. 'You're still late.'

'Probably got lost,' said Private Staines, sniggering nastily. 'Country bumpkins!'

Ginger heard the two gruff guards scampering away, continuing to grumble and then laughing a bit too loudly, like they wanted to make someone think they were laughing at them.

'How do yer like that, now?' Ginger heard Bumfluff say. 'Bumpkins, so, is it?'

'I'll give them bumpkins in their bum, like,' said Fleabomb.

'Boys,' hissed Ginger at them. 'Can we please concentrate on what we're supposed to be doing here. Did you have any luck with any of the other guards?'

The two rats appeared in the dim light of Ginger's cell.

'Nigh,' said Fleabomb, '"luck" is a very interesting word. It reminds me of a man I knew who was asked why he was always so lucky. "It's funny," he said, "the more I practise at something, the luckier I get."'

'Aye,' said Bumfluff, '"luck" implies a lack of skill,

whereas I think you'll find we are two very highly-skilled rats.'

Ginger sighed and would have rolled her eyes, but she was very nervous. 'Well, did you have any *skill* with any of the other guards then?

'Oh, aye,' said Fleabomb. 'There's one there who's just rushed off to the loo with a very nasty case of food poisoning. He must have eaten something that wasn't rotten.'

'And there's another,' added Bumfluff, 'who's just heard news that his mother down the other end of the sewer needs a hand fouling her nest.'

'Very good,' said Ginger. 'And …'

'She's about to ask about the bus timetable,' said Bumfluff. 'Just yer listen. That's what she's going to ask. And about the sunglasses, you'll see.'

Now Ginger did roll her eyes. 'Well, did you get them?'

'Get what?'

'The bus timetable and the sunglasses?'

'Ha!' said Bumfluff, giving Fleabomb a wink. 'Didn't I tell yer she'd be asking about them, so?'

Then he caught the look on Ginger's face and said hurriedly, 'Sure now, didn't I leave them just where yer said? At some great danger to meself, I might add. The place is fairly crawling with cats up there.'

'So the posters worked?'

'Something worked alright. That old boss cat of yers, Sue Narmi, she nearly ate me. I hope yer will take account of that when considering my compensation.'

'Compensation?' said Ginger.

'Payment.'

'Payment?'

'Wages, like.'

'Here you go,' said Ginger. 'How about I get rid of your sworn enemy, have a good percentage of my stolen goods returned to you, and then how about I *don't* eat you. How does that sound for compensation?'

Bumfluff appeared to be thinking about it so Ginger pushed passed him with another sigh. She'd crawled a metre up the tunnel before she heard the sound of his voice again.

'Good luck, yer big ginger cat girl, yer,' he said.

'Aye,' said Fleabomb. 'What he said, like.'

Ginger turned and thanked them. Then she said maybe one day she'd see them back at the farm. If she did, she'd be true to her word, and never eat them.

WHAT A HERO!

Tuck worked hard through the night. First, he worked at keeping the other cats calm, now that he'd convinced them of the Pong's perfectly poisonous plans for the pussies in their perilous penitentiary.

'We should be quiet,' he said quietly.

'We should whisper,' he whispered.

'Ssh,' he shushed.

But the other cats just ignored him. Principessa Passagiata Pawprints from the posh part of Palermo was particularly perplexed.

'Me-a!' she sobbed. 'That anyone should-a wish to kill-a me-a! Do they not-a know-a my lineage?'

Butch, meanwhile, was arguing with fat-cat Matt about how they should escape.

'Maybe we should keep our voices down?' said Tuck. 'After all, I already know how to escape.'

Suddenly all was silence as the other cats turned and stared at him.

'Do you really, sweetheart?' said Butch.

'Er, I think I do. But you all have to be very quiet or else the Pongs will come back and discover we're alive.'

Well, poor Tucky soon wished he'd said nothing at all. For now, as he worked away on his second task of the evening, he had multiple pairs of eyes watching his every move. And more than three dozen mouths asking what he was doing and how it was going and why wasn't he done yet? Ooh, how **extreeeeeeeemely** unhelpful! Because, let me tell you, dear reader, watching someone do something is the most sure-fire way to make them make a mistake. If you don't believe me, ask your resident adult to explain how to park a car next time they're parking the car. Ask them to describe in detail how they're doing it, what they're looking out for, what their hands and feet are doing. I bet they make a mistake—and I bet they blame it on you! Ha, ha! Oh, sorry.

Bendyfenders, imagine how poor little Tuck felt. Everyone was watching him and he couldn't afford to do anything wrong. It's a good job all of his intelligence lay in his physicality or the chances of him succeeding would have been even smaller than they already were. The first thing he did was push his paw through the wire between him and Bunk and stretch and stretch and **STREEEEEEEEETCH** with all his might to reach his friend.

'He can't do it,' he heard fat-cat Matt say.

'He can't do it,' he heard Butch say.

'Oh, of course he can't-a do it!' he heard Principessa Passagiata Pawprints say.

But that only made Tuck even more determined and he pushed and pushed and **puuuuushed** until he was just shy of Bunk's neck. Then he extended one of his magnificent black claws and looped it around Bunk's collar. He pulled on it hard until the collar popped open and he could drag it back towards him.

'He did it!' said Butch.

'He did it!' said fat-cat Matt.

'Of course he-a did it!' said the Principessa.

Getting the right pin out of Bunk's collar was easy for Tuck, but using it to open the lock on his cage door was maybe the most difficult thing he'd ever done. You see, he had to remember the instructions from ever so many chapters ago, and he wasn't that kind of clever. He remembered not to swallow the pin this time, and he remembered he had to pick up the pin and put it in the lock, but he had no idea what he had to do next.

'Try wiggling it,' said fat cat Matt.

'Try-a niggling it,' said the Principessa.

'Try jiggling it, darling,' said Butch.

And so Tuck wiggled and niggled and jiggled and, just like that, the lock on his cage popped open.

'Me next, me next, me next!' shouted all the cats, until Tuck told them whoever spoke next would have their cage opened last. Well, mute moggies, that worked well. All the cats sat silently, giving him those eyes cats give you when they want something. And to a degree this worked (as it so often does), for it made Tuck walk up and down the rows of cage to see, for the first time, quite how many cats he had to set free. Yikes, there were loads! Tuck didn't even know where to start. But the closest cage to him was Butch's, so Tuck jumped up and, hanging off the cage by his claws, wiggled and niggled and jiggled the pin in the lock until his mouth was sore. But sure enough—**click!**— Butch's lock came open. No sooner had it done so than

Butch was out of the cage like a cat out of hell. He didn't even say thank you. He just pushed past Tuck, ran out of the barn door and into the night. And so it went with all of the cats Tuck set free that night. They were so excited at being freed that they all completely forgot their manners. Only Principessa Passagiata Pawprints from the posh part of Palermo made any acknowledgement of the service she'd received.

'*Mille grazie*,' she said, before jumping down to the ground and bolting for the barn door. 'One shall-a remember you-a in the birthday honours list-a.'

Then, like all the other cats before her, she disappeared into the dark night. Well, I jolly well hope you're thinking what I'm thinking! I'm thinking about my dinner. Oh no, not that bit. I mean, I'm thinking: '*How* **ruuuuuude!**' and '*What about teamwork?*' and '*Couldn't they have stuck around and helped Tuck open the other cages?*' I mean, it's come to a pretty sorry state of affairs when the PP from the PP of P is the only one minding her P's and Q's. I do hope that if *you* had been one of those cats you'd have hung around, not only to say thank you, but also to help free the others.

However, unlike me and (maybe) you, Tuck was not thinking this at all. He was just thinking that he had to carry on working and finish what Bunk had set out to achieve: to free the other cats. On and on and on he worked, so deep into the night that it was officially the next day. When he'd freed the very last black cat, a skinny black tom who'd been in custody so long he was halfway institutionalised, Tuck collapsed in a heap. His jaw ached, his claws ached, but most of all his heart ached for, unlike all the cats he had set free, he had nowhere to run to.

He stood slowly and, without knowing why, used his sore and tired mouth to pick up the pin for the last time. Then he walked back down the row of cages and wiggled and niggled and jiggled it in the lock on Bunk's cage. Except, of course, when the cage door popped open, Bunk didn't push past him to escape. He didn't move at all. Tuck couldn't say why, but it seemed wrong to leave Bunk there alone in the cage. Who knew what the evil Pongs would do with his body? Whatever it was, Bunk deserved so much more, so Tuck climbed into his cage, grabbed him by the scruff of his neck and dragged him slowly out. He dropped him to the floor of the barn, then dragged him all the way to the huge doorway and out into the farmyard. Then, without any idea of where he was going, he carried on walking backward, dragging Bunk through the snow.

WHAT AN ENTRANCE!

The tunnel that led from her cell seemed much longer than the previous time Ginger had crawled along it. Bumfluff and Fleabomb had told her all she had to do was head straight on until a sharp corner turned towards a major junction. Then all she had to do was turn right. That way she would be sure to find the exit she wanted. But now, with her eyes accustomed to the dark after so many days underground, she saw lots of offshoots she hadn't noticed on the way down. Sometimes, an entrance to one of these offshoots appeared when her tunnel was curving, so that neither way was really straight on. Or maybe this offshoot was the junction the two rats meant? What if she took the wrong turning and got lost? What if she was destined to perish down here, whether King Rat and his guards found her or not? Ginger stopped and shook these negative thoughts from her head. All she had to do was to keep calm and carry straight on until she found a large junction.

After ten minutes she still had not come upon any guards, and she was at last convinced that the two country rats had done that part of their job properly. Still, she knew there would be guards soon enough and she crept slowly forwards, barely able to see where she was going at all, her ears and nose and eyes alert. Soon enough she heard a scuffling noise and then, as if it was right next to her, a voice squeaked: 'What was that?'

'I didn't hear nothing,' squeaked another voice.

It was as if the two rats were either side of her, or right in front of her, or just behind her. Ginger froze, and then listened as the rats spoke again.

'How's your mum?' said the first.

'Same as ever.'

'And the kids?'

'Vermin, the lot of 'em.'

The voices were definitely ahead of her after all, and so Ginger took another step forwards. As she did, she felt the wall of the tunnel push into her and she realised it was turning sharply. The rats must be just ahead, out of view. Ginger took a deep breath, steadied herself and ran around the corner. There were the rats alright and, at the sight of this great ginger monster appearing beside them, they both gave out piercing squeals. Ginger bared her teeth and they turned and ran, squeaking loudly as they disappeared down the tunnel, shouting for help at the top of their voices. Bumfluff McGuff and Fleabomb McGee must have heard them for, as agreed, they too started squealing at the top of their voices.

'Prisoner on the loose, like!' shouted Fleabomb.

'That big ginger cat there has got away, so!' squeaked Bumfluff.

Now Ginger lost no time. She looked quickly around her and saw offshoots and tunnels running in every direction. This had to be the junction the two country rats had told her about. She went back the way she'd come, around the sharp corner to be completely sure of her bearings. This part she could not afford to get wrong. She came back to the junction again, turned right into a wide flat tunnel and ran along it as fast as she could, not worrying about the wet ground below her paws. Soon she saw two guard rats barring the passage.

'Just let me go,' she shouted running towards them. 'You don't have to get eaten. Grrr!'

Well, that was enough for one of the guards and he shot into a side tunnel and away into the dark. But the other stood his ground. It was Binjuice Jones, the rat with the sharpened front teeth and the leather cap who had guarded her on her first night in the tunnel.

'Come on then' he said. 'You don't scare me. Let's s—'

But that was all he got to say because next thing he knew (or, more likely, didn't know) was that his head had been bitten off. It was fear as much as anything that drove Ginger to such drastic action. Binjuice Jones was such a big and scary rat she wasn't sure she could have beaten him in a fair fight—at least, not quickly enough to escape the other rats who soon would be on the scene. Thankful for her fight training and the fitness it had given her, Ginger ran on, the tunnel widening around her until it became a huge drainage pipe, the dirt beneath her paws now replaced by concrete, along which ran a steady stream of water. Not to mention a steady stream of Ginger. There was concrete on the walls and ceiling of the pipe too and it echoed every noise. At first, this was just the splashing of Ginger's paws as she ran quickly through the water, but soon, Ginger heard, it was also the scampering of hundreds of rats.

'There she is!' The unmistakeably rasping voice of

Corporal Punishment echoed up the tunnel. 'Cut her off at the next opportunity!'

Now Ginger ran faster than ever. She pushed herself on and on through the darkness, the noise of the rats behind her growing steadily louder until—just as she was beginning to lose hope—she saw a bright pinprick in the distance. It had to be the large tunnel mouth Bumfluff and Fleabomb had told her about. The sight of it drove Ginger on, gasping for every breath, until the pinprick of light grew into a blinding ball of light and her eyes were unable to cope with the white gleam from the moonlit snow on the ground beyond the mouth of the tunnel.

Ginger was desperate to carry on running out through the wide opening and into fresh air at last. It was only by using that ingredient which is required for all success— self-discipline—that she managed to resist. Half a metre from the tunnel's bright and snowy mouth, she sat and turned, panting heavily and sucking in the fresh air, and looked down along the pipe behind her. For the first few metres, the water that ran along the tunnel's floor caught the light of the moon outside. After that, there was nothing to see but darkness. Turning back to look outside, Ginger studied the creek which ran into the tunnel. She didn't know exactly where she was, but she knew from Fleabomb and Bumfluff that she had to look for a shopping trolley and exit the creek there. With the brightness of the outside world in her eyes, the massive hole behind her looked black and empty. But Ginger's ears were not deceived: they heard nothing but scratching and scampering and shouted orders. Corporal Punishment had misjudged how fast

Ginger could run and was telling her underlings where to go. Which offshoots to use to intercept Ginger, which ones to take as short cuts. Louder and louder the noises came as the army of sewer rats approached. Then, at last, Ginger saw movement. It looked at first as if the tunnel floor was oozing a thick tide of mud. But then she blinked again and saw it was oozing with a thick tide of rats. Thousands of them, only metres away, and at the head of them, the small white rat who was their king. His teeth were bared and his pink eyes were bright. Suddenly, he spotted Ginger. He sat up on his haunches and shouted out, his squeaky little voice echoing all around.

'Tear her to pieces! Two weeks of meat for whoever brings me a morsel of her!'

Spurred on, the carpet of rats moved faster than ever. Still Ginger forced herself to stand her ground. Ten one thousand, eleven one thousand, twelve one thousand. Only when the first rats were a metre away from her did she turn and run. Thirteen one thousand, fourteen one thousand. She ran more quickly, worrying she would be late. She spotted a rusty old shopping trolley ahead of her, ran up to it, and jumped up out of the creek and through a hole in the fence which ran around this part of the waste ground. But that was no deterrent to the rats. They broke ranks at last, hundreds of them scampering up the side of the creek and under the fence; a thousand rats fanning out after her, like a deadly wake chasing a boat. On and on Ginger ran, until she could hear the noise of the crowds ahead of her. She glanced back quickly to see if the rats had heard it too and gasped at the sight behind her. There were thousands and thousands of rats, as far as she could see in every direction, the nearest of them much closer than she had imagined. She could hear their murderous squeaks of 'Let me at her!' and 'The reward is mine!' and 'I'd kill that cat for free!' and remembered how rarely a rat has a chance to gang up on a cat.

From the darkness on her left, a huge grey rat appeared in a Riff Raff jacket, jumping through the air with his teeth ready to snap at her neck. She didn't waste time in fighting him, just dodged him and ran on. She had stopped listening to her bellies and didn't know what time it was, but she could hear the crowds in the darkness and prayed that would be enough to save her. Maybe Bumfluff and Fleabomb had got the message wrong, or maybe she had underestimated the distance? But just as she was wondering how much further she could actually run, she heard a tannoy system turn on and the unmistakeable voice of Sue Narmi booming from the speakers.

'Toms and she-cats. I give you … Ginger Jenkins!'

At that very moment, as planned, the streetlamps circling the wasteland were turned on, illuminating the snow-covered ground below. A huge cheer went up from the darkness all around as the amassed cats of the city watched Ginger run into the light. And then, a huge growling started as the amassed cats of the city saw the amassed rats of the city, who, at last, took their focus from Ginger and looked around in confusion, wondering what all the light and the noise was about.

WHAT A
WAKE-UP CALL!

Meanwhile, back at the farm, the thick clouds that had hung heavy all night, began to break up, revealing plinky stars in the inky-black sky. It was as if the clouds had chickened out of snowing after all, and had scattered in all directions before anyone could accuse them of even thinking about it. They left behind a freezing night, lit by a dull and tired moon. Tuck had dragged Bunk as far as the stables, leaning against its new glass front wall, barely glancing at the shiny machinery that stood inside. He couldn't explain why he'd dragged Bunk out of his cage. He just couldn't bear to see his friend's poor limp body lying there in captivity.

Tuck listened to the sad chimes of distant church towers over the hours and spoke to his poor dead friend. He wondered out loud where all the cats they'd helped now were, or where they were going. If they were cold too, or if running home was keeping them warm. He spoke of how he hoped their owners would welcome them back, and imagined the warm welcomes each of the cats would receive. But that subject made him feel more lonely than ever, and so he tried to think of happier things. This became easier when the dark in the eastern sky began to fade, and the birds began to sing and, before Tuck knew it, a beautiful pink-and-gold sunrise had started to form in the sky above the Great Dark Forest.

Then Tuck heard a sound that was new to him. It came from the farmhouse to his left, high up in the attic. It was a clanging, ringing sound, which was suddenly silenced and soon followed by the loud yawning of a female human and the nasty nasal tones of a male human. Tuck had forgotten all about the Pongs. They must have been sleeping up in the attic of the farmhouse, where he and Minnie used to sleep.

'*Uh-oh,*' he thought. '*Now the Pongs are going to come and find what Bunk and I have done. And they'll probably kill me. Oh well.*'

He was so depressed and tired and upset that this thought didn't spur him into any kind of action. Instead he just sat there, still making the odd comment to Bunk's limp and lifeless body, as he listened to the Pongs moving around and making their breakfast.

Sooner than he had expected, he heard footsteps on the stairs of the farmhouse. Then, the tall and skinny frame of Mr Pong appeared in the gap left for a front door in the half-built farmhouse wall. He was wearing a pair of pinkish spotty pyjamas. Mr Pong looked at Tuck, and Tuck looked at Mr Pong. Before either of them could say a word, Mrs Pong appeared wearing a flame-proof nightie patterned all over with fire-breathing dragons. She gave a huge yawn, the rays of the early morning sun glistening on her yellow teeth, and then, like her husband, she spotted Tuck and Bunk. As Tuck watched, both Mr and Mrs Pong looked towards the barn.

WHAT A CURIOUS PHENOMENON!

At roughly the same time, miles across the Great Dark Forest, down the river and to the left a bit, cat owners across the city were experiencing a strange phenomenon. Every single one of them was used to waking up and finding their cat alert and ready—not to mention somewhat impatient—for their breakfast. But on this morning, every single one of them found their cat—if they found their cat at all—snoring away, content and seemingly well-fed. In every street of every suburb, in houses, apartments and converted warehouses, in studios and flats and bungalows and townhouses; anywhere where cats and humans lived together, there was nothing to be heard but the sound of forks tapped on tins and shrill cries of 'Din-dins!' All to no avail. This sound was then replaced by the noise of cat food scraped back into tins and—in a thudding that sounded like distant thunder—fridge doors closed in disappointment. Because not a cat in the city needed breakfast that morning. Rats, after all, are very filling.

Other parts of city life went on as normal. Humans went to work as normal (albeit a little concerned for the health of their puddy-wuddy darlings and making notes to call the vet); dogs peed on lamp posts as normal; the birds tweeted about everything and nothing as normal. And, at half past five, the first number 37 bus set off from the central bus depot as normal. It had only one passenger: a rather large ginger cat who barely said hello to the bus driver as she paid her fare, and who wore a large pair of sunglasses throughout the journey. She didn't say much, just one word the entire trip. This was when the bus driver, a chirpy, chummy, chubby chatterbox called Charlie from Chichester asked if she was going far.

'Home,' she said.

Then she turned, sighed, and looked out of the window.

WHAT A GRUESOME WAY TO GO!

'**Noooo!**' screeched Mrs Pong in her thick and throaty tones. '**Noooo, noooo, noooo!!!**'

'Horrors!' yelled Mr Pong in his nasty nasal voice. 'What horrible awful evil cats! How dare they be so devilishly dishonest about their deserved deaths!'

Tuck sat listening to the Pongs screech and scream and watched the sun rise in the pale blue sky. Maybe it was the reflection of the sunshine off all the glass behind him, or more likely it was the increasing fury of the Pongs as they cursed, clamoured, and kicked cages around the barn, but he was beginning to feel rather hot under the collar. Then he remembered he wasn't wearing a collar. All the same, he felt little nervous.

'My coat!' he heard Mrs Pong screech to the accompaniment of a cage being thrown against a wall.

'My plans!' he heard Mr Pong yell as another cage was smashed to the floor. 'Those furballing felines will tell everyone! How can I give out free tasty treats if everyone knows they're toxic?'

'My coat has escaped!' wailed Mrs Pong. 'The ungrateful evil cunning and wretched thing. Every sleeve, every cuff, ever lapel, all gone! Not even a pocket left behind.'

Then there was a sudden silence from the barn which made Tuck look towards it. There, in its huge doorway, stood tall and skinny Mr Pong with short and dumpy Mrs Pong panting beside him.

'All except two!' they said together. And with that they marched across the farmyard in their nightwear towards Tuck and Bunk. Tuck let them pick him up. After all, what else could they take from him, but a life he didn't care about? Ginger was gone, Minnie was gone, Bunk was gone. Then Tuck saw Mr Pong kick Bunk's body roughly to one side and he scratched and spat at him. But **ow-ee!** Even when you're happy to die, it still hurts like billy-o when a human gives you a shake to stop you scratching. And **ouchy-oo!!!** It hurt Tuck even more when Mrs Pong snatched him from Mr Pong, holding him at arm's length so he couldn't scratch her.

'Turn on the skinning machine!' she shouted to her husband.

'Oh, Frances, what's the point?' said Mr Pong sadly. 'We've only got one cat left.'

'It's better than nothing,' said Mrs Pong, breaking into a smile which revealed her horrible yellow teeth. 'I'm going to skin this little monster. If I can't have a coat, I can at least get a fetching little belt.'

'Oh, darling!' cried Mr Pong, his eyes alight. 'How I love you. You're right, let's do it!'

Tuck struggled and kicked, wiggled and writhed, but

Mrs Pong had held him in such a way that his legs kicked only at cold fresh air and his claws caught only the morning sunlight. He watched helplessly as Mr Pong opened a glass door in the glass wall of the stables and walked inside. Then he heard the huge silver machinery inside begin to throb and hum.

'How will we kill him first?' Mr Pong shouted out over the noise.

'We won't,' laughed his wife. 'We'll throw him in alive!'

Then, skipping with surprising grace, she followed her husband into the glass-walled stables and held Tuck over a huge funnel which stuck out of the end of the silver machine. Tuck looked down into it and saw blades slicing in a circular motion below him.

'*One last look at the farm,*' he thought to himself, lifting his head to look out through the glass wall before Mrs Pong dropped him to his certain death. '*I just want to see ... WHAT THE—??? WHAT??!!!!*'

Now, admittedly, it wasn't often Tuck managed to think of anything for long enough to finish his sentences, but on this occasion he had interrupted himself quite deliberately. For outside, in the farmyard, he had seen a sight he had given up on ever seeing again. Not the farmyard itself, he'd been staring at that all night. And not the barn, that looked the same as ever, perhaps a little more upright than it used to be. But, there, where the farmyard met the driveway, he saw nothing other than a fit ginger cat arriving home. And not just *any* fit ginger cat, but a cat called Ginger who was fitter than he'd ever seen her, looking around at all the changes that had taken place since she'd been away. Tuck blinked and blinked again until he was super-duper certain it really was her.

'*Oh!*' he thought. '*Oh, there is a reason to live! Phew, just in time.*'

And with that he sunk every one of his teeth into Mrs Pong's podgy right hand, which she had let linger conveniently close to his mouth.

'Agh!!' she yelled. 'The little monster's dealt me a welt. Let's melt him into a belt of pelt!'

But she wasn't able to drop Tuck into the skinning machine. Oh painful pincers, no. For Tuck was still attached to her by his teeth. Mrs Pong waved her arm around in all directions, whizzing Tuck through the air as he tried to extract his teeth from her hand.

'Do something, William!' Mrs Pong screeched at her lanky husband, who was hopping from foot to foot at the sight of his irritated wife and her gyrating strife. 'Get him off **meeeeeeeee!!**'

But Mr Pong didn't need to do anything for, exactly at that moment, Tuck managed to excise his incisors and went flying through the air. Now, if this scene had happened in your house (or in your stables come to that), Tuck would have slammed straight into the large wall of glass through which he'd spied Ginger. But this is a fantastic adventure book, and, as we all know, in fantastic adventure books heroes go smashing straight through glass. Which exactly what Tuck did. And if this had been your glass, or my glass, come to that, Tuck would have cut himself to pieces almost as much as if he'd been thrown into the skinning machine. But this is not your glass, nor mine; this is the glass in a fantastic adventure book, and so, no sooner had Tuck smashed through it, metallic cross-frames and all, than he executed a roll which Bunk would have been proud of and stood up with barely a scratch on him.

'Ginger!' he yelled as he ran towards her. 'Ginger, don't come any closer, it's dangerous!!'

Well, smashing smithereens, imagine this from Ginger's point of view! There she is, sauntering up to the farm and wondering how on earth she's going to explain all her adventures to her friends who, in the meantime, have only known a simple life in the countryside, when Tuck comes smashing through a window which wasn't even there when she left, executes a roll like he's in the FBI or CIA or something, and then comes running towards her telling her not to come any closer. Goodness. I think that's the longest sentence in this entire book. (Not the 'Goodness' one, the one before that—do keep up!) Well, even Ginger struggled to remain calm in the face of such an unexpected welcome. Struggled, but succeeded.

'Yeah, hello Tuck,' she said, sighing and rolling her eyes. 'Don't be so dramatic. Have you been eating mushrooms again?'

'Run, run, RUN, RUN, RUN!!!' said Tuck. 'Oh hi, by the way. You're looking good. Now run, run, RUN, RUN, RUN!!!!'

And with that he pelted past her. But, after all she'd

been through (i.e., a long bus journey), the last thing Ginger felt like doing was running. She thought Tuck had probably been frightened by Minnie scowling at him, or a big snail, or his own shadow on the farmyard. Which was strange, Ginger thought to herself, for now as she looked at the farmyard, it looked like there was a shadow of Tuck still lying there, almost completely still.

Tuck had run almost a quarter of the way up the drive before he realised Ginger wasn't with him. He turned to see her sitting there, squinting towards Bunk.

'Come on, Ginger, please!'

But no sooner had he shouted this than he regretted it. For Ginger turned to face him and remained that way, rolling her eyes and sighing again, not noticing at all the tall skinny form which now stepped out of the stables holding a large black-cat-catching net.

'Don't be so silly, Tuck,' said Ginger. 'After all I've been thro—'

'Ginger, look out! Behind you! Oh, please, run! Everyone else managed to escape, apart from poor Bunk; why can't you escape too? Please! Or, at least, look behind you!!'

Tuck watched Ginger roll her eyes again and, then—as if only to keep him happy—she turned and looked. But it was too late. She had barely drawn a breath to say 'Really?' when Mr Pong swooped and caught her up in his net.

'No!' Tuck yelled. 'No, take me, take me. Let her go!'

Without a second thought, he ran straight at Mr Pong and climbed up him with all his claws until he reached his long and skinny face. Tuck opened his mouth wide and was just about to sink his teeth into Mr Pong's huge nose, when he felt himself grabbed from behind.

'Thought you'd bite, did you?' he heard Mrs Pong say. 'Well, we'll see who's biting who!'

And with that she sank her horrible yellow teeth into Tuck's back leg.

'**YEEEOWWW!**' he screeched. But then, before he could screech again, he found himself thrown into the net beside Ginger.

'Much happen while I've been away?' she asked.

WHAT A TO-DO AND A HOO-HA!

Yes, yes! I know! I'm supposed to keep you in a more stressful state of suspense than a boy who's forgotten to wear underwear and is relying on a very old pair of braces to keep up his trousers. But, ooh, I just can't bear to do it. I'm desperate to find out what happens next. After all, let's admit, it doesn't look good. True, the weather's picked up a bit, which is always nice, especially when you're out in the countryside and the birds are singing like there's no tomorrow. Which—if you think about it—is weird, because if there was no tomorrow, I'm quite sure I wouldn't feel like singing; but there you are, that's birds for you.

Manyways (to end the story), let's fast forward to two minutes later. I warn you, though, it ain't pretty. Stringy Mr Pong has still got the skinning machine going; tubby Mrs Pong is chortling in a somewhat deranged manner and each of them is holding a cat. Mr Pong has Tuck by the scruff of his neck and Mrs Pong has Ginger by the scruff of her neck. **Youch!** Being held by the scruff of your neck is fine when you're a kitten, but no fully-grown cat likes to be held like that, let alone lifted like that, let alone dangled over the funnel of a throbbing skinning machine like that.

Poor Ginger. After everything she'd been through, taking on King Rat and his entire army and beating them, busting the biggest underground crime syndicate the city had ever known, escaping the clutches of not only the Gertrude Street Fur Girls, but also the Citrus Street Sourpusses. To have managed all of that, only to return home to be skinned alive.

And poor Tuck. Thinking he had nothing left to live for, thinking his death would be a sadness to no one, and now having Ginger die too.

'Ho, ho, ho,' chortled Mrs Pong over the noise of the skinning machine. 'I'm going to make a black belt and ginger mittens! It will be **sooooooo** tasteful.'

'Then we'll run away and deny we were ever here,' said Mr Pong, revealing his plans in the way baddies always do. 'We'll adopt new identities and be free to develop and distribute our delicious, deadly din-dins and free the world of cats forever!!!!'

The throbbing from the skinning machine seemed to grow louder still, as if there were two machines now running, and Tuck and Ginger each looked through the broken glass wall at the beautiful day outside. Then they looked at each other.

'Goodbye Ginger,' said Tuck.

'Goodbye Tuck,' said Ginger.

And then, as the second throbbing noise got even louder and seemed to change a bit, and then got even louder still, they each closed their eyes. Then they heard a voice neither of them had heard in a very long time.

'Welcome to a special addition of *Back To Your Roots,*' they heard this voice shouting through a megaphone. 'You are live on national television!'

Ginger was the first to open her eyes. Immediately she shut them again because she thought she must already be dead and dreaming. Then she remembered you can't dream when you're dead (so do it now, folks!) and opened them a second time.

'Tuck,' she said. 'Tuck, did I miss a meeting?'

For there, outside the window, was the explanation of the second throbbing noise. It was a huge helicopter with its side door open to reveal a great big television camera. Beside the camera in noise-cancelling headphones and holding a huge microphone between her paws was a curvaceous cat with a multi-coloured coat of unusually long hair. She was elbowing a smaller, similar-looking cat out of the way.

'My name is Minnie Themoocha Ripperton-Fandango,' she shouted into the microphone. 'Welcome to my special—'

But Minnie said no more, for she suddenly realised the camera wasn't even pointing at her. Instead, the cameraman was filming the owners of the country's largest pet food company holding two fully-grown, and very much alive, cats over the mouth of a throbbing skinning machine.

Dear reader, I must confess that at this point in my interviews with the cats involved, it became very difficult to get reliable information about the course of events which followed. Ginger and Tuck had their eyes closed half the time, Minnie was unavailable for comment, and Dora refused to speak without an upfront fee.

Fortunately, I have managed to retrieve the original television footage. It, at least, clearly records the reaction of the Pongs to this surprising development. The phrase 'stunned mullets' comes to mind, were it not for the fact that neither of the Pongs wore a mullet nor was a mullet. Not to mention the fact that I've no idea what a mullet is, stunned or otherwise. Let's say they were frozen by shock. Mortified. Petrified. Anything which involved them not moving until slowly, very slowly, Mrs Pong—who was holding Ginger—began to loosen her grip.

It seems this was the point at which everyone in the helicopter, other than the cameraman, realised what was happening in the stables/ skinning room (and never has a slash (/) been more appropriate). The footage shows Dora, in the foreground, grabbing the microphone from Minnie so that the viewers at home could hear her shout down to the Pongs: 'No! You no do it! The whole country watches!'

Well, possessive pussies, Minnie clearly is not a cat who, even during a potentially gruesome catastrophe, likes to have a microphone taken from her. She grabbed it back and shouted down to the Pongs, 'I demand you put my friends down right now!'

Given all the noise that was going on, what with the helicopter whirring and the skinning machine throbbing, you have to be a bit of a lip-reader when watching the footage to see what happened next. Fortunately, modern technology (i.e. a book) allows us to zoom in, watch in detail, and do a bit of lip-reading.

Firstly, we can see Ginger give Minnie one of her most gingery looks before rolling her eyes, sighing slowly and saying something I really can't repeat here, but which did include the words: 'stupid thing to say.'

Then we can see Mrs Pong come to life, stare at the camera so hard I'm surprised it didn't break, and mouth the words: 'Watch me.' Mrs Pong then turns to her husband to say something which cannot be made out, but to which he clearly responds: 'OK, Frances, let's do it.'

Slowly, Mrs Pong loosened her grip on Ginger, while Mr Pong loosened his grip on Tuck. Once more the two cats squeezed their eyes shut and said goodbye to each other.

'The nation is watching a tragedy unfold before its very eyes on my own special show,' they heard Minnie say. 'Keep watching after the commercial break.'

But, suddenly, there was another change in noise. No, not another helicopter. What do you think this is, an air show? No, the noise was less now, not more.

'Tuck,' said Ginger. 'Tuck, look! Open your eyes and look. Who on earth is *that*?'

But Tuck was too scared to open his eyes. All he noticed was that he could no longer hear the throbbing of the skinning machine.

'**Nooo!!**' shouted Mr Pong. '**Nooo!!** Foiled again! There are supposed to be less cats, not more. How did that one become alive again?'

Now Tuck opened his eyes. It couldn't be? Could it? He turned his head in all directions until at last he saw what had stopped the skinning machine. It was a very tired and very droopy Bunk, who was holding a power cable between his teeth, its plug drooping at one end where he'd pulled it from the wall.

'Bunk!' shouted Tuck. Then he shouted '**Aaagh!**' as Mr Pong at last dropped him into the mouth of the now silent and harmless machine. Then '**OOFFEEE!**' as Mrs Pong dropped Ginger in on top of him.

'Bunk, Bunk, you're alive!' Tuck yelled out of the funnel. 'I'm so sorry I left you. I'm such a clot, leaving you to rot outside in the snow. Will you ever forgive me?'

Bunk's surprisingly small head with its surprisingly huge yellow eyes appeared over the edge of the funnel and he looked down at Tuck.

'Me to rot?' he said into the pot. 'You a clot? No, you're not! Have you lost the plot or what? It was the perfect spot during the perfect slot, bang on the dot; I mean it a lot. This bot got hot in a jot, like a tot in a cot in a sunny yacht. I recharged in the sunlight because of you, Tuck. You saved the day. Tuck, you're a hero!'

'Bunk's alive!' Tuck said to Ginger through tears of joy. 'And you're back. And Minnie's here … and … and …'

'Tuck,' said Ginger. 'How about we get out of this deadly machine before you tell me any more about how happy you are to be alive?'

And for once, folks, Tuck saw the sense in action now and words later.

WHAT A SET UP FOR A SEQUEL!

W ell, what more is there to say? Oh, an ending, I suppose. Man, you have to get every little ounce out of me, don't you? OK, here goes. William and Frances Pong were arrested that very night. During their trial, the judge, Justice Justin Justus, was outraged at Mrs Pong's outright denial of any wrongdoing. Even when confronted with the video evidence, which of course the entire nation had also seen, she tried to pretend it was someone else who looked a bit like her. Mr Pong sat and sobbed throughout the entire event and kept saying how sorry he was. Which explains, perhaps, why Mrs Pong got sent down for a far longer stretch than Mr Pong did. Or perhaps not.

You see, Mrs Pong was so busy denying she'd ever done anything wrong that she refused all compromises, concessions or courses of correction. Mr Pong, on the other hand, was not so arrogant. He agreed to partake in a rehabilitation program known as *The Feline's Mutual*, a course specifically designed for 'humans who haven't learned to love cats yet'. Can you imagine how disgusted he was when he first arrived at the Cat Correction Centre? Really, can't you? Well, do try a bit harder. He was **tremblblblblbling** with disgust.

But after a week or so, William Pong realised the reason cats always scratched and bit him was only because he didn't like them. Through exposure therapy and kitten counselling, he soon learned that if he relaxed around cats and stopped trying to kill them, they actually were quite furry and purry and not in a hurry to hurt him. He's still in prison—you don't get out that easily—but I've heard he is now a big cat fan and actually planning on opening a cat sanctuary when he finally gets out.

Nobody knows what Frances Pong wants to do, or, indeed, if she'll ever get out of prison. She is, you see, stuck in a solitary confinement cell until she learns not to be such a big fat liar. Or a short fat liar in her case.

As for the cats, well, I'm sure you can guess the end. Can't you? Oh, come on, I'm getting really tired of writing this book. Next you'll be wanting me to read it to you. Or maybe a video game, how about that?

Endsontheway, this is what happened to the cats: Minnie and Dora's career sky-rocketed after their explosive exposure of the Pongs. Everyone wanted to know who this glamorous duo was and Micky Manx's publicity department wasted no time in telling them. Soon Minnie and Dora were receiving offers from around the world to perform their songs, dance their dances and even to be judges on *The F Factor*. Naturally, neither of them let this go to their heads because, of course, in their heads they already were huge, huge stars and deserved to be treated like it every second of the day. Naturally, they continued to fight about who precisely was the bigger star, who had the most talent and who got to wear which outfits. But, underneath all the cattiness, they knew they needed each other. So they stuck together through all their dysfunctional co-dependent back-biting—because that's show business, folks.

As for Bunk, he quit the CIA. He might have been a catbot, but catbots need love too. And they don't need sending back into dangerous situations where they are considered expendable. So Bunk scratched off the homing beacon on his collar and made sure he lay in the sun for as long as possible each day. Just like a normal cat, really. And where did he lie in the sun? Why, on the farm, of course! Because that's where his best friend was.

At first, Tuck thought the Pongs really had ruined the farm and that he didn't want to live there anymore. But then Ginger pointed out that they had also left behind lots of new walls and roofs, which would come in very handy during the winter. Tuck still wasn't convinced until a few days later. He was showing Bunk around the parts of the farm Bunk hadn't seen before. Inside the farmhouse, beside the stables, up in the attic. It was behind the newly upright barn that they made their discovery. The huge high-sided lorry which had once held the cats in captivity was still there. But instead of holding cages, it was now packed to the brim with Pongs Pet Food.

'It's probably poisonous,' said Tuck.

'No,' said Bunk. 'Remember, they didn't think they'd discovered the perfect poison until yesterday. This must have been for Mrs Pong to bring her food from. Besides,

I've used my toxicity sensor and I can confirm the food in these tins is not only tasty, but also perfectly healthy. I calculate there is enough food here to feed you and Ginger for … twenty-seven years, five months and four days.'

'But what about you?' said Tuck. 'Don't you need to pretend to eat chocolate?'

Bunk looked at him and gave a strange underbite smile.

'As long as I stay here,' he said, 'I never have to pretend anything ever again.'

Ginger wanted to stay too. She decided that she'd had enough adventures to last her a lifetime. And, just as importantly, she'd also paid her dues. Before leaving the city, she'd left a note for Sue Narmi and the Fur Girls telling them they could keep half the food they'd find waiting for them in the sewers beneath the wasteland. Now, with Bunk and Tuck's discovery, she was able to send them a message on Furbook telling them they could keep it all (minus ten per cent for Bumfluff and Fleabomb). Which meant no one went hungry that winter.

So Tuck and Ginger and Bunk stayed at Dingleberry Bottom, welcoming in any cat who might be passing by and had any news to share. When tour schedules permitted, they welcomed Dora and Minnie too—along with their entourages of seven limousines, twelve hat-boxes, three wardrobe assistants and five fluffers each. And even Bumfluff McGuff and Fleabomb McGee visited sometimes, sharing their stories of rat life and how much better it was now that King Rat was no more.

And they all lived happily ever after. Until, one day, two very evil witches—whom the cats had battled in an earlier book—came back to life with a **kerbang!**

But that, as they say, is another story.

THE END

We really hoped you enjoyed *Cats Undercover!* If you did, please give the book a positive review - this will help us to write more books in the future. THANKS SO MUCH!

For information on future books sign up to Tuck & Ginger's mailing list: **www.tuckandginger.com/contact**

FIND OUT WHERE IT ALL STARTED...

CATS ON THE RUN
Tuck & Ginger's hilarious
first adventure!

FIVE STARS!
Scholastic Reader Review Crew

Available at Amazon, Kobo, Nook, iBooks, Tolino, the BookDepository and all good bookstores.

Printed in Great Britain
by Amazon